The last mutie raised its head and crooned at the sky

It was a new and different kind of hoot that none of the companions had ever heard before. Almost immediately, a distant hoot answered.

"Dark night, it's calling for help!" J.B. gasped, dropping a spent clip and slapping in a spare. "What is going on here?"

Even as she frantically reloaded, Mildred considered the matter, and knew that she had no possible answer. Nobody knew for sure where the stickies came from in the first place, whether they were accidents of Nature caused by the nuclear holocaust, devolved humans, escaped genetic experiments, bioweps or what. But there was one singular, unarguable factor about the mutants. They lived, and anything alive always tried to improve itself, to make the next generation stronger.

Mildred shivered at the idea. Stickies with weapons. Oh, dear God in Heaven, protect our mortal souls....

**Other titles in the
Deathlands saga:**

JAMES AXLER

DEATHLANDS®

Shatter Zone

THE COLDFIRE PROJECT
BOOK I

A GOLD EAGLE BOOK FROM
W❂RLDWIDE®

TORONTO • NEW YORK • LONDON
AMSTERDAM • PARIS • SYDNEY • HAMBURG
STOCKHOLM • ATHENS • TOKYO • MILAN
MADRID • WARSAW • BUDAPEST • AUCKLAND

To my parents

First edition September 2006

ISBN-13: 978-0-373-62585-7
ISBN-10:   0-373-62585-5

SHATTER ZONE

Printed in U.S.A.

For man also knoweth not his time: as the fishes that are taken in an evil net, and as the birds that are caught in the snare; so are the sons of men snared in an evil time, when it falleth suddenly upon them.

—*Ecclesiastes* 9:11–12

THE DEATHLANDS SAGA

This world is their legacy, a world born in the violent nuclear spasm of 2001 that was the bitter outcome of a struggle for global dominance.

There is no real escape from this shockscape where life always hangs in the balance, vulnerable to newly demonic nature, barbarism, lawlessness.

But they are the warrior survivalists, and they endure—in the way of the lion, the hawk and the tiger, true to nature's heart despite its ruination.

Ryan Cawdor: The privileged son of an East Coast baron. Acquainted with betrayal from a tender age, he is a master of the hard realities.

Krysty Wroth: Harmony ville's own Titian-haired beauty, a woman with the strength of tempered steel. Her premonitions and Gaia powers have been fostered by her Mother Sonja.

J. B. Dix, the Armorer: Weapons master and Ryan's close ally, he, too, honed his skills traversing the Deathlands with the legendary Trader.

Doctor Theophilus Tanner: Torn from his family and a gentler life in 1896, Doc has been thrown into a future he couldn't have imagined.

Dr. Mildred Wyeth: Her father was killed by the Ku Klux Klan, but her fate is not much lighter. Restored from predark cryogenic suspension, she brings twentieth-century healing skills to a nightmare.

Jak Lauren: A true child of the wastelands, reared on adversity, loss and danger, the albino teenager is a fierce fighter and loyal friend.

Dean Cawdor: Ryan's young son by Sharona accepts the only world he knows, and yet he is the seedling bearing the promise of tomorrow.

In a world where all was lost, they are humanity's last hope....

Chapter One

The blowing dust of the Manitoba desert tinted the air red, as if the world had been painted in fresh blood.

Patches walked carefully among the tall barbed cactus plants, a small knife in his weathered hand. The wep was a homie, just a piece of window glass repeatedly rubbed against stone until it was razor-sharp, with a piece of rat skin wrapped around the bottom to make a handle. The wrinklie remembered once seeing a baron with a steel knife. But then the ruler of that ville had also carried a working blaster, a wheelgun with live brass. The glass knife would be useless in a fight against a black-powder handcannon like that, but it served him well enough for the harvesting.

Stopping his slow progress near a tall cactus, Patches eased his hand into a cluster of the barbed needles and cut free a fat purple globe. As the juicy fruit fell, he neatly caught it with his other hand, and tucked it away into the patched canvas bag hanging at his side. The bag was almost half full and Patches smiled at the thought of how happy his wife would be knowing that they would eat this night.

The cactus plants replenished the harvested fruit

very quickly, but always in new patterns, and he had never found another way of harvesting the fruit except by wandering through the deadly grove. There were many much larger fruits still nesting inside the cluster of needles, ripe and ready for the taking, but all of them were too big to retrieve without getting his arm punctured.

A fluttering from above caught his attention and the old man looked up to see a bird of some kind land on top of a tall cactus and start pecking at a fruit. Patches salivated at the thought of fresh meat, but he knew it was already too late.

Suddenly the little bird gave a horrid squawk and reared back with a quill sticking out of its wing. As it shook the wing, the needle fell out and the bird went happily back to the plump fruit.

"Three," Patches whispered softly. "Two, one…"

Violently shuddering all over, the bird went limp and toppled off the cactus, bouncing from limb to limb of the plants. Then the aced bird was gone from sight, lost somewhere deep inside the overlapping needles covering the spreading arms of the tall cactus.

Goodbye, meat. With a sigh, Patches thumbed the desert sand from beneath his eye patch, then returned to the arduous work at hand.

The air of the desert grove was sweet, rich with a tangy infusion of citrus from the clusters of plump red fruits hanging from the flowering sides of each green cactus. A few of the plants lacked flowers, and those he simply avoided as a waste of time. No flowers meant no fruit. Although the venom in the needles of those cacti was much stronger, perfect to tip the arrows of his crossbow. A man didn't have to be a very good shot with one of those on his arrow. Shoot a slaver in the leg and before he finished cursing, the flesh peddler would go stiff and topple over, a new passenger on the last train west.

It had been a long time since Patches last saw a slaver in his little valley, and that was just fine by him. Every day that he didn't hear the crack of a leather whip or feel the cold of steel around his wrists was a good day. He wouldn't even have put chains on a rad-blasted mutie, the shambling mockeries of men that wandered mindlessly from the desert. Strange they were, and triple deadly with sharpened teeth, claws and suckers on their fingers. Thankfully, no big muties came here. This tiny grove was his world, his private domain, unwanted by anybody, except himself and his wife.

The flowery grove stretched to the end of the valley, hundreds of yards long and equally wide. The warm ground beneath the cactus plants was covered with the decomposing bodies of small rodents, birds, reptiles and even some large insects with four wings. Once he found the skeleton of a norm, but the bones were so old even the clothing was gone, not even a zipper or button remaining. The corpse might have been lying there since predark days, who could say? But since there had been nothing to scav, Patches had moved onward and left the dead alone. Finding a bunch of bones was nothing new. Dark fire, there were ruins of predark villes carpeted with gleaming white bones, the predark skulls still staring skyward, sightless eyes forever looking at the nuke death raining down upon them.

Shaking off the grisly memories, Patches went back to work. Slow hours passed as the long day wore on. The old man became drenched with sweat, more from the effort of staying perfectly still than from the rising desert temperatures. Once, his ragged shirt snagged on a barbed needle and the breath caught in his throat, his heart pounding wildly. Turning ever so slowly, it took Patches a good hour to cut himself loose. Too tired to turn about again, he simply continued on in the new direction. There was food in this part of the grove, too. There was always fruit here. It was why they stayed.

Then again, he added ruefully, maybe Suzette had caught a lizard today. Meat for dinner! She hadn't caught one since the last acid rain, over a dozen moons ago, but there was always hope.

Soon, another plump fruit was added to his bag and Patches snorted in mild annoyance at the memory of finding it. The leather bag seemed perfect for the job of harvesting. However, the faded lettering on the side read "Mail," or so his wife said. And since he was the male she reasoned it should be his job to gather the fruit, even though she was much smaller and could slip through the lethal needles with much greater ease.

They had argued over the matter, of course, but Suzette was the granddaughter of a whitecoat, and much smarter than him. He went into the grove to gather fruit while she went into the sand dunes with their crossbow to hunt rats and lizards. The rats weren't edible; the meat would put a man on the last train west.

"You playing or working in there, old man?" Suzette called from the direction of their hut.

Their home was a predark wag of some kind, the tires long gone and the engine a rusted lump block. But the body was a big box of metal that even the spring sandstorms couldn't get through, and with the door shut tight, the howlers couldn't seem to find them. If they kept very quiet.

"You back already?" Patches demanded suspiciously, craning his neck to try to get a glimpse of his wife. But the cactus completely blocked his view. "Hunting that bad?"

"That good!" she retorted happily. "Besides, it takes a long time to skin a lizard."

A lizard? Hot damn, meat for dinner!

"Then don't waste time talking to me. Get back to your cooking!" Patches laughed, returning to his own task. With luck, there might even be enough of the lizard to spare some for Trio.

His mind on dinner, the old man started to gather another plump globe when his rat-skin moccasins slipped on the loose rock in the sand. Jerking back to try to stay upright, Patches went motionless at the cool touch of a needle pressing against his wrist. *Nuking hell! If the tip broke the skin...*

Moving with glacial speed, the wrinklie moved

away from the needle until he was clear. Then he stood perfectly still for a few minutes, waiting for his heart to stop pounding. Idiot! Fools always die, that was rule number one. Stay alert, stay alive.

Taking a small fruit from the bag, Patches allowed himself a tiny bite as a reward. The juicy pulp was as sweet as canned peaches, but with none of the metallic aftertaste. Licking his cracked lips clean, Patches tucked the fruit away and began his slow creep toward the edge of the grove and his waiting wife. There was no fast exit from among the plants, so he might as well gather as much food as possible along the way.

Patiently, slowly, the one-eyed wrinklie worked his way through the grove of death, gathering the tiny harvest of life.

WITH THE RED DUST WIND blowing around him, the outlander stood on top of the rocky hill watching the four horsemen of the apocalypse ride along the horizon. Delphi almost smiled at the literary reference. Then he did smile at the idea that he was probably the only person in ten thousand miles who did know the allusion.

Except for Tanner, Delphi added, the smile quickly fading. Professor Theophilus Algernon Tanner. "Doc" to his friends. Experimental test subject No. 14 to his former captors.

High above the lone man, the polluted clouds in the fiery sky roiled and rumbled with endless thunder, the sheets of heat lighting cutting across the orange clouds like an executioner's ax, bright and sudden, then gone, leaving nothing behind.

Formerly a lush woodlands, this section of the wasteland was now only a barren desert of hard rock and windblown sand. However, in the secluded valley below this hill there was a small forest of succulent cacti. Two old people were living in a rusted courier service truck that hard-crashed at one time, and seemed to have learned how to safely harvest the edible fruit growing on the deadly cactus.

Reaching into a pocket, Delphi pulled out a cigarette and tapped the end on the back of his hand. A moment later the tip glowed red and he drew the thick sweet smoke deep into his artificial lungs.

It was a good location, Delphi admitted. The rad pits were few and far between, plus there was even a small creek of clean water trickling from a rent in the side of a nearby mesa. In comparison to the rest of the shattered world, this was almost an Eden, a lost paradise. Such a pity that somebody else wanted it, too.

Allowing the pungent smoke to trickle out of his nostrils, Delphi tilted his head at the sound of singing coming from the old woman skinning a fat Gila monster. Singing. Now that was a very rare sound these days. Or rather, happy singing was uncommon. The cannies often cut their victims in special ways to make the people scream in what they called death songs. But Delphi didn't approve of cannibals, and killed them on sight, despite the standing orders from his superiors at TITAN to never hurt a gene-pure norm. Orders were orders, yes, but there were limits to his tolerance. And to his grudging obedience.

Briefly he wondered if the people in charge of TITAN even knew that Department Coldfire existed. Wheels within wheels. A secret wrapped in a mystery, a conundrum lost in the fog, and everything cloaked in total denial. As far as Delphi knew, only about a dozen people in the world had ever known what his department was trying to accomplish—nine of them were operatives, and one was a test subject who had gotten away. Doc Tanner. But if all went well...

A movement on the horizon caught his attention and Delphi turned to focus his silvery eyes on the four horsemen galloping along the desert at full speed. Their bodies were bent low over their animals as they whipped the beasts on to greater speed.

So they understood wind resistance. Good. They aren't as stupid as they look, Delphi thought.

The four men rode without saddles or bridles, using only blankets and ropes. Although they were heavily armed, no sunlight glinted off the weapons in their hands, the ax blades and one blaster were wrapped in cloth to prevent any reflection that might reveal their presence too soon.

That was also good, Delphi admitted, removing the cigarette to exhale slowly. They were smart, but cautious. And the four moved well, working together as a unit. Excellent.

Hopefully these four coldhearts would be the end of his search. The previous thirteen groups Delphi had tested all proved to be useless. They were always too eager, too bloodthirsty or too stupid. Delphi needed operatives who could be trusted. Soldiers to be where he could not be, and to do what he was not allowed to do. Although perhaps the more colorful term of mercenary was more accurate for their job description, though "mercie" was the current term. From mercenary to mercy, what a misnomer! The irony was delicious.

Suddenly a blaster shot rang out and Delphi saw the old woman fall to the ground, blood pouring from her shoulder. All four horsemen began to whoop a war cry as the rest fired their crossbows. The flight of arrows missed the woman as she stumbled into the truck, the shafts stabbing into the loose sand all around her.

Crossing his arms, Delphi frowned. Was she seeking refuge?

Then the woman reappeared with her own crossbow and fired. The arrow just missed the lead rider and struck the second horse just below a shoulder. It was only a glancing blow, nothing of importance. But the animal abruptly slowed and began to shake all over, foam dripping from its mouth. The convulsing horse stumbled, throwing its rider. The big man with a bald head hit the ground hard but came up rolling, completely undamaged. But minus his crossbow. With an expression of incredible fury, he reared up, brandishing a steel knife.

As the coldheart charged straight for the wrinklie, she struggled to reload the crossbow. But by now the others had arrived. Swinging their weps like clubs, they rode past the woman, knocking the crossbow from her hands and smashing her about the face.

Giving a startled cry, the woman dropped to the ground. The big man with the knife descended upon her and started to hack wildly. Blood sprayed at every stroke. Trapped beneath the coldheart, the struggling wrinklie began to shriek once more, then went completely still.

Circling the box canyon, the three riders joined their companion. Stepping away from his grisly work, the big man gave a cruel laugh, then lifted up the patched skirt of the aced wrinklie.

Horrified, Delphi furrowed his brow. Surely they weren't going to rape the corpse!

Laughing, the man used the skirt to clean his gory knife, while the three riders trotted over to the fallen horse. The Appaloosa-colored mare lay motionless on the hot sand, its eyes wide in terror, foam flecking the black lips. There was no doubt that it was chilled. Turning away from the sight, the man with the knife spit on the aced wrinklie.

Just then, a spotted dog jumped out from the cab of the truck and raced toward him, moving incredibly fast on just three stubby legs. Crying out in surprise, the man dived out of the way. But the dog ignored him to stop alongside the corpse of its still master. The animal gave a little bark, as if waiting for a reply, then raised its massive head and snarled in bestial rage, baring sharp white teeth.

But the pause had been a mistake, and the riders feathered the dog with arrows. Mortally wounded, the bleeding animal limped toward the first man, yipping and barking. With his back to the grove of cactus plants, the man reached for his knife, but found the sheath empty. Lunging forward, the coldheart grabbed the dog by the throat and throttled it with his bare hands. The dying animal fought to the end, snapping its jaws and clawing for the hated enemy with its three stubby legs. But it couldn't reach the man, and eventually the dog eased its attack to go limp. With a guttural curse, the man tossed the corpse away and went looking for his dropped knife.

From his hilltop refuge, Delphi watched as the three men dismounted from their horses to spread out and recover the used arrows. Armed once more, the tall man with the bald head stood guard while the others looted the interior of the truck. Apparently there wasn't much of interest inside, but the four men shared the collection equally. One of them found a bag full of dried meat and started to take a bite when the smaller man with a ponytail shouted a warning and slapped it to the ground. As the others listened, he spoke harshly to them, and used a dirty handkerchief to retrieve the dropped jerky and put it back in the bag.

So that one knew about mutie rat meat, eh? Delphi chuckled and lighted a fresh cigarette. Better and better. Maybe these four would be acceptable after all.

Going over to the chilled horse, its former rider gently stroked the long neck, then walked over to the dog and began butchering it on the sand. One of the riders, a large man with a pronounced barrel chest, started a fire using the stack of tree limbs. As the dog was cut into joints, the barrel-chested man put the meat on a spit and began cooking.

Delphi watched with marked interest as one of them kept glancing at the grove of cactus plants, then finally loaded his crossbow and walked over to the edge of the prickly forest. From his high vantage point, Delphi could see the old man standing hidden inside the deadly grove, his thin shoulders shaking slightly from silent weeping. Ah, he had almost forgotten about the fruit harvester.

What will you do, old man? Hide and run away? Or try to avenge your fallen mate?

Tilting his head as if listening, the tall man raised the crossbow and fired. The wrinklie cried out and dropped to the ground. Resting the crossbow on a shoulder, the tall man turned his back on the grove and went to join the others.

"Now that was an excellent shot," Delphi whispered. Maybe his search was at last done with these four killers. Then he frowned. No, damn it, the word was chill, or ace, in this place. Apparently nobody used the word kill anymore, and abstract terms such as murder were completely unknown.

Down in the box canyon, the coldhearts separated without discussion, each to his own task. The bald man reloaded the black-powder blaster and stood guard, while the tall man and the fellow with the ponytail dragged the aced woman by her skirt over to the dead horse. Then both of the norms started digging a hole large enough to hold the two bodies.

A dry breeze whipped the loose sand around his polished boots, as Delphi nodded in satisfaction. Excellent. They weren't going to butcher the horse for meat because it had served them well—and they'd be sated by the dog—but they also understood that an exposed corpse would only spread the smell of death onto the wind and summon every mutie beast for miles. They were tough and smart. These four could kill strangers without hesitation, even helpless old men and women. Plus, they were loyal, but without being sentimental.

Raising his right hand, Delphi glanced at his palm and saw their names scroll along the nanotech monitor embedded into his pale flesh. John, Robert, Edward and Alan. The Rogan brothers.

Yes, these men would do fine.

Chapter Two

The tumultuous sky above the U.S. Virgin Islands was a solid bank of moving gray clouds. The roiling heavens split asunder as sheet lighting flashed on the horizon, leaving an ionized trail of purple across the ravaged clouds. Huge waves rose to white crests and crashed onto the rocky shoreline of the tropical island with triphammer force.

Dotting the white-sand beaches were the rusted hulks of predark warships, their massive metal forms lolling sideways, the armored hulls split open like dying animals to expose the complex interiors to the savage pounding rains. The corroded remains of cannons and missiles lay in plain sight and thousands of small blue crabs moved freely among the wreckage, consuming anything organic that was to be found: bones, boots and uniforms. Fluttering in the harsh rain, the faded remains of a flag hung from the end of the mast of a yacht. The cloth was bleached white, the crumbling keel covered with barnacles, the smashed hull charred badly in spots from numerous lightning strikes.

"This nuking storm is never going to end," Ryan Cawdor stated, staring angrily at the savage ocean.

Impulsively, the one-eyed man reached up to adjust the worn leather patch covering the ruin of his left eye. His own brother had taken the organ in a knife fight, and given him a long ugly scar on the right cheek to go with it. But Harvey was under the dirt now, while Ryan was still sucking air, and that was all that truly mattered. The ancient marks of violence on his face were merely two small memories among countless others decorating his hard, muscular body.

Ryan's hand rested comfortably on the checkered grip of his SIG-Sauer autoloader safely secreted in a hip holster. A large panga in a curved sheath balanced the deadly weapon on his other hip, and a bolt-action longblaster with a telescopic sight was slung across his wide, muscular shoulder.

"Yeah, hell of a storm," J. B. Dix agreed, lowering the brim of his fedora as if for a bit more protection.

A good foot shorter than his friend, John Barrymore Dix was wearing a mixture of predark clothing: U.S. Army boots, fatigue pants, OD T-shirt and a leather Air Force bomber jacket. His weapons shone like new, lovingly polished and oiled every night by the master armorer. An Uzi machine pistol was draped across his chest, an S&W M-4000 shotgun slung across his back. However, the munitions bag that carried his stash of plas and grens was hanging flat at his side. The canvas satchel was sadly empty, aside from a few loose rounds of brass and a couple of predark civie road flares of questionable service.

Standing in the access tunnel of the underground redoubt, the two men were safe from the touch of the deadly acid rain outside, yet they carefully watched as the chem-rich water fell like a yellow curtain across the mouth of the passageway. The acid rain was mixing with normal rain, orange clouds mixing with black in the violent sky overhead. They hoped it was a good sign for the future, that the acid rains were starting to fade away. But that didn't lull them into a false sense of security. In less than a minute, the deadly yellow rain could strip a shrieking man of flesh down to his raw bones, in spite of being weakened by the presence of the clean water shower. Of course the strength of the acid rain depended on many factors, one of which was a person's location in the Deathlands.

"Seen worse." Ryan grunted, rubbing his smoothly shaved chin. "But not by much, that's for sure."

With all that useless water outside, the salty ocean and the acid rain, it had seemed amazing to the companions that the machinery of the redoubt had been still able to deliver all the crystal-clear water the companions wanted the previous night. Everything Ryan was wearing, predark combat boots, denim pants and matching shirt, were in the unusual state of being thoroughly clean. Even his heavy fur-lined coat had gone through the wash, the accumulated blood, mud and food stains purged by the gently chugging laundry machines down on the fifth level. The companions were showered and shaved, warm and clean, a rare treat for anybody these days, and everyone except Krysty Wroth had had his or her hair trimmed.

"I hear ya," J.B. said, blinking at the tempest through his wire-rimmed glasses. "Dark night, remember that big wash in Tennessee? That was nothing compared to this mother of a storm!"

"And those ruins are so damn close," Ryan muttered darkly, tensing as if about to take a step outside. But then he relaxed and frowned.

"Mebbe if we had an APC we could chance a run," J.B. added, crossing his arms. "But I'd sure hate to be the first to try!"

Sullenly, Ryan grunted in agreement. Yeah, a man would have to be pretty damn desperate to risk going into the hellish downpour. Even this deep in the tunnel, the reek of the chem storm was thickly unpleasant. Only the cool breeze coming from the open door of the redoubt behind allowed them to stand this close to the reeking miasma of the rain.

Just then, a huge wave crashed on the rocky shoreline and lightning flashed again, the strident discharge briefly illuminating the area. In the blue light, just for a split tick, Ryan and J.B. could see the ruins of a predark city filling the eastern side of the island. Tall skyscrapers of glass and chrome were still standing downtown, apparently undamaged by the nuke war or the ravages of time. Five, six, some of them even ten stories tall! And scattered about the buildings could be seen the steady unblinking glow of electric lights. Powered by resilient nuke batteries, the old beacons were still giving a warning for airplanes that had ceased to exist a hundred winters earlier. There weren't many of the lights, only a precious handful. But the beacons shone bright as hope in the tropical storm.

Hunching his shoulders, Ryan frowned. But there was something there even more important than the electric lights. Surrounding the buildings on every side was a thick forest of green trees, the oddly shaped leaves shiny-slick from the combination of rain and ocean spray. Leaves, trees…it was almost fragging unbelievable, given the acid rain and all.

Standing in the access tunnel near the somber men was a beautiful redheaded woman leaning against the brick wall of the passageway, her left arm moving steadily as she brushed her teeth. The long hair hanging to her shoulders flexed and stirred against the direction of the breeze coming from the redoubt as if the crimson filaments were endowed with an independent life force of their own.

"Think we're still in Deathlands?" Krysty Wroth asked, once again dipping the toothbrush into an open box of baking soda.

Her cowboy boots shone with polish. She'd traded in her jumpsuit for denim pants and a crisp white shirt, found sealed in a plastic box. Around her waist was a police gunbelt supporting a .38 revolver, a deadly compact blaster that had seen many battles. But very few of the ammunition loops of the gunbelt held any live brass, mostly they were filled with spent cartridges waiting to be reloaded.

"Nuking hell, we could be anyplace," Ryan answered gruffly. "No way of telling through this drek."

He paused at a peal of thunder, then added, "But it doesn't resemble any area I've been to before."

Folding back his collar, J.B. touched the minisextant hanging on a chain around his neck. "And without a clear view of the sun, there's no way for me to get a reading. We might be in Europe or Brazil for all I know."

"That memo we found on the trash bin mentioned the Virgin Islands," Ryan reminded him, glancing sideways.

J.B. shrugged. "Yeah, but that doesn't mean this is them. Mebbe the guy was planning on going there when the world ended."

With a dissatisfied grunt, Krysty went back to scrubbing her molars. Thankfully, the pain wasn't too bad today. She had the beginning of a major cavity, and was fighting off the day when it would be necessary for Mildred to use pliers and yank the rotten tooth out by the roots.

How odd, death I can face, Krysty thought privately as she scrubbed diligently away. But not pain. Have I experienced so much that I am getting weak? Mother Gaia, help me, if that ever happens!

Suddenly the sound of boots rang on the concrete behind them, and the three companions turned to see a stocky black woman walk out of the redoubt.

"Aw, hell, still raining," Mildred Wyeth said angrily, contorting her face into a dark scowl. "Damn it, we're never going to get a sample of those trees!"

The short physician was dressed in Army fatigue

pants, an officer's white shirt and a loose denim jacket.
Clipped to the front of her canvas web belt was a
Czech ZKR target pistol, and draped over her shoulder was a canvas bag with the faded letters M*A*S*H
on the side. The predark field surgery kit had never left
her possession since she'd recently found it. The medicine was long gone, but the few surgical instruments
it contained were beyond price.

"Nobody's going anywhere, Millie," J.B. said
kindly, curling an arm around the woman's waist.
"Sorry."

Mildred moved a little closer to the Armorer, savoring the warmth coming off the man. "Who would have
thought it ever possible," she muttered, squinting into
the storm. "Plants, living green plants immune to the
acid rain!"

"Some new mutation, probably," Krysty said, tucking the toothbrush and box of baking soda into a pocket
of her bearskin coat. "Not every mutie wants to eat people."

"Just most of them." J.B. snorted in droll humor.

"Mebbe these plants feed off the rain," Ryan said
unexpectedly, his brow furrowed. "We know for a fact
that the predark whitecoats were working on making
things that could survive skydark."

The companions grew silent at that comment. They
had encountered the experiments of the crazy whitecoats before, the bioweps, genetically altered creatures
that could withstand certain hostile conditions, some
even surviving the deadly rads in the blast craters.

"If only I could get a sample…" Mildred muttered, easing away from her lover.

For a moment there flashed in her mind the legend of Johnny Appleseed from the eighteenth century, how he traveled across North America scattering apple seeds and creating entire forests of fruit trees, changing grasslands into beautiful forests. She could do that with just a few cuttings from the strange plants out there. Mildred would just have to plant a few sprigs everywhere the companions went. Oh, she would never see the final results, but someday, in a hundred years, the continent could be green again. Deserts turned into forests. It would work! The Deathlands could be defeated! If only…

Lost in her reverie, Mildred started forward when a gust of wind from outside washed along the access tunnel and she flinched at the sharp stink of the rain. If only we had an APC, she thought. But would even an armored personnel carrier, or a U.S. Army tank be safe in this downpour? Probably not.

"They are as unreachable as the stars, madam," Doc Tanner rumbled, his voice sounding deeper than the thunder.

The four companions turned to see their other friends amble through the open doorway of the redoubt. With nobody standing in the way anymore, the multiton door slid closed, the titanic slab of metal easing into the adamantine wall as silent as a knife in a dream.

Tall and lean, Doc Tanner was dressed as if from another century with a swallowtail jacket and frilly shirt. But the impression of gentility was beguiled by the strictly utilitarian .455 LeMat handcannon on his gunbelt, the grip of the massive black-powder weapon worn from constant use. Tucked under one arm, Doc carried an ebony walking stick with a silver lion's head for a handle. Hidden inside was a rapier of the finest Toledo steel.

"NASA has sent probes to the stars, you old coot," Mildred snapped irritably.

"Indeed, madam, so you say," Doc continued unabated. "But they brought nothing useful back that we know about, and so shall it be again this time, I am afraid. We can look, but not touch."

"Just like in vid," Jak Lauren stated, brushing back his snowy-white hair. The albino teenager was wearing camou-color clothing. His jacket was a deadly weapon, as bits of razor-sharp metal had been sewn into the fabric here and there. If anyone grabbed him by the collar, the person would lose fingers. A number of leaf-bladed throwing knives were hidden about his person, and a massive .357 Magnum Colt Python was holstered at his side.

"What vid was that?" Ryan asked over a shoulder.

Jak shrugged. "Dean and I saw in another redoubt. *Victory for Victoria,* mebbe. Skinny man standing in snow look through window at fat baron in a gaudy house stuffing self with food." The teenager frowned. "Not follow story after that. Boring, but only vid that still played on comp."

"*Victor/Victoria,*" Mildred corrected him with a wan smile. "Yes, I wouldn't think that a musical comedy would be to your liking."

Jak arched an eyebrow. "Why say? Like music vids. Always lots of food, pretty girls."

"And that, my young friend, is as good a description of paradise as any in these draconian days." Doc sighed. Slipping the walking stick out from under his arm, Doc strode to the very end of the tunnel, stopping only a few feet away from the damp spot on the floor where the rain had been blown inside.

"Most people, I believe, shall never see, a poem as lovely as... What was that line?" Doc whispered softly, then spun fast. "Ryan, we simply must have those trees! Surely something can be done. That city cannot be more than a league away. Maybe less."

A league? "We wouldn't last ten feet in that," Ryan stated gruffly, hitching up his gunbelt. As the lightning flashed once more, the big man turned his back on the storm. "Come on, we've wasted enough time. Let's go."

"But..."

"Cut the gab," Ryan snapped impatiently. "We agreed to wait a day for the storm to end. Well, it's still here and the day is gone. Time to go. You zero that?"

"Yes, my friend, I understand," Doc rumbled in acquiescence. "It has, indeed, been a full day, and fair is fair."

Going to the entrance of the redoubt, Ryan tapped a code into the armored keypad set into the doorjamb.

There was a brief pause, then the huge black portal ponderously slid closed. Ryan gave one last look toward the nameless city and its surrounding forest. *Trees that could withstand the acid rains.* With a grimace, the one-eyed man turned and entered the redoubt. The rest of the companions stayed close behind.

As the group walked along the entranceway of the redoubt, they heard the massive nukeproof door slide shut with a subdued boom of compressed air.

Running stiff fingers through his black hair, Ryan tried not to let his anger show. Shitfire, this base had been a triple zero. No food, no ammo, no exit. Oh, sure, all of the basic stuff in the base worked, everybody had washed their clothing and soaked in hot baths until they felt clean again. Hell, J.B. had even found a pair of decent socks, and Doc had located a tiny plastic vial of silicon lube. The stuff was made for comp printers, but worked just fine on the sword hidden inside his walking stick. But that had been the lot. The rest of the redoubt had been stripped clean, bare to the walls. And worse, their food supplies were getting dangerously low again. The companions had six days' worth of MRE packs left. After that, they'd be eating stewed boot if they couldn't find anything in this redoubt. There really was no other choice. The companions would have to jump again, whether they wanted to or not.

Exiting the passageway, the somber group crossed the vast parking garage and retrieved their backpacks. All around them, the painted lines on the concrete floor of the garage were empty and waiting. This was where the staff of the redoubt would have parked over a hundred wags: civie cars, motorcycles, Hummers, APCs, trucks and even the occasional tank. But the garage looked brand-new, as if it had been built and then abandoned. There wasn't a single tool on the pegboard racks behind the workbenches, only the tape outlines of where each tool should be placed after it had been used. The drawers were empty, the supply closet vacant, and there wasn't a single stain in the grease pit. Even the fuel storage tanks were bone-dry, the seals on the new pumps intact and unbroken.

As the companions crowded into the spotlessly clean elevator, J.B. hit the middle button and the cage swiftly descended to the center level of the redoubt. When the doors parted with a sigh, the companions trundled along the corridor and dutifully checked the straps on their backpacks and the loads in their weapons. The corridor was lined with doors on each side, and when the companions had arrived the previous day, every one of them had been closed and locked. One at a time, each door had been carefully opened, only to reveal a deserted room or office, without so much as a piece of furniture or a candy wrapper on the carpeted floor. It had taken most of a day for them to go through the entire base before finally admitting that the place was as empty as a mutie's pockets. This wasn't the first redoubt they had found in this condition, but it seemed to be happening more and more often. Was somebody looting the underground forts besides themselves? It was a sobering thought, and one that left the companions apprehensive and uneasy. The redoubts had been their lifeline more times than could be counted.

Reaching the door for the control room, Ryan pushed it aside and strode past the banks of humming comps. This was the heart of the redoubt, or more correctly, the brain. These were the machines that controlled the mighty fission reactors deep down in the subbasement for the life support systems, air-recycling, water sanitation, the freezers, the front door and the all-important mat-trans units. Without the comps, the base instantly became an airless tomb.

After passing through the anteroom, Ryan drew his 9 mm SIG-Sauer blaster before further pushing open a door to a room surrounded by armaglass. As the vanadium portal swung aside, he gave the chamber a quick scan with his weapon at the ready. The companions weren't the only people who knew about the secret mat-trans units, and more than once they had found evidence of others just leaving the gateways.

However, the entry chamber was uninhabited. With his blaster leading the way, Ryan warily stepped through the doorway into the next room. The hexagonal chamber was a deep red in color, sprinkled with flakes of a hundred colors. The gateway chamber in each redoubt was a different color, supposedly for the purpose of identification. But if there was a chart to show what the colors meant, they had never found such a thing. The wall of this chamber vaguely resembled the terrazzo flooring used in most government buildings and major shopping malls, only with a much greater depth of color.

"It's clear," Ryan announced, holstering his blaster.

The others filed into the chamber, past Ryan. As he closed the door behind them, something rolled out of the shadows at the far end of the control room. With its two metallic antennas quivering, the boxy device rushed to the main computer and urgently extended a probe to quickly connect with the master control panel.

HALFWAY ACROSS THE WORLD, Delphi suddenly felt a vibration inside his left wrist, and flipped his hand over to see a message scrolling along the palm monitor. Excellent! The prey had been found at last!

Quickly typing instructions on his bare wrist, Delphi waited impatiently as the droid accessed circuits undisturbed for a century. Come on, come on…

Now, a roster of available redoubts was displayed. Frowning at the list, Delphi chose one at random. It was a base he had never been to before because it was on the Forbidden list. But this was a day for breaking the rules, and once the process had started he saw little reason to be cautious now.

"Get ready, traitor," Delphi muttered, his heart quickening to the thrill of the hunt. "Here I come…."

RYAN CHECKED to make sure that everybody was safely inside the unit and seated on the floor.

"Ready?" he asked.

"Yeah, ready as we'll ever be," J.B. mumbled, removing his glasses and tucking them safely away in a pocket. The jumps always hit the companions hard, often sending them to the floor puking out their guts from the shock and pain of the instantaneous transference. Doubling over, J.B.'s glasses had once bent when they flew off his face and someone had stepped on them. It had taken him days to repair the frames, and he subsequently swore that sort of triple-stupe mistake would never happen again. His backup glasses were functional, but unflattering.

"Once more into the breach, dear friends," Doc said in that singsong quality that meant he was quoting something.

Mildred merely snorted at the Shakespearean reference, and Ryan slammed the door shut. As he hurried to sit next to Krysty, a fine mist swirled upward from the disks on the floor to engulf the companions, mists from the ceiling descended upon them. They braced themselves for the expected snap of tiny sparks to crackle over their exposed skin. But instead, there was only a soothing warmth that spread through their bodies as the thickening mist began to swirl faster with every heartbeat.

What in nuking hell? Ryan thought in confusion. Something didn't feel right. After so many jumps, there was a certain "sameness" that the companions had come to expect. So anything out of the norm was suspicious. Was the mat-trans broken? Were they being sent somewhere, or worse, were they going nowhere?

Mebbe the computer was having a malfunc. Nuking hell, he had to stop this jump!

Frantically trying to stand to reach the door, Ryan felt the floor drop away and he knew that he had been just a split second too slow. The jump had begun.

As gently as falling through a cloud, the terrified companions descended into the artificial forever of the matter transfer, and vanished from sight.

Chapter Three

But even as it started, their fall came to a relaxing halt and the companions were able to watch as the electronic mists faded away to leave them unharmed and unruffled in a new mat-trans unit.

"Son a bitch," Ryan muttered, drawing his blaster without conscious thought.

"We not dead," Jak mumbled, sounding slightly shocked. With a gesture, a throwing knife slipped out of his sleeve and dropped into his waiting hand.

"No," a hoarse voice whispered.

Turning, the companions saw Doc cringing against the wall, braced as if for a blow. His hands twisted the silver-lion's head on the walking stick, exposing a few inches of the stainless-steel sword hidden inside the hollow sheath.

"You okay?" Mildred asked, reaching out a hand.

"Not again," Doc rambled, eyes darting about madly. "No hardship means a controlled jump. That means they...they have found me. *Operation Chronos has found me again!*"

"Are you sure—" Ryan began slowly.

Suddenly a new light came into Doc's wild eyes and

his face went pale as he closed the stick with a solid click. "No, by the Three Kennedys, they haven't found me, the bastards have found *us!*" he gasped. "But they can't have you. I wouldn't let them get their hands on you, too!"

Whipping out his ebony stick, Doc lunged toward Krysty. Even though the sword stick was sheathed, the redhead twisted aside. But it hadn't been necessary. The bottom of the stick missed her by inches, as intended, and stabbed the Last Destination button on the control panel.

Recoiling at the sight, everybody braced for the torture of instantaneous travel, but nothing happened. The mat-trans unit didn't respond to the signal from the emergency LD button.

"Nuke me," J.B. said hoarsely, putting on his glasses. "Well, that never happened before! We should have gone right back to last redoubt. The LD button has never failed to work before!"

"I don't think it failed now," Krysty said, her hair flexing unhappily about her tense features. "I think we're not being allowed to leave."

"You mean, that maybe Doc is right," Mildred returned, "and that this might have been a controlled jump?"

"Could be, yes."

"Mutie shit," Jak muttered. "Just malfunc."

Ryan slid the Steyr SSG-70 longblaster off his shoulder and worked the bolt.

There were only four 5-round clips remaining for

the Steyr, but the neckered-down brass packed a hell of a lot more punch than the fat 9 mm Parabellum rounds in the SIG-Sauer. Anything could be behind that door, from a squad of armed whitecoats to a sec droid hunter. Once, very long ago, Ryan had chilled a cougar with his bare hands, and the Deathlands warrior would rather do that again than face a sec hunter droid even if he was armed with a predark bazooka. The damn machines were almost impossible to stop once they started coming after a target.

"If you're feeling nervous," Ryan added, "then start us on a jump." The man was listening hard to the redoubt, getting the feel of the place, the gentle hum of the air vents, the muffled noises of the water pipes and high-pitched whine of the fluorescent lights overhead. Everything seemed normal, not a thing was different or strange, and that was scaring the nuking hell out of the warrior.

Keeping his handcannon level, Jak reached for the keypad and tapped the LD button to no result.

"Okay," the teen stated angrily. "We trapped."

"No, please, we must jump again," Doc begged, dropping the ebony stick. Pushing the others aside, he hit the controls in a fast sequence. "We cannot let them find you…you have no idea what they can do…will do to you…we have to leave right now!"

Mildred reached out a hand, but the time traveler dodged out of the way.

Closing a fist, Doc started pounding on the keypad. "Work, damn you, why will you not work!"

The startled companions exchanged worried expressions at the outburst, but before they could do anything Doc slipped to the floor and started to weep uncontrollably, his face buried in his hands.

The sight of such weakness shocked Ryan for a moment, then he suddenly understood, and felt like a fool. It had to have been all of those jumps that had scrambled Doc's brain and made him so forgetful. Pieced together from various conversations, Ryan knew that the agents of Operation Chronos had trawled dozens of people from the past and brought them into the twentieth century. But Doc was the only person to ever survive the process sane. The predark whitecoats had nearly turned the poor Vermont scholar inside and out trying to solve that vital mystery.

Then one day, Doc was deemed too much trouble to deal with and was sent into the future, to arrive in Deathlands. The agents of Operation Chronos immediately regretted the decision and took off after him in hot pursuit. But there was no way to track the old man in the vast wasteland that was the Deathlands. The agents of Chronos had long ago given up the chase as impossible, but Doc kept running. Finally he wandered, dazed and confused, into some serious nuking trouble with a lunatic baron before accidentally encountering the companions.

"Sweet Jesus, look what they've done to him," Mildred said softly. Kneeling by the sobbing man, she tenderly stroked his hair. "Doc might annoy the hell out of me at times, but he's no coward. The old coot has proved that a thousand times. The horrors he must have endured at the hands of those whitecoats...."

Doc had once claimed that Operation Chronos was a subdivision of Overproject Whisper, the group that built the redoubts and invented the mat-trans units. Was that, in fact, true? Were there perhaps other unknown groups prowling through the redoubts of the world? There was very little about the bases that they knew for certain. Except that everybody they met was usually an enemy.

Kneeling, Jak handed Doc the dropped sword stick, and the trembling scholar hugged it tightly to his heaving chest.

"Sorry," Doc whispered in a hoarse voice, tears on his cheeks. "I seem to have...lost control there for just a moment. I will be fine in a trice. Really, I will...."

"Theophilus," Ryan said, stumbling over the name.

Sluggishly, Dr. Theophilus Algernon Tanner looked up in shock at Ryan's scarred face. It was the very first time he could recall the man using his Christian name.

"If those nuke-sucking whitecoats are coming, then we'll face the entire fragging lot of them together, old friend," Ryan stated, offering a scarred hand.

A long minute passed as Doc breathed deeply, the color slowly returning to his features. Then the silver-haired gentleman reached out and clasped Ryan's hand in a powerful grip. It always caught the one-eyed man by surprise that Doc looked sixty, but really was only in his late thirties and as strong as a horse. His mind had been damaged but not his body, and not his fighting spirit.

"Together," Ryan said, helping the man to stand.

The two stood for a moment, hands tightly clasped.

"Together, my friend," Doc vowed, his voice as strong as ever. As he released the hold, he softly added, "And please allow me to apologize for my earlier… lapse. You see, I—"

"Frag it," Ryan said bluntly, glancing over his shoulder at the closed door. "It don't mean drek."

"Doesn't," Krysty corrected him. "And anybody who says they've never been scared is a liar. Gaia knows we've all been there."

"Fuckin' A," Jak chimed in, slapping Doc on the shoulder.

"Nuke them till they glow, then shoot them in the dark," Mildred added impulsively.

The rest of the companions chuckled at that, but Doc threw back his head to roar in laughter. "Indeed, madam! Well said. Cry havoc, and let loose the dogs of war, eh?"

"Oh, stuff it, you old coot."

"Well, as long as we're not going anywhere," Ryan said grimly, striding across the chamber's cold floor, "then we better get ready for company. Get hard, people. If the whitecoats do come for us, it's going to be bloody."

"I hear ya," J.B. stated, leveling his Uzi machine pistol and walking across the chamber to join his old friend. The fleeting moment of camaraderie was past. Back to the grim business of staying alive.

This new mat-trans unit was the same as every

other, a hexagonal room made of seamless armaglass, with small hidden vents near the ceiling, one door with concealed hinges, and an operating lever to open it. The only difference was the color. Nothing else.

As the rest of the companions prepared to leave the mat-trans unit, J.B. eased the M-4000 shotgun off his shoulder and passed the weapon to Mildred. Tucking away her ZKR revolver, the physician expertly racked the scattergun to chamber a 12-gauge cartridge.

"I wonder why they haven't hit us already?" Krysty said, checking the load in her wheelgun. Five rounds, two of them predark, three reloads. All of the soft-lead ammo had been split into dumdums to maximize their destructive power. The slugs would go in like a finger but come out like a fist. But only on flesh. Against a machine, or a biowep, they were about as useless as spitting.

"Why? Not need," Jak growled, swinging out the cylinder on his weapon and removing some of the brass cartridges. "Where go? Trapped like rats in shitter." The Colt Magnum blaster had the unique attribute of being able to hold both .357 rounds and .38 rounds, which doubled the kind of brass he could use. Jak really couldn't understand why everybody didn't use this type of blaster. Just made good sense.

"Any grens?" Doc asked, checking the load in his LeMat. The black-powder weapon had nine chambers in the main cylinder, but only six were loaded at the moment. In the bulging pouches of his gunbelt, Doc had plenty of black powder, and .455 miniballs, but it

had been a long time since he had found any fulmi-
nating mercury "nipples" needed to ignite the Civil
War blaster. Without those caps, the deadly LeMat
was reduced to nothing more than an oddly shaped
club.

"No grens, plas or pipebombs," J.B. replied, setting
the firing switch on the Uzi to full-auto. "If we happen to run into a sec hunter droid, just aim at the eyes
and stay out of the reach of its blades."

"Good luck with trying that tactic," Doc commented.

Removing the last .38 bullet, Jak tucked them carefully into a jacket pocket, then thumbed in the more
powerful .357 rounds. If they were facing whitecoats,
he wanted a sure chill with every stroke of the trigger.

"Here," Mildred said, pulling a plastic bottle out of
her med kit. She splashed some of the homie shine on
a strip of cloth normally used for a bandage, then tied
it around her mouth.

"In case they try to use sleeping gas," she said, wetting another strip and passing it along. "I don't know
how much it'll help, but this should buy us a little
time."

Everybody took a mask and tried not to make a face
as the sharp smell of the homebrewed alcohol filled
their nostrils.

Keeping a close watch on the door, Ryan checked
his weapons one last time. He had three full clips for
the SIG-Sauer, plus four for the Steyr longblaster.
After that, it would be hand-to-hand with the panga.

In preparation, Ryan loosened the knife in the leather sheath on his belt.

"Okay, I'm on point," Ryan stated. "Jak and Krysty, cover me. Mildred and Doc, hold off as backup. J.B., you bring up the rear." The one-eyed man had almost issued instructions to Dean, too, but his son had left the group a few months ago. His absence left like a ragged wound deep inside Ryan, but pain was part of life, and he accepted it as such. Only the dead felt nothing.

As the other companions moved into positions, Ryan pressed an ear against the door, listening for the sounds of any movement beyond. The silence was thick and heavy. Gingerly, he ran his hands along the jamb, searching for boobies. J.B. then stepped forward and ran a small pocket compass along the surface of the metal. The magnetic needle didn't quiver once to indicate a hidden magnetic switch or mass proximity fuse.

Mildred tried to snort at the sight of J.B. studiously moving the tiny plastic compass along the door frame. The compass was a recent acquisition, found inside a cereal box in the ruins of a predark convenience store. It was a toy, nothing more, laughably inaccurate compared to a Boy Scout compass or a military-issue model. However, most of the predark compasses the companions found had been demagnetized by the EMP blasts of the nukes that burned down civilization. Incredibly, the toy still worked, and that alone made it invaluable.

"Looks clean," J.B. said hesitantly, tucking away the precious compass and stepping back. "At least, no traps that I can find."

Out of the corner of her eye, Mildred noticed that Doc's hands were shaking a little as he set the selector pin on the LeMat.

"Sure that you can shoot straight?" she asked bluntly.

"Shoot? Absolutely," Doc replied, assuming a firing position with the Civil War revolver. "As for straight, that is another matter entirely."

"You know, they may not have attacked us yet," Krysty said unexpectedly, "because they don't know we're here."

Thoughtfully sucking at a hollow tooth, Ryan considered that notion. "Fair enough. Let's try for a night-creep first," he suggested, inspecting the SIG-Sauer's acoustical silencer. "We go soft and silent. No blasters until absolutely necessary. Jak, get ready."

The albino teenager holstered his Colt Python and flexed both hands. Leaf-bladed throwing knives slid from inside his camou sleeves. He flipped the blades once in the air, catching them by the handles, then nodded. "Ready."

"Triple red," Ryan ordered, advancing to the door and pulling the lever. As the door swung aside, he slipped into the anteroom, then the control room with his blaster leading the way.

Nobody was in sight.

Whistling softly, Ryan waited as Jak and Krysty

moved into the control room. Then the three companions quickly spread out so that they wouldn't offer a group target for any snipers. Moving in unison across the control room, the three listened hard, but couldn't hear a thing except for the soft mechanical hum of the giant, wall-spanning comps, and their own harsh breathing.

Reaching the opposite door, Ryan whistled and the other companions entered the control room, their blasters searching for any possible dangers. Staying close to the rear, Doc seemed uneasy, the scholar constantly switching his black-powder blaster from hand to hand to dry his palms on a pant leg.

"Nothing here—" Ryan started to say, then abruptly spun around and fired from the hip. Across the room something exploded in the shadows under the main console, spraying out bits of plastic and wiring.

Advancing slowly, Ryan scowled at the smoking device, wondering what the hell it could be. Then his eye went wide as the pieces lying on the floor began to ripple through an array of colors to finally match the pattern of the floor. But the effect only lasted a few moments before the smashed electronic circuitry of the broken device gave an audible click and the plastic faded into a neutral beige.

"Shit," Jak muttered, tucking away a knife. "Seen lizard do, but…machine?"

"That is a probe droid," Doc said, the wall vents gently sucking away the acrid smoke rising from the debris. "A robotic hunter for Operation Chronos."

"Like dog?" Jak asked.

"Exactly. It is just one of their many…toys," Doc finished with a sour expression. Standing straight, the scholar looked around with a scowl. "But if I recall correctly, a probe droid is for true emergencies only. By gad, where are we, their headquarters?"

"Does the place look familiar?" Krysty asked, frowning, her long hair coiling tightly in response to her tense nerves.

"They all do, dear lady," Doc said angrily, thumbing back the hammer on his handcannon, only to gently ease it down again. "I always assumed that was done deliberately as another of their endless defenses. If an enemy force jumped in, they would still have to waste precious time making sure they were at the right location before attacking."

"The way we do," J.B. said unhappily.

"Exactly."

"Shit."

"Any chance two of them?" Jak asked urgently, watching the shadows in the corner for any suspicious movements.

Askance, Doc raised an eyebrow. "Two? Good Lord, no. You're looking at about several million dollars' worth of advanced robotics lying in pieces on the floor. They never even sent one of these after me before. I learned of them only by accident when I was crawling through an air vent in one of their insufferable prisons."

"That during an escape attempt?" J.B. asked, reaching into a pocket and pulling out half a cigar. He tucked the stogie into his mouth and chewed it into place.

"During one of my many attempted escapes," Doc corrected, his face going neutral. "They caught me that time, and…punished me severely. Then the scientists decided I was too much trouble, and, well, you know the rest."

"A hunting probe," Ryan growled, rubbing his chin. "If the whitecoats didn't send one after Doc, then we can damn well guess what it was looking for this time."

"Us. The whole nuking group," Krysty said grimly, her hair flexing in agitation. "I thought there had been something watching us in the redoubts for a while."

"Well, they found us at last," J.B. agreed, tilting back his fedora.

"No, they haven't," Mildred corrected, kneeling alongside the broken machine. Fumbling among the wreckage, she lifted a flexible cable into view. "See this? It's a USB cable, and I don't see any radio inside the probe."

Moving the end of the cable closer to the master control board, she point at a USB port set about a foot off the floor. "That's where this goes," Mildred stated, holding the cable near the input jack, then she moved it slightly farther away again, just to be safe. "So maybe this droid knows we're here, but it never got the chance to tell anybody."

"Mebbe," Ryan said darkly, his face unreadable. "On the other hand, if they were here, they'd be using the sec vid cams in the walls and not some fancy robot."

"So the whitecoats must be in another redoubt."

"Yeah."

"Makes sense," Krysty agreed, looking at the hallway door. "But there's only one way to be sure."

Crossing the control room, Ryan went to the exit and yanked open the door. The outside hallway was empty, all of the doors along both sides of the passageway closed as usual. The floor was spotlessly clean, the air from the vents warm and clean, smelling ever so slightly of disinfectant chemicals. Personally, Ryan would have been more comforted by a few scorch marks from explosions and some decaying corpses. A redoubt full of dead he could comprehend. Why the predark mil had removed all of the supplies and left the bases stripped bare had never made any nuking sense.

"Stay triple red, people," Ryan commanded, proceeding along the hallway. "Chill anything that moves against us."

Chapter Four

The desert night air was cool and sweet, scented with the flowers from the nearby cactus grove. The roiling polluted clouds overhead had broken, allowing the crescent moon to shine a silvery light across the landscape, turning the box canyon a stark black and white. The only source of flickering color came from a small cookfire. Squatting around the crackling flames, the four Rogan brothers licked their fingers and wiped greasy mouths on grimy sleeves.

Hawking and spitting on the ground, Alan Rogan cut loose a satisfied belch. "Now that was a good dog." He chuckled, scratching his belly. "Don't you think so, bro?"

The elder Rogan scowled at his brother. "Shaddup," John snapped, tossing a gnawed leg bone onto the fire. The impact stirred up a cloud of red embers that lifted into the air and danced about to float away on the breeze.

Alan frowned. "Hey, I was only—"

"Go water the horses," John ordered, licking his fingers clean. "This shithole didn't have anywhere near the number of people we were told. We ride at dawn."

"Hopefully to a ville with some sluts," Robert groaned in a horrible, barely human voice. The large bald norm then broke a bone in two and sucked out the dark marrow. A dirty silk scarf was wrapped around his throat, almost hiding a long puckered scar that completely encircled his neck, the classic telltale mark of a hangman's noose.

Dropping the pieces of bone into the flames, Robert rubbed a greasy hand across his bald head and smiled ruefully. "Been a long time since I showed some gaudy slut the ceiling," he croaked. "Too goddamn nuking long."

"We still have the shovel," Alan said, jerking a thumb at the darkness outside the nimbus of the firelight. "I'm sure if ya really wanted to you could still find the wrinklie. Mebbe the ants haven't eaten much of her good stuff yet."

John snorted a laugh at that, but Robert lowered his head as if about to charge like a rampaging bull. "I'd do you before a rotter," he growled in mock warning.

Without any expression, Alan gestured and knives slipped from his sleeves into each hand. "Any time you wanna try, big brother," he replied softly, turning the blades slightly so that the feathered edge of the steel reflected the reddish light of the campfire.

Moving back slightly, Robert raised his hands as if in surrender, and Alan now saw that one fist was holding a pipebomb, the fuse smoldering and spitting sparks.

"Come to Poppa," the bald man snarled, gesturing closer.

"Cut out the fragging drek and get to work," John ordered, dismissing them both with a wave of his scarred hand. "Alan, the horses. Robert, go spell Ed."

Grinning broadly, Robert licked two dirty fingers and pinched out the fuse, then pulled the string from the pipebomb and tucked it away into his voluminous jacket. The bomb itself went into a pouch on his belt. "Sure thing. No prob, bro," he croaked, and stood to walk away into the night.

"Why is he always on my ass like that?" Alan complained, tucking the blades away again. "I was only joking around."

"He's bald as a rock, and you got a ponytail down to your balls. Figure it out yourself," John said, sneering contemptuously. "Now water the fragging horses, or do ya wanna try that knife trick on me?"

Angry, Alan started to shoot back a taunt, but then saw his elder brother's face and thought better. John was in charge of the gang because he was the smartest, there was no denying that. But also because the other brothers were terrified of him, and there was no denying that, either.

Forcing a smile onto his face, Alan strolled away into the night, kicking at the sand to raise little dust clouds as he moved toward the remaining horses.

As Alan vanished into the gloom, Edward appeared and sat on the ground. Taking a haunch of roasted meat from a rock near the crackling flames, the barrel-chested man started tearing off pieces like a wild mutie. In spite of the cool evening, he had his shirt mostly unbuttoned, and a grisly necklace of shriveled "trophies" hacked off his enemies was clearly visible.

Lighting a handrolled cig, John sucked in the sweet dark smoke of the zoomer, nodding in satisfaction that he finally got the mixture of tobacco, marijuana and wolfweed just right. A little too much of the tobacco and you didn't get zoned. Too much of the mary and it tasted like drek. Some people chatted about shine as if it had tits and an ass, but weed was the cure for what ailed a man.

"Any more?" Edward demanded as a question, trying to crack the bone apart for the marrow. But the bone splintered in his enormous hands and he cast the greasy mess into the flames. The glowing charcoal sputtered and started to give off thick smoke.

"Nope, we each got a quarter," John said, letting the zoomer dangle from his lips. "Share and fair alike, as always, bro."

"I'm bigger," Edward complained, thumping a fist onto his hairy chest. "I should get more."

"Would, should, could. Don't mean shit to me."

"Ain't fair," Edward rumbled dangerously.

Blowing out a smoke ring, John debated getting rough, when there was an unexpected flash of light. For a split tick, he thought he was having a vision from the drugs in the cig. But then the light came again, softer, whiter, and rapidly expanded to fill the entire box canyon as if it was high noon.

"Son of a bitch!" Edward cursed, reaching behind his back and pulling out a short hatchet. "What the hell is this?"

Dropping the zoomer, John rolled backward off the rock he had been sitting on and grabbed the blaster from his bedroll. Clicking back both of the hammers on the double-barrel longblaster, the elder Rogan looked frantically about. The weird light completely filled the box canyon, all the way up to the rocky ridge above. But it seemed to stop there, as if it were a pool filled with shiny water.

Now how the nuking hell can that be possible? You can't carry a bucket of light! he pondered.

Glancing down, John felt his gut tighten at the sight of no shadows on the ground, not even behind the rocks set around the crackling fire. Experimentally, he tilted a boot, and there was no shadow underneath. That was impossible. Mother-nuking flat-out impossible. Light had to come from somewhere. Air didn't fragging glow! He paused at that. Actually, yes, it did, but only at the bottom of blast craters thick with rads.

Looking for his brothers, John saw Robert standing over by the truck with the loaded crossbow in his hands, the bald man's eyes darting about madly. Alan was walking toward the horses...

John blinked and looked again. No. Alan was backing away from the horses, and there was an outlander strolling toward them!

The fellow was slim and pale, and his hair was slicked down flat to his head, the soft face as smooth as a young girl's. The outlander was wearing some sort of white outfit, kind of like a robe that draped from his shoulders down to the silvery moccasins. Oddly everything he wore was spotlessly clean, damn near looked brand-new. Now, that was weird enough, but even more bizarre was the fact that the outlander didn't have any weapons. There wasn't a sign of a blaster, blade or a bomb. Yet he was smiling broadly as if he had just won a big hand of poker in a friendly ville.

"Feeb," Alan whispered, raising both knives.

"Loon," Edward retorted, leveling his wep.

"Hello, Rogans," the outlander said with a friendly wave. "My name is Delphi, and we should talk."

"Frag that," Robert snorted, frowning at the use of their family name. "Take him!"

Grunting in acknowledgment, Edward instantly fired, the arrow from the crossbow flying straight for the outlander. But a few feet away from the man, it smashed apart in midair, as if hitting a brick wall. The broken pieces tumbled to the sand.

What the nuke? With a snarl, John raised his blaster and cut loose with both barrels, just as Alan jerked his hands forward. But the spray of birdshot and the knives impacted the same invisible barrier around the outlander and ricocheted away.

"Done yet?" Delphi demanded, impatience flashing in his silvery eyes.

This damn mutie is laughing at us, John realized in cold shock. Laughing at the Rogan brothers! As if we were children playing games!

Just then a large rock slammed onto the shield, or whatever it was, around the outlander, and shattered into pieces. Breathing heavily from the exertion, Edward stared at the stranger more in puzzlement than fear.

"Let me know when you're done," Delphi said, sounding annoyed. "We have business to discuss."

Muttering a curse, Robert threw the pipebomb. It landed behind the pale outlander and detonated, the blast throwing out a death cloud of sand, pebbles and iron shrapnel. The entire grove of cactus shook, dropping a hundred pieces of fruit, and just for a single moment there was clearly defined shape around the outlander, some sort of glass ball or transparent sphere. Then the force of the blast faded away, the rolling noise echoing into the open desert.

Not glass, John realized, squeezing his weapon in frustration. But some kind of shield. There was an invisible wall as hard as iron around the newcomer. Was this some form of mutie mind power or predark tech? His bet would be for tech. But there was no way to be sure.

"Enough," Delphi said, making a gesture. A blue light engulfed Edward and the big man dropped to the ground as if poleaxed.

Rushing over to the sprawled form of his brother, Robert saw that the huge chest was still rising and falling. His brother was only knocked out, but Robert had no doubt that the outlander could have aced Edward if he wanted. Shitfire, the outlander could chill them all at his whim.

"What…who are you?" Alan asked in a strained whisper. His hands flexed as if reaching for more of his hidden knives, but no blades came into sight.

Tilting his head slightly, Delphi gave a half smile as if enjoying a secret joke. "I have already told you my name," he said in an even tone. "And as of this moment, you now work for me."

"Yeah?" Robert growled, notching another arrow into the crossbow. "What if we don't wanna?"

Turning slightly, Delphi stared hard at the big man. "You have no choice," he replied, making a gesture at the horses.

Lashed to the bumper of the predark truck with knotted lengths of old rope, the three animals shook violently all over, then slumped to the ground with red blood gushing from their slack mouths. The brothers stared in horror at the chilled horses and slowly turned back to Delphi. The outlander was still smiling, the expression tolerant, almost amused. It sent a shiver down their spines.

"Don't fret about your beasts. You shall receive exemplary compensation for this assignment," Delphi continued smoothly, tucking his slim hands up the loose sleeves of his robe. "Transport, reconnaissance, heavy ordnance…"

Having no idea what half of those words meant, John said nothing, his fingers aching to reload the longblaster, but knowing it would be seen as a sign of fear. Forcing his hands to obey, the elder Rogan rested the weapon casually on a shoulder. In any negotiation, especially when the other fellow held all the blasters, a man had to stay cool and calm. If all you had was words, then try not to use any. That always threw off the other fellow and helped even the balance a little.

Chuckling softly, Delphi seemed to be extraordinarily pleased by the lack of action for some reason, as if a pet had done a particularly clever trick and deserved a treat.

"Okay, you got our attention," John stated, taking a step forward. "What's the job, Whitey?"

"Something has been lost," Delphi said, anger crossing his pale face for the first time.

"And ya want us to find it." Alan snorted in disdain. "Easy enough. What is it that you're looking for?"

"Salvation," Delphi growled as a strange humming filled the air and white mists suddenly appeared to engulf the four coldhearts. "Salvation!"

Clawing for their weps, the Rogan brothers felt themselves drop into the ground, as the desert disappeared, replaced by an infinite panorama of burning stars.

TWO HOURS LATER the companions were halfway through their inspection of the redoubt.

Starting at the bottom, the companions did a fast recce on the humming nuclear reactors behind the thick walls of unbreakable glass, although Mildred sometimes called it Plexiglas. Then came the life support rooms, where the hundreds of pumps and filters kept the base clean, warm and uncontaminated from the rad-blasted hellzone outside the redoubt.

Everything was functioning normally and seemed to be in perfect working order. But all of that changed once the companions reached the storage and barracks areas. On that level, the redoubt was as bare as the last one they had visited. Every room, every closet, was completely empty. Even the beds in the barracks were devoid of mattresses and pillows. There wasn't a pencil in a desk drawer or a roll of wipe on the toilet.

"If the last redoubt never got its supplies delivered or was stripped clean," Ryan muttered, walking along a corridor, "then this one was still being built."

"You can load that into a damn blaster," J.B. agreed, his fingerless gloves tight on the Uzi machine gun. Some of the sections seemed unformed and still rough along the edges. It was just little things, doors out of plumb, keypads off kilter, details that nobody would ever notice, unless they had been in a hundred other redoubts.

Pausing at the next closed door, the companions took combat positions. With Jak keeping cover, Krysty pushed open an unlocked door. The walls were unpainted, and in the next room the floor was only bare concrete, without even linoleum tiles in place.

"Never seen so much nothing," Jak drawled angrily, the heavy Colt staying tight in his grip.

"I agree with your double negative," Doc rumbled pensively, easing down the hammer on his massive LeMat pistol. "This is most curious indeed."

After checking out the entire level, the companions went to the elevator and pressed a button for the cage. When it arrived, they checked for traps, then piled inside. Using the tip of his SIG-Sauer pistol, Ryan started to press the button for the garage at the top of the redoubt, but then paused and hit the button for the next level upward instead.

"Impatient, lover?" Krysty asked, tilting her head.

With a tiny vibration, the elevator started smoothly upward.

"Worried," Ryan answered honestly. "Sure. If the blast doors are remotely locked by whitecoats, then we're prisoners."

"Trapped without food," Mildred said, frowning as she leaned against the bare metal wall. "Damn, I hadn't thought of that possibility."

"Starvation is a mighty slow way to be chilled," J.B. noted, removing the unlit cigar, only to put it back in place once more.

"Eat blaster first," Jak stated coldly, tilting his head slightly forward so that his snowy hair fell across his face, hiding the features.

"Then again, maybe Operation Chronos only wants us trapped long enough to get weak, and then they capture us alive," Ryan guessed, voicing his dark thoughts. Why fight an enemy at full strength when you can wait a few days and clamp on the slave chains without resistance?

"Alive," Jak growled. "Like for experiments?"

"Sure. Why not?"

"Nuke that," Jak muttered, tightening the grip on his blaster.

Just then, the elevator gave a musical chime and the doors parted. As the companions stepped into the corridor, they became instantly alert. In spite of the warm breeze from the wall vents, there was a dry chill in the air. This was something they had encountered only once before, a long time ago.

"Just like that redoubt in Zero City," Ryan said as a warning, bringing up the barrel of the Steyr longblaster. The two blasters were rock-steady in his hands.

"Just as long as it isn't another Alaska," Krysty added grimly, her hair tightening in response. The old madman in charge of that redoubt had a lot of funny ideas about breeding, and the companions had been triple glad to leave that place far behind. A recent visit had spooked them all.

Easing along the corridor, the companions saw only bare, blank walls until taking a corner. A huge steel door stood at the far end of the next passageway, the metal-and-ceramic surface touched with patches of snowy frost along the edges. There was no doubt that this was the source of the cold.

"A deeper," Jak stated, stopping in his tracks.

Ever so slowly, Ryan gave a nod. Yeah, definitely looked like a Deep Storage Locker. He remembered the first time the Trader had told him and J.B. about such things. Just another legend, they'd thought at the time, only this one happened to be true. A deeper, a Deep Storage Locker, was a special vault filled with dead air—inert gases, Mildred called them—and then made colder than winter ice. The combo was supposed to keep everything from aging, suspended animation was the whitecoat term. The ammo would be live, the canned food fresh, the blasters in perfect condition, the medicine still potent. The companions had found only one of these before in all of their travels, and that deeper had been guarded by a sec hunter droid.

"How much C-4 do we have, John Barrymore?" Doc asked, using his left hand to pull back the massive hammer of the LeMat. It locked into place with a solid click, the single-action revolver now ready for immediate firing.

"Plas? Not a scrap left," J.B. said around the cigar. "I'm down to road flares and bad language."

"Mebbe we should check the blast doors first, lover," Krysty said hesitantly. "Just in case we have to run."

There was logic to that, Ryan had to admit. But there was also no denying the fact that somebody had rigged their last jump, and he'd sure as hell feel a lot better about that with some spare brass jingling in his pocket.

"We keep going," the one-eyed man growled, hefting his longblaster. "But spread out more. We'll need space if there's a sec hunter droid inside the locker."

"What we'd need is a freaking bazooka," Mildred muttered under her breath, shifting her grip on the scattergun.

Proceeding warily along the corridor, the companions took their time and checked every room along the passageway in turn, making sure there wouldn't be any surprises left behind them if the locker proved to be guarded.

Once past the last door, the companions gathered in front of the icy portal and studied it carefully. There was a painted curve on the floor to show the swing of the armored slab, and a keypad on the wall offered easy access.

Holstering the SIG-Sauer, Ryan started forward, but the moment he crossed the painted line, a siren started to bleat, and a red light began to flash above the icy locker.

"Warning!" a mechanical voice blared from the ceiling, rattling the tiles. "Warning! Intruder alert! Intruder alert! All security personnel to Section 9! Repeat! All security personnel to Section 9!"

Swinging the Steyr upward, Ryan blew the speaker apart with a single shot and blessed silence returned to the hallway.

"Stupe machines," J.B. commented, using the barrel of the Uzi to push back his fedora. "Can't tell the difference between—"

The Armorer never got to finish the statement as there came a soft hiss and the corridor behind them was suddenly closed off by a grid of steel bars that dropped from the ceiling to violently slam onto the floor. If anybody had been standing under the gate, he or she would have been mashed into bloody pulp.

"Good thing…" Ryan started, then felt cold adrenaline flood his body as a second sigh sounded. On impulse he dived forward. While in the air, something smacked into his left boot, sending the man tumbling. He hit the wall hard, gritting his teeth against the pain shooting through his ankle. Nuking hell!

Looking backward, Ryan scowled at the sight of a second gate sealing off the corridor, the other companions now trapped between the array of steel bars. Caged like rats.

Her hair flexing wildly, Krysty started to speak, but then jerked her head toward the ceiling as panels swung open and a Vulcan minigun dropped into view. The deadly rapidfire was covered with armored cables and enclosed in cascading ammo feeds.

"Drop your weapons!" a voice boomed through the speaker mounted on the Vulcan, the volume almost deafeningly loud. "Drop your weapons, or die!"

Wasting no time, Ryan ignored the pain in his ankle and stood up to grab with both hands the electrical wiring attached to the bottom of the minigun. He pulled with all of his strength, and the smaller wires easily snapped free. But the larger cables were sheathed in flexible metal and only bent under his weight.

"Alert! Alert!" the speaker loudly announced as the robotic weapon swiveled, trying to target its attacker. The barrels began to spin and the Vulcan cut loose, the armor-piercing rounds chewing a path of destruction along the floor. The tiles disintegrated, spraying out rubbery pieces in every direction and exposing the hard concrete floor underneath. But hanging suspended directly underneath the Vulcan, Ryan stayed just outside its range.

Ricochets flew everywhere, several of the slugs zinging off the steel bars of the security cage holding the companions prisoner. In response, J.B., Krysty and the others shoved their blasters through the cage and hammered lead at the shielded control cables of the deadly rapidfire. The incoming barrage tore the flexible casing apart, and Ryan dropped to the floor with two fistfuls of sparking wires. Instantly the deadly Vulcan stopped firing and the spinning barrels slowed until they went completely still, the metal ticking as it radiated away the tremendous heat of the brief barrage.

"Anybody hurt?" Ryan demanded, tossing away the circuitry. As the wires hit the floor, miniature computer chips broke off from the ends. He had never seen tech like that before. Curious.

"No blood in sight," Mildred reported, glancing quickly about as she slung the shotgun over a shoulder. "Damn, that was lucky!"

"Lucky my ass," Krysty retorted, grabbing the steel bars and trying to shake them. The metal grating didn't budge. "We're locked in tight, and you're trapped between this and the door."

Walking the perimeter of the cage, J.B. studied every section. Steel bars closed off both sides of the corridor, and more had slid into existence along the walls when he hadn't noticed, probably when the Vulcan was blasting.

"There's no way out of this that I can see," J.B. said in disgust. "There's no lock to pick or keypad to short out."

"Pity young Dean is no longer with us," Doc said slowly, biting a lip. "He could have easily slipped out between these bars."

"What good would that do?" J.B. demanded. "We need to liberate everybody, not just one of us."

Jak dropped his backpack and started to remove his boots, then the rest of his clothing. In a few moments the teenager was stark naked and forcibly throwing himself at the smooth bars. Sheer momentum got Jak halfway through before he became stuck. Wiggling, the teenager gained another inch, but then stopped, unable to advance or to retreat.

"Exhale deeply," Mildred directed. "Contract your chest."

Grimacing unhappily, Jak did as requested as J.B. put two hands on the teenager's shoulders and started to push. Both of them began to curse from the exertion. Then, with a lurch, Jak came free and tumbled down the corridor.

"Well done, lad!" Doc stated with a sharp nod. "The legendary Count of Monte Cristo could not have done better!"

"Now what?" Jak demanded, rubbing his scraped chest. The albino's skin was already starting to show a few bruises.

"Head for the garage and find a crowbar," J.B. suggested as Krysty passed the teenager his clothes, the Colt and the gunbelt.

"I don't think a crowbar will lift these," Ryan said with a dark frown. "And there's no way you could drive a Hummer down here to try to ram the bars, even if there is one on the garage level."

"Got no choice," Jak said as he dressed. "Best light candles." Turning, the teen started at an easy lope down the corridor toward the waiting elevator.

"Use gloves if you got any!" Ryan shouted through cupped hands.

Pausing at the corner, Jak waved in understanding, then dashed out of view. A moment later there was a soft chime from the closing elevator doors.

"Candles?" Mildred asked in confusion, then her eyes went wide. "Oh hell, he's going to try to cut the power to the whole redoubt!"

"Think that will also open the Deep Storage unit?" Krysty asked tersely, reloading her revolver.

Frowning deeply, Ryan turned to stare at the giant portal. "Sure as frag hope not," he muttered, sliding off the Steyr and checking the rotary clip inside the long-blaster. "But we better get hard, just in case."

Long minutes passed as the companions prepared for a close-quarter firefight. If the locker door automatically opened and a sec hunter droid came rolling out, Ryan was the only person in real danger. The droids weren't armed with distance weps—that they knew about, at any rate. Protected by the thick steel bars, everybody would be safe from the deadly war machine, except Ryan. Trapped between the cage and the locker, the one-eyed man would only have a few yards in which to try to outmaneuver the kill bot. His only defense would be the combined firepower of the trapped companions.

"All for one, and one for all," Doc muttered in a singsong manner.

"Do we look like the Three Musketeers?" Mildred snorted rudely.

"There were four of them, actually," Doc corrected with a smile.

"Oh, I know that. Keifer Sutherland, Oliver Platt, Charlie Sheen and the other guy."

Doc blinked. "What in the name of God are you babbling about, madam?"

Suddenly the ceiling lights flickered and went out.

"Here we go," Ryan growled softly as the air vents slowly stopped blowing and a deafening silence filled the subterranean mil base.

Chapter Five

A flicker of light stabbed into the darkness as Ryan applied the flame of his butane lighter to a wax candle stub. As the wick caught, he set the candle near the wall and the reflected illumination cast flickering shadows across the people in the cage.

Reaching into her med kit, Mildred pulled out a survivalist flashlight and worked the small pump on the handle to charge the old batteries, then she flicked the switch and the device gave off a weak yellow glow. She had gotten the flashlight from a baron quite a while back as a reward for saving his son's life. The battery was rechargeable, but there were no spare lightbulbs and the last bulb was starting to die. However, the flashlight still gave off ten times the power of a wax candle.

As Krysty and Doc also retrieved butane lighters and got more candles going, J.B. fumbled in his munitions bag and pulled out a predark road flare. Twisting off the cap, the Armorer scraped the magnesium nubbin underneath and the stick sputtered, almost seeming to go out for a moment. But then the chemical flame returned bright and strong, the flare giving off a tremendously bright reddish flame, along with a great amount of dense sulfurous smoke.

"Good thing the fire detectors aren't working," Mildred joked, shying away from the sputtering flare. "Jeez, that thing stinks!"

"Still works, though." Reaching through the bars, J.B. tossed the flare outside the cage and the thick smoke rose upward to pool on the ceiling, the dark fumes flowing along the white tiles like a living thing.

"Okay, let's see if we can hoist this," Ryan said, grabbing two of the bars in his big hands. The man twisted his fists on the smooth steel to try to get a good grip. "Ready?"

Just then there came a loud gurgle, as if some horrible beast had been awakened. The companions froze, then gave a nervous laugh when they realized it was merely the water pipes draining inside the walls.

"All together now," Ryan ordered, bracing his boots on the floor. The man tensed his legs and back. "One…two…three!"

The companions heaved with all of their combined strength and the gate slammed into the ceiling it lifted so easily and without resistance.

"Son of a bitch," J.B. said, releasing his grip. "The grating must use a mag lock! With the power gone, it's dead easy to open."

Stepping into the cage, Ryan let the gate slide back down, then crossed over and experimentally lifted the other side with a single finger.

"Come on," Ryan said. "We need to find something

strong enough to use as a prop under these. With the juice turned off, we can't use the keypad to get through the door of the locker. Besides—"

There was a metallic crash from somewhere and bright lights came on overhead, flooding the corridor with rods of sharp illumination that marked the exit door to the stairwell and a couple of empty wall niches that probably should have held fire extinguishers.

"Yeah, backup power," Krysty said, casting a glance at the closed door. "Sometimes I forget that the redoubts clean and repair themselves. The main power will come back on anytime."

Leaving the candles on the floor, the companions headed for the stairs. Along the way, J.B. pulled out his butane lighter and lit the end of his cigar. He knew that Mildred really disliked the habit, but there was a rare time when a man needed a good smoke. Ah!

Their blasters at the ready, the group started up the stairs with Mildred giving J.B. a stern disapproving look that the Armorer did his best to totally ignore.

Reaching the top level, Ryan checked for any traps, but found the entrance clear. Pushing open the partly closed metal door with the barrel of his handcannon, Ryan stepped into the garage and looked around, his scarred face slowly smiling.

The emergency lights were working here, too, casting a zigzag pattern of illumination. He could see that the entire floor was filled with mil wags, all of them parked in a wild jumble over the neat lines on the concrete flooring. Several of the vehicles seemed to have collided near the exit tunnel, their hoods crumpled and headlights smashed. But the rest of the wags were intact, including several Hummers and a LAV-25 armored transport. He didn't stop to wonder why such a barren redoubt had so many vehicles in its garage.

Moving past the maze of vehicles, Ryan went to the wire enclosure of the storage room, shot off the padlock and yanked open the mesh door. Inside were dozens of spare tires and burnished steel rims in assorted sizes, along with stripped engine blocks, cases of headlights, sealed pallets of nuke batteries, and everything else needed to keep the fleet of mil wags in proper working condition. Along with about a dozen heavy-duty jack stands.

"Everybody take a pair," Ryan directed, grabbing a couple of the heavy stands. "These things will hold about half a ton. Those gates can't be putting out too much more pressure than that, or else the floor would crack. A dozen of these should do the job."

"Sure hope so," J.B. muttered judiciously, slinging the Uzi across his back to take a pair of the bulky triangular stands. The things were damn heavy, but even with his backpack he could handle the weight.

Holstering their weapons, Doc and Krysty each took two stands. Awkwardly, Mildred managed to lift one, cradling it to her chest and obviously struggling to keep from dropping it.

"Set it down, Mildred," Ryan directed, starting for the elevator. "One of us has to stay armed."

Grunting from the strain, the predark physician

thankfully set down the jack stand, and straightened her back. "No problem there," Mildred wheezed, pulling out her ZKR revolver and thumbing back the hammer.

Back in her own time period, before she got frozen in a cryogenic chamber and woke up almost one hundred years later, Mildred had rated in the marksman class with the target pistol. That took a lot of skill, not brute force. Besides, physicians didn't need big muscles.

Returning to the cage on the lower level, the companions easily lifted up the powerless gates, lined up the jacks on the floor and set the gates into place.

"I shall go inform Jak," Doc offered, pulling out the LeMat before heading for the stairs.

The other companions waited impatiently. But pretty soon, the fluorescent lights strobed in the ceiling and then came back on at full force. In gradual stages, the emergency lights died away and the two gates along the walls crashed back down into position. However, the row of jack stands across the corridor only groaned as two main gates tried to forcibly descend once more. There came a soft whining noise from the ceiling and the jack stands groaned, but nothing else happened.

"Bet that intruder alarm would be howling like crazy now," J.B. said, taking out the stogie and blowing a smoke ring at the smashed ruin of the speaker.

"You can load that into a blaster," Ryan agreed, warily studying the cage and stands. For just a second, they seemed to quiver, but then it was gone. Probably just a trick of the fluorescent tubes. Damn things pulsed in the weirdest way sometimes.

"Those appear to be holding," Mildred said slowly, worrying a lip. "What do you think?"

Pivoting, Krysty kicked the steel bars as hard as she could with the heel of her cowboy boot. The metal rang from the impact, but nothing more.

"Yeah, that'll hold," J.B. said, puffing in satisfaction.

Inhaling deeply, Ryan grunted at the news, then lay down and crawled along the floor between two of the jack stands, across the cage and out the other side. Standing, he waited for the others to pass through. A few minutes later Doc and Jak arrived, and slipped through to join the rest of the companions.

"Good work," Ryan said.

"No prob," Jak muttered.

Going over to the broken Vulcan minigun, J.B. checked the enclosed feed and yanked out a cotter pin. Something disengaged and the Armorer removed the rectangular tube of louvered steel. Removing a cartridge from inside, he inspected the brass, then used a knife to cut off the lead bullet and poured the powdery contents of the round into his palm.

"We can use this," J.B. stated, fingering the granules. "Even if the deeper has been looted, at least we'll have some reloads. Two, mebbe three hundred rounds."

"Good," Jak said, standing. Then the teen pulled out his Colt Python. "Let's open door."

As the companions approached the frosty portal, a wave of cold swept over the group, but this time it only generated a sense of excitement. Pulling out some tools, J.B. did a pass over the door jamb and declared it clear of boobies and sensors.

Without a word, Ryan went to the keypad and tapped in the usual sequence that opened blast doors that led to the outside world in all redoubts. The indicator on top of the keypad flashed red, yellow, then green. A series of heavy thuds banged around the rim of the door as the internal locks disengaged. Next came a powerful sigh of working hydraulics, and the truncated door noisily disengaged to ponderously swing aside. With a mighty exhalation, a bitterly cold mist flowed out to block the sight of the companions for a few anxious moments. Ryan and the others tensed impatiently as the warmth of the corridor slowly dissipated the chilling fog.

The interior of the locker was pitch-black.

Pulling out his last road flare, J.B. started to scratch it alive when lights rippled across the ceiling of the locker. Row after row of bright tube lights came on until the inside of the deeper was fully illuminated. The glare was almost painful.

"Bingo," Mildred whispered softly as dozens of packing crates came into view. Dozens, hell, there were hundreds!

The locker was stuffed full of stored equipment, the plastic shelving along the walls packed solid with military cases designed for long-term storage, and air-tight ammo drums, fifty-five-gallon barrels that held a lifetime of brass for most villes. Wooden crates wrapped in thick plastic sheeting were stacked to the ceiling in huge pyramids, and banks of cabinets formed orderly rows along the spotlessly clean floor.

Staying in combat formation, the companions eased into the locker, their weapons searching for targets. Just because a sec hunter droid didn't come rolling out instantly, didn't mean a hundred of the machines weren't waiting for them somewhere.

"Blasters, food, grens," J.B. stated, reading the serial numbers off the sides of the assorted containers. "This place has a hundred times more supplies than the Alaskan redoubt!"

"Thank Gaia! And no madman in charge trying to ace us," Krysty added in a pleased tone of voice. A smile touched her full lips.

"Okay, everybody stay in pairs," Ryan directed, shouldering the longblaster. "Just because something didn't try to stop us at the door, doesn't mean we're safe. Hunt for grens first. After that, go for ammo. Then food, you all know the list."

Placing two fingers into his mouth, Jak gave a sharp whistle. "Got 'em!" he announced, pulling out a knife and slicing through the tough plastic sheeting around a stacked tray of mil grens. The clear polymer resisted, but the teen finally hacked through and started to yank the resilient sheeting aside.

Gently lifting off the top tray, Jak beamed in delight at the neat rows of colored spheres resting in gray foam cushioning. The color of the stripes said these were high-explosive grens, steel shrapnel. Excellent! Those were the best kind to find because the grens could be used for everything from chilling muties to fresh-water fishing. Mildred had once told Jak about a type of mil gren that had used plastic shrapnel that could not be seen on an X-ray machine. Weapons designed to maim, not chill. The concept was beyond foul, somehow it felt almost cowardly.

"Dark night, now we're talking," J.B. said happily, removing his cigar and grinding it out on the floor before approaching the massed explosives.

Grinning eagerly, Jak started passing out the grens. Everybody tucked several into their backpacks and then a few more into their coat pockets. When the rest of the companions were done, J.B. went to the next tray down and added a dozen more spheres to his munitions bag. The weight of the grens felt reassuring after being absent for so many months. The Armorer always felt vulnerable when he was out of explos. There were few problems in the Deathlands that couldn't be solved with the adroit application of high explosives.

"Ammo next," Ryan stated, brushing back a strand of his long black hair.

"I'm going to hunt for medical supplies," Mildred countered, taking off at a run among the stacks of crates.

"Stay in pairs!" Ryan barked.

Shrugging his bag into place, J.B. said, "I got her

six." Checking his blaster, the Armorer followed after the stocky woman already racing into the maze of green metal cabinets.

Cutting open the seal on a sturdy trunk, Krysty hesitantly lifted the heavy lid. Inside were shiny metallic envelopes.

"MRE packs!" the woman shouted, raising a Mylar envelope. "Hundreds of them! Enough for an army!"

"Excelsior!" Doc cried, lifting a burnished aluminum box.

Laying the container on a worktable, the scholar began pulling out sealed plastic jars of grainy black powder, and clear plastic jars of fine-grain gray gunpowder, the slick material appearing almost oily as it moved. There were several boxes of lead rods for melting into bullets, and even a small assortment of premade balls. None of them were the right caliber for the LeMat, but Doc had enough for a couple of reloads already. He wisely took some extra lead, and all of the copper percussion nipples that he could find.

"Why not get real blaster?" Jak said, looking over the man's shoulder. He pointed to an open cabinet filled with cardboard boxes. "Boxes of .44 wheelguns over there. Plenty of brass, too."

"Let the artist choose his own brush," Doc rumbled, his hands busy purging the spent chambers of the LeMat as a preliminary to reloading. "This has served me well, and I seek no other mistress."

This was an old argument between the two, and the teen shrugged as always at the impossibility of convincing the scholar otherwise. Going to a row of cabinets, Jak began opening each door and checking inside for anything good. There were a lot of mil uniforms, combat boots, gas masks, night goggles and a few items that he couldn't readily identify.

Have to ask Mildred about those later, Jak decided, closing the door to continue his recce of the locker.

"Besides, being able to fire nine rounds without stopping, this has startled more coldhearts than I wish to remember," the time traveler muttered to himself. For a split second Doc recalled the day when he'd faced that wolfweed dealer in the dusty streets of the burning New Mex ville. Doc had known the other fellow was out of range and so he'd fired the LeMat six times, then only fanned the hammer a couple of times to make the Civil War blaster click loudly. Grinning in triumph, the dealer had charged straight at Doc and raised his ax for a fast chill. When the dealer got within ten feet, point-blank range, Doc had raised the LeMat and fired three more times, ending the coldheart's regime of terror forever.

"Nine is fine," Doc chuckled, closing the fully loaded cylinder with a solid, satisfying click.

Prying a board free from a packing crate, Krysty whistled softly at the sight of the brand-new HK G-11 caseless rifles nestled inside. The plastic boxes alongside obviously contained spare ammo blocks. There was a score of them, perhaps more. The woman started to reach for one of the angular rapidfires, then frowned and closed the lid. Dean Cawdor had really liked this weapon, in spite of its faults. Actually, the caseless rapidfire only had a single flaw. It worked too efficiently. All by himself, Dean had once stopped a pack of muties with the dire weapon, only to discover that the rapidfire was empty. The boy had used the entire ammo block of a hundred rounds in only a few heartbeats. The priceless weapon had been abandoned in the street, useless without a replacement block.

"Find something?" Jak asked, draping a bandolier of ammo clips across his leather jacket. The teen was holding a MP-5 submachine gun, repeatedly pulling the bolt to work out the stiffness of the predark spring. The gun had been properly packed in anticorrosive gelatin, but that was easy to wash off with the accompanying solvent.

Wordlessly, Krysty shook her head and continued to search. She truly missed Dean. Such a pity that he was gone forever.

"Well, I'll be damned," Ryan whispered with a smile, lifting a peculiar-looking gren into view. A whole case of implo grens!

This was the find of a lifetime. Not even Mildred had any idea how the things worked. The tech involved was far beyond her understanding of twentieth-century science. The burnished gray sphere looked like a standard mil gren, but instead of a C-4 explosion, or thermite blast, it somehow generated a massive gravity field for a split second that destroyed anything caught within the collapsing zone. An implo gren could stop a tank, and would smash a sec hunter droid like the angry fist of God.

Judiciously deciding between weight and mobility, Ryan finally took four of the implo grens and added a fifth to his jacket pocket. For the first time since they had arrived, the Deathlands warrior allowed himself to relax slightly. Whatever came their way now could be aced. Norm, mech or mutie, nothing could stand against an implo gren. That was good enough. He wanted more—who wouldn't?—but the first hard lesson learned in the Deathlands was that having too many weps was just as bad as not having any. It made you slow, and a single moment wasted trying to decide what to fight with could easily be the deciding factor between living another day and ending up in the hot belly of some slavering mutie beast.

Slowly, the long hours passed as the companions expertly combed the Deep Storage Locker for all its precious treasures. Carrying bundles of equipment, they started forming neat stacks in a clear area near the open door and began to organize the materials into piles. Calling a halt for food, Ryan passed out some MRE packs, and the hungry companions devoured the predark meals of beef stroganoff with sour cream and noodles, with the usual nut cake for dessert. It was just food, nothing more. But there was also coffee, wonderful coffee for dessert. Greatly refreshed, the companions returned to the work of choosing supplies and weapons. New backpacks were found to replace their old patched ones. Mil bedrolls were exchanged for the civie versions dug out of a collapsed department store in a distant land.

Neat piles of ordnance were formed, and decisions made. Some of the simpler blasters were set aside as possible trade goods, in case there was a ville nearby. But for once, the companions didn't need anything from the outside world. There was food and clothing galore, plus enough weps and brass to fight the most powerful baron in the land if necessary. Ryan took a new pair of combat boots. A case of U.S. Army socks and underwear was greeted with cries of delight, and everybody helped themselves. Placing aside her med kit, Mildred sat on a box of landmines to exchange her socks right on the spot. The stiff cloth was cast aside, and the new soft socks were gratefully pulled on, her toes wiggling almost sensuously in the clean cloth.

After a couple more hours, the companions broke for dinner, MREs again; chicken stew with dumplings. It was better than the beef stroganoff, and the packs were licked clean.

Fed and fully armed for the first time in a long time, the companions left the Deep Storage Locker, closing the door in their wake. It had been a long day, but there was still a lot to do before sleep could even be considered.

Chapter Six

As the terrible throbbing in his head slowly eased away, Edward awoke groggy on a grassy field, with the bright sun high overhead. Forcing himself to move, the man groaned from the herculean effort. His head hurt, his gut was roiling, and every bone felt as if it had been removed, then shoved back in again.

"Well, it's about nuking time you came around," John snapped irritably, walking closer. The elder Rogan was holding a tin cup full of something that gave off wisps of steam and smelled incredibly like coffee. "We were starting think you'd gone on the last train west, ya lazy bastard."

It took Edward a few times to get his throat working. Blind norad, he felt as if he'd been run over by a baron's war wag!

"Where—" Edward broke into a rough cough and tried again. "Where the frag are we? And is that coffee?"

"The Zone," Alan said as he joined his brother and passed him a canteen. "And yes, it is, bro. But this will do you more good."

Eagerly taking the canteen, Edward really didn't

care what the contents of the container was, as long as it was wet. He all but ripped off the cap and poured the cool water down his parched throat.

The other Rogans said nothing, waiting for their brother to get fully awake. There was a lot to discuss.

Finally lowering the canteen, Edward sighed then gave a loud belch. "Okay, where are we?" the man repeated, scowling at his younger sibling. "The Zone, ya said? But that's halfway around the rad-blasted world!"

"Not quite," Robert croaked in his mangled voice, the sound vaguely similar to a chuckle. "But close enough."

Weighing his thoughts, Edward took another long drink from the canteen. "How fragging long have I been out?" he demanded curiously.

His face revealing nothing, Alan crossed his arms. "Since last night," he said. "About half a day."

A single day and they had reached the Zone? Rising stiffly to his feet, Edward took another swig from the canteen and warily looked around. Desert, sand, cactus were all gone. Now the brothers were in a grassy field, a glade really, with a smoky campfire crackling away in a small pit. An iron pot was sitting on a flat rock near the flames, its dark watery contents bubbling softly and giving off the aroma of black coffee. Tall green trees surrounded the glen and there was the sound of splashing water from somewhere nearby. A concrete building of some kind stood nearby. Then the man froze as his gaze fell upon the machines.

Bikes! Four big bikes, unlike any two-wheelers he had ever seen before.

The sleek motorcycles were sitting in a pool of the bright sunlight, all of them painted a deep satiny black, the chrome trim edging the frames shining mirror-bright. Shuffling closer, Edward couldn't take his sight off the beautiful vehicles. He had seen a lot of different bikes when he'd traveled with the Hellrider gang in the Southwest, but those were patchwork monsters held together with baling wire and duct tape. These machines gleamed as if brand-new, and they were huge, much larger than any two-wheeler he had ever seen.

Pouring some of the water from the canteen into a palm, Edward scrubbed his face and walked straight past the cookfire, heading for the bikes. Every thought of the hot coffee was gone. Wags...

The predark machines were in perfect condition, he saw, abso-fragging-lutely perfect! Strapped across the rear fender were large cargo pods, molded to the frame as if installed there when the bikes were manufactured before skydark. The lids were open on the pods, and Edward stared inside to see rolls of clothing, self-heat cans of food, knives in sheaths, boots and grens. The loot of a ville! A baron's ransom!

"Where and when did we steal those?" Edward asked, running a hand across the cushioned leather seat of a bike. It was the softest thing he'd ever felt, and blacker than midnight.

"Advance payment from Delphi," John said, joining his brother at the bike. "We each get one."

The barrel-chested man frowned. "Delphi? What did the triple-damn outlander hit me with anyway, a gren?"

Tucking both thumbs into his new gunbelt, John shrugged. "Who knows," he replied honestly. "There was a flash of light and you dropped like a wrinklie with his knees blown off."

"No shit," Edward growled, feeling a touch of fear flicker in his stomach. "So…uh, how did we get here?"

John shrugged again. "Beats the living shit outta me, bro."

"Here, this is for you, little brother," Robert said, thrusting a longblaster at the puzzled man.

"More jack from Delphi," Alan added with a humorless smile, pouring fresh coffee into a steel cup without any dents.

Taking the complex wep, Edward couldn't believe his eyes. It was a rapidfire, and also in perfect condition! Not a scratch or a fleck of rust on the metal. Just like the bikes. There were two barrels, two triggers, and a crosshair scope on the top. He'd never seen anything like them in his life.

"Delphi called them an M-16/M-203 assault rifle combo," John said, reaching out a finger to point. "You press that to get the ammo clip out, or back in."

Clumsily moving his big hands along the blaster, Edward did as directed and released the clip. Pulling it free, he gasped at the full load of predark brass. Thirty greasy rounds.

"The big thing underneath is a gren launcher," Robert explained, lifting up a 40 mm shell for display.

"You slide that part forward and shove in this, then close before firing."

It shot grens as well as lead?

"And that Delphi guy just gave us this?" the man whispered in awe. Then he curled a lip. "Wait a tick, you called it 'advance payment.' Okay, what does he want done?"

"We gotta chill a guy," Alan said, draining the cup in his hand.

Hoisting the longblaster, Edward snorted in amusement. "That's all?"

"Nope. We also capture some wrinklie alive, and haul his ass back to Delphi," John growled, sounding annoyed. "And alive is the big word. If we chill the wrong person, if the wrinklie gets aced by mistake, Delphi is gonna…." John turned away. "He…showed us some stuff while you were out."

"Trust me, bro, we do not wanna screw this up," Robert urged in his broken voice.

Pulling back the arming bolt of the rapidfire, Edward let it snap back with a satisfying crack. "Chill a man and captured a wrinklie alive. Big nuking deal." He chortled, starting to adjust the canvas sling for his large shoulders. "And for that we got the bikes and blasters? Delphi is a feeb."

"No," John said in a low and dangerous voice, glancing about fearfully. "No, he isn't. And don't say that again."

"Why in nuking hell not?" Edward demanded with a laugh, hanging the rapidfire across his wide chest.

"Because Delphi said he'd be keeping a watch on us," Alan said quickly in a low voice, placing the cup aside. "So keep your fragging yap shut. Or else."

The two brothers exchanged knowing looks for a minute, and Edward finally nodded agreement. Okay, the outlander had really rattled his brothers. But he still had a score to settle with this Delphi, and when the time came, he wouldn't hesitate for a bloody second.

Climbing onto a bike, Edward twisted the throttle and the dashboard came alive with glowing green lights. But there was no sound from the engine between his thighs, only a soft gentle vibration. The engine was as silent as a grave. Looking backward, Edward could see that there weren't any exhaust pipes or mufflers. And there was no drive chain, either. Some kind of an enclosed transmission seemed to connect the engine to the wheels, sort of like how a wag worked. He grinned at the possibilities of a silent two-wheeler. Hot damn, these would be great for a night-creep!

"So who do we ace?" Edward asked, then he started to sniff. What was that smell? There was some sort of a sharp a tang in the air, very similar to how wind smelled after a lightning strike, and it seemed to be coming from the engine. Did these things run on lightning?

"Some mutie lover named Ryan," Robert said in his mutilated voice. He reached over and turned off the bike.

"Why'd you do that?" Edward asked petulantly.

"Saving juice. These things run off sunshine, and they need a couple of hours of just sitting every day to reload. Recharge, refuel, whatever the fuck it's called."

"Sunshine?"

"That's what Delphi said."

"Then we never have to steal shine, or fuel?"

"Nope, they don't use it. Just daylight."

"Well, shit." Shaking his head at the concept, Edward climbed off the machine and carefully backed away so that his shadow wasn't touching the metal. "S'kay. We got any idea where to find the people we're after?" he asked, shifting the rapidfire across his back to a more comfortable position.

"Supposed to be somewhere in the Zone," Alan said, giving some assistance. "Here, rig the combo blaster this way. Better?"

"Yeah, thanks, bro."

"No prob."

Looking around the glen, Edward rubbed his jaw. The Zone, eh? But that was where they were right now. Okay, so this Delphi wasn't a total feeb. "Better and better." Edward grinned. "And who's the other guy we gotta do? Or it is a slut?"

"Some wrinklie called Doc," John snapped, taking the big man by the jaw and forcing him to look directly into his eyes. "Doc Tanner. And we capture him alive, feeb. *Alive.* Remember that."

Although almost twice the size of other man, Edward had no wish to ever cross his brother. The older man enjoyed giving folks pain, and Edward had gotten more than his fair share when they were all growing up together in the ruins of Border ville.

"Yeah, sure, no prob," Edward relented, shaking free. "Alive. Sure. Whatever ya say."

"Don't forget again," John warned, then his voice softened. "Hey, it'll be a slice. They travel together like us. We find one, we find the other."

"Are they kin, too?"

"Who gives a hot damn?" John said, walking to the campfire and pouring himself more coffee.

"Just asking." Edward felt and heard his stomach rumble. "Well, I gotta eat before we roll anywhere. My gut is so empty, I feel like I've been drinking acid rain."

"Yeah, thought so." Alan chuckled, hitching up his ammo belt. A wide belt of leather pouches across his chest bulged with clips for the rapidfire, along with a couple of spare shells for the gren launcher. He was hauling a lot of metal, but felt like the baron of the world. "You've never skipped a meal in your life. I'm surprised you are still alive, what with missing breakfast and all."

"Lots of grub in the saddlebags," Robert said, jerking a thumb in that direction. "All you want."

"We can eat on the way," John said, looking directly at the sun. Taking one last swallow of the coffee, he poured the rest on the grass and tossed the dirty cup into the cargo pod on the rear of his bike. "I want to get this over as soon as possible."

"I can load that into a blaster," Robert agreed wholeheartedly, cracking his oversize knuckles. "Where do we start looking for this Ryan?"

"First, we got a little task to do," John said, closing and locking the cargo pod. "A private matter."

"Yeah?" Alan asked hesitantly, then his face brightened. "Check, we're in the Zone. We're gonna visit Dempster."

Removing his combo longblaster, John slid the wep into a cushioned holster set along the black frame. Then getting onto the bike, John started the whispering engine. "Visit? Yeah, that's one way of putting it," he muttered, giving a hard smile devoid of any warmth. "Now, let's move out!"

LEAVING THE DEEP Storage Locker, the companions shoved their backpacks underneath the grating and out the other side. J.B. was the last to go, and paused for a few minutes inside the cage to rig a trip wire between two of the jack stands, the end of it connected to a U.S. Army Claymore mine.

"Think that's really necessary?" Mildred asked, loosening the heavy bandolier across her chest.

"Boobies are never necessary," J.B. said, releasing the arming switch and crawling to the next pair to do it again, "until one saves your ass."

"Besides, we're fairly sure Operation Chronos is looking for us," Ryan added, hiding another Claymore under the ruined Vulcan minigun. "Might as well give them something to find."

Now that last sentiment Mildred did agree with, and while the two men were busy setting their boobies, she dutifully checked her new blaster. Ryan had found an entire cache of automatic weapons—M-16 assault rifles, M-16/M-203 combinations, Thompson .45 machine guns, and such. It was quite an arsenal. After some heated debate, Mildred, Krysty and Jak all decided on the compact 9 mm Heckler & Koch MP-5. It was very lightweight and used the same caliber ammo as the SIG-Sauer and Uzi, which was always a good thing.

Doc, the odd man out, had disdained accepting one, espousing his dislike of rapidfires. But the Vermont scholar did agree it would be sensible to augment his firepower, and reluctantly took a Ruger .44 revolver. The stainless-steel hogleg was resting in a military police web belt around his waist, two side pouches taut with spare ammo speedloaders. With those, he could reload the Ruger in a matter of moments, unlike the LeMat, which took a minimum of ten minutes to fully repack each of the nine chambers.

"Okay, that should do it," J.B. announced, standing and dusting off his hands. "Set off one, and all four will blow. That's enough to turn a sec hunter droid into a grease stain."

"Then add two more," Jak said in deadpan humor.

Chuckling, Ryan carefully studied the area. "Looks good," he announced. "Can't spot a thing." The one-eyed man then looked at the ceiling. "Now let's see if we can get out of here," he added grimly, "and find out what is waiting for us outside."

Continuing the interrupted sweep of the redoubt, the heavily armed companions found the upper levels as devoid of anything as the lower ones. Strange that the Deep Storage Locker should be so full and the rest of the base so starkly empty.

"Should take LAV," Jak commented as they rode the elevator to the topmost level. "Not tank, but close."

"That's for damn sure," Ryan agreed.

Just then the elevator chimed and all conversation stopped.

As the doors parted, the companions spread out across the garage, but nothing seemed to have changed since their last visit. They had encountered many empty redoubts before, most of the installations were deserted, but this was the first in a long while packed with weapons.

Traveling down the zigzag tunnel, the companions reached the exit without incident. At the blast door, Krysty tapped in the exit code on a keypad. As the last digit was entered, Ryan pressed down on the lever and the whole tunnel shook slightly as the seamless expanse of black metal began to move with a rumble of distant thunder.

That brought everybody to attention. Normally the blast door was silent, or gave only a low growl, but not loud grinding. Was it broken? Had the base been nuked? Ryan and J.B. checked the rad counters on their lapels, but the devices weren't registering anything.

As the door came away from the wall, everybody

stepped aside when a trickle of water began to come through the crack, the flow quickly becoming a cascade and then a torrent as the blast door slid unstoppable to the side.

"Gaia, we're under water!" Krysty cried, trying to hold on to the keypad for support. The flood was pushing hard against her boots, and the woman was having trouble standing. Frantically, she punched the code into the keypad again to try to get the door to cycle closed. But the automatic process couldn't be interrupted, and the door continued onward until the exit was completely wide open.

Incredibly the flood began to slow and finally eased to a meager wash rippling along the floor. Moving in swirls, the dirty water began to gurgle into a series of drains set along the walls, and stopped spreading after only a few yards. At the sight, Mildred clucked her tongue in admiration. The designers of the redoubts truly had thought of everything.

When the door finally responded to the command code and began to close, Ryan sloshed closer and tried to glimpse outside. The light from the fluorescent tubes of the access corridor only reached a short distance down a long, flooded, brick tunnel.

After the portal sealed with a resounding clang, Ryan waved a hand. "Open it again, lover," he directed.

As Krysty fed in the code again, then jerked the lever, more water came into the redoubt, but nowhere near as much before. Going to the very edge of the doorway, Ryan squinted into the darkness but couldn't see an end to the tunnel. Dropping to one knee, he studied the water, then experimentally dipped a finger into the fluid. There was no burning sensation or reek of sulfur. This was just water, not a pool of acid rain. But how deep did it go?

"Doc, try using your stick," he suggested.

Joining his friend at the entrance, Doc withdrew the steel sword from inside the ebony stick and eased the tip into the dark water. The blade went all the way to the handle before it stopped.

"Nearly three feet deep," the scholar said, retrieving the sword and wiping it dry on a handkerchief before sheathing the blade again.

"Shallow enough for us to wade through," Ryan muttered thoughtfully, rubbing his chin. "But we're not going in without more light."

"Gators like shallow water," Jak said, furrowing his brow. "Snapping turtles, eels, snakes, all sorts of things."

"Damn straight."

"We're also going to need a depth gauge of some kind," Krysty added. "Mebbe we could use a wrench tied to a length of rope and toss it ahead of us along the way."

"Light, I can give you," J.B. said, pulling out one of the flares he found in the locker. As the stick burst into life, the reddish light showed deep into the watery tunnel, and still no end was in sight.

Swinging his arm back and forth, J.B. built momentum and threw the flare down the brick tunnel. It went flying for a good twenty feet before splashing into the water. As the flare sank, the light became muffled, a riot of bubbles forming around the magnesium flame, but it didn't go out. The flare dropped a few feet and stopped on the bottom, hissing and burbling furiously. The radiant pool clearly showed the brick bottom of the tunnel in distorted relief. If there was anything alive in the water, it stayed in the black shadows outside the range of the dying flame.

"The ground must have sunk during a nuke quake," Mildred guessed, tugging on a beaded strand of hair. "Then ground water filled it over the years."

Ryan scowled at that. A nuke quake? Now there was a nasty thought. Quickly, he checked the rad counter on his lapel again, turning in different directions, and grunted in satisfaction when it registered only the unusual amounts of background rads. The tunnel wasn't hot.

"At least it's fresh water, which means we're not going into the ocean," Krysty said. Then she frowned. "That is, unless this leads to one of the Great Lakes. Those are oceans!"

"Ocean, lake or reservoir, makes no damn difference," Ryan said bluntly. "We can't use the mat-trans, which leaves this as the only way out."

"Could be boobie," Jak said, scowling. "If Chronos put here, want us leave this way."

"Fully armed?" J.B. countered, patting his bulging munitions bag. "That makes no sense."

The teenager shrugged. "Whitecoats never make sense."

In wry remembrance of a hospital administrator, Mildred barked a bitter laugh at the comment. Doc said nothing, but his personal opinion on the subject was clearly readable on his somber features. If Operation Chronos gave them weapons, then it was a trick, and the guns were simply there to lull the companions into a false sense of security so that they'd be caught off guard when the real trap was sprung.

"Even paranoids have enemies," Doc said softly.

"The Hummers and the LAV can go through water this deep," Ryan stated with conviction. "No prob there."

"Although if the water gets any deeper, they both sink like stones going to Hell," Mildred added truthfully.

"I say we take the LAV," J.B. countered. "I like having some armor around me. Reminds me of the days we rode blaster with the Trader."

Resting the stock of his blaster on a hip, Ryan almost smiled at that reference. "Fair enough. We'll recce the wags, and if the LAV is usable we take it. If not, that big GMC truck we saw will do."

"Truck?" Jak drawled out of the side of his mouth. "No armor a'tall."

"But plenty of room for cargo," Ryan replied. "The 4x8 truck was wedged in pretty good among the other wags, be a triple bitch to get out. But the smaller, 4x6 was in the clear. Tires were flat on the LAV, but that we can fix." Everybody in the group was becoming a pretty good mech out of sheer necessity.

"Okay, a truck, and a couple of the Hummers as escorts," J.B. nodded. "But we try the LAV first."

"Fair enough," Ryan said, then scowled. In the sputtering light of the dying underwater flare, something large moved within the murky shadows. Taking a hesitant step closer, he blinked, unsure if he had actually seen anything. The flare was throwing crazy shadows everywhere.

"You know, I could have sworn..." Mildred started hesitantly.

But the physician was cut off as shiny wetness reared up from the water. Backing away, the companions stared at the giant thing, whatever it was, some form of amorphous mass, sort of like a gigantic jellyfish. There were no details, no eyes or ears or fins, only the smooth shimmering body that constantly changed shape.

"What is this Hellenic kraken?" Doc whispered, a hand on his LeMat.

The blob turned toward the scholar and a ripple of shimmering light moved through its body, briefly revealing a bizarre metallic framework inside the creature. As the flexing array of struts moved, the translucent body followed.

Sniffing, J.B. made a face. "Ozone," he said. "Just like—" His eyes went wide. "Just like a Cerebus cloud!"

As if knowing the word, the front of the impossible thing split apart as if slashed with a hot knife to reveal a red gaping maw lined with stubby protrusions. With an echoing roar, the inhuman guardian charged.

"Ace it!" Ryan snarled, firing the SIG-Sauer from the hip. But the soft lead rounds smacked into the jelly and simply passed through to hit the brick wall behind and ricochet away.

Suddenly the four rapidfires began to pepper the shapeless thing, but the combined hail of hot lead had the exact same effect as the subsonic 9 mm Parabellum rounds.

"Fireblast! We can't even touch the thing!" Ryan raged, frantically reloading. *Exactly like a Cerebus cloud.* The nuking creature had to be another guardian of the redoubts! Just some type they had never encountered before. Or was this the trap?

Releasing the Uzi to hang from its shoulder strap, J.B. pulled around the S&W M-4000 pump-action shotgun, and unleashed its fury. Loaded with steel slivers instead of buckshot, the barrage of fléchettes cut deep into the quivering mass and struck the moving framework inside at several points. A few of the twinkling lights died, several flared brightly. The titanic guardian now swiveled toward the Armorer.

"Keep firing!" Krysty shouted, throwing herself toward the keypad. Mother Gaia, that metal framework was some kind of skeleton for the creature. It was a nuking cyborg!

Moving fast, Krysty slapped in the memorized code, and in a muted rumbled, the massive adamantine slab started to slide across the entrance.

Instantly, the black guardian seemed to dive into the water, only to flip its backside over the top, then repeat the process as it rolled with frightful speed.

Moving with the closing door, the companions stayed behind the protective metal, constantly firing their weps, as the guardian loomed ever closer.

Holstering the SIG-Sauer autoloading pistol, Ryan clawed for a gren, uncaring what kind it was. Jerking out the ring, he flipped the handle and threw the bomb hard at the shiny mass. The mil sphere smacked into the guardian and bounced off to hit the brick wall and splash into the water. Incredibly, the cyborg lurched to the opposite side of the tunnel as if it knew what a gren could do. Flattening itself against the bricks, it began undulating for the narrowing opening in the blast door just as a fireball blossomed under the water. Steam and muted thunder expanded to fill the tunnel and a whole section of the guardian turned gray and pebbly, closely resembling rotten meat.

The blast door was almost shut, but the concussion pushed through the crack to shove the companions backward, the searing heat singeing their hair and clothing. Covering their faces, the companions hastily retreated down the tunnel, getting off a few last shots until the door boomed shut. The thermal wave was abruptly cut off.

"Thank God." Mildred sighed, leaning wearily against the wall. "This has really been one hell of a—Oh shit, look!"

There on the floor inside the redoubt was a small

piece of the guardian, black tendrils stretching from its shaking form to the blast door. The cyborg had obviously tried to get through the closing portal and a chunk got nipped off. But even as the companions started closer, the bent skeleton inside the blob reared upward and a new red mouth formed to howl in unsuppressed fury.

"Fuck!" Jak snarled, triggering his rapidfire. But the rounds went through the jelly and hit the blast door to come back and ricochet down the zigzag access tunnel.

Snarling a curse, J.B. tried the scattergun again, but missed the smaller skeleton completely. In response, the cyborg folded itself into a ball and started rolling forward.

"Elevator!" Ryan shouted, turning to run as fast as he could. Hot nuke, they needed some combat room to tangle with this thing, and the narrow access tunnel was about as bad a place for a firefight as he had ever seen. There was no room to dodge, and nothing to duck behind for cover.

Dashing down each leg of the zigzag tunnel, the companions maintained a constant barrage at the rolling guardian. Doc tried a gren, but it bounced off the jelly and landed behind the cyborg to harmlessly detonate in its wake.

Erupting into the garage, the companions spread out through the collection of wags, heading for the elevator. They didn't know what Ryan had in mind, but they trusted his combat instincts.

Reaching the door to the stairs, Krysty started to reload the rapidfire when she saw Ryan across the garage scramble over a civie wag. Veering sharply around the imposing LAV, Ryan went straight for the fuel pump. Yanking the hose free, he squeezed the control in a short burst and made a puddle on the concrete floor. Now that he knew the rate of flow, the one-eyed man flicked his butane lighter to life and knelt to ignite the fluid. The condensed fuel immediately caught, the bluish flames dancing above the dwindling pool of predark juice.

Suddenly the guardian rolled into sight from behind the LAV, and Ryan squeezed the handle again, wide-open this time. A powerful lance of fuel shot out of the nozzle to touch the shrinking puddle and instantly burst into flames. The guardian paused at the sight, and Ryan lifted the makeshift flamethrower to sweep the burning column across the pulsating cyborg.

The creature was covered in flames, its red mouth appearing once more, only this time to keen in unmistakable agony. Sluggishly, it tried to move away, but Ryan advanced to the end of the hose, arcing the spray high to keep the rain of fire centered on the horrid thing. The outer skin was already gray and pebbly, and thick ooze was dribbling from the cracked expanse. Greenish smoke was rising from the cooking jelly, the air vents in the walls of the redoubt audibly increasing their suction in a valiant effort to clear the atmosphere.

The skeleton inside the jelly tried to roll away, but the cooked flesh began to crumble. The lights inside the darkening mass took on a frantic pace and then winked out. Sagging to the floor, the cyborg lay quiescent. Not trusting the thing, Ryan kept the flames on the bubbling mass until there was nothing left but the charred and slightly melted frame of its skeleton.

Releasing the hot handle, Ryan tossed it aside and sagged against a Hummer, gasping for breath. The fragging handle on the hose wasn't designed for that kind of punishment and had conducted the heat right back to him. His hands felt as though they'd been cooked to the bone. It hurt to move them even a little bit.

Somewhere an alarm began to clang, and the water sprinklers in the ceiling cut loose with white foam to quell the blaze. Not water this time, but fire-retardant foam that would smother a grease fire.

Rushing through the bubbling downpour, Mildred and J.B. went to check Ryan, while the others hurried directly into the supply closet. Seconds later they emerged with sledgehammers and proceed to loudly make sure that the bastard skeleton would never function again. As the blaze died away, the ceiling slowed its outpouring of white foam until it stopped completely. However, the hammering continued for quite a while.

"How bad," Ryan asked through gritted teeth.

"You'll be fine," Mildred said as she started to rummage through her med kit. "I know that it hurts, but there's no permanent damage. And I have an ointment that'll fix you up in a few days." Opening the tube, she got busy.

"Don't…have…days." Ryan grunted at the application of the salve. Then his face eased and he sighed in relief. "The mat-trans is dead, there's a cage in front of the deeper, and a guardian at the exit."

"Yeah, I know," Mildred said angrily. "Somebody does not want us to leave this redoubt alive."

"Which is why we have to get out immediately," J.B. stated, resting his sledgehammer on the sticky white floor.

"How can we?" Krysty asked, her soaked hair struggling to move under the weight of the foam. "The minute we open the blast door, the other half of this thing is going to attack."

"Or worse, my dear lady," Doc noted, pulling out his sword. Experimentally, he prodded the smoldering mass on the floor, but invoked no response.

Krysty scowled. "What do you mean?"

"While our Stygian blob has joined the choir invisible," Doc said, sheathing the blade, "its *pater familias* will most likely be waiting to ambush us."

"You think it's that smart?" J.B. asked, removing his glasses to wipe them clean.

"Quite right. A Cerebus cloud is, so we would be fools to evaluate this with any less intelligence."

"Mebbe try again?" Jak asked, tilting his head at the fuel pumps. "I'll do next."

Rising slowly, Mildred went to the pump and wiped the faceplate of a gauge clean, then rapped it with a knuckle. "Plenty of juice left," she stated.

"No need," Ryan stated, carefully flexing his hands, and wincing slightly. "I have a better idea."

Chapter Seven

The sun was just rising over the horizon, casting a clean pearlescent light across the world, highlighting the deadly orange clouds of chems and toxins that crackled with thunder.

A dry wind drove twirling dustdevils across the ground, the miniature tornadoes spinning madly and then vanishing when they reached the strip of hard-packed dirt that formed the local highway.

Sitting on their silent two-wheelers, the Rogan brothers rolled along the road, handkerchiefs tied over their lower faces to hold out the ever-present dust that always carried the taste of some ancient foulness. The big men and their bikes were streaked with dirt, the halogen headlights resembling a line of full moons moving through a cloudy night. The Rogans passed a lizard sleeping on a rock without disturbing its slumber. There was only the soft crunching sound of the ground compressing under the weight of the motorcycles as the four coldhearts moved toward the little desert ville ahead.

The landscape around the ville was rippled, as if molten stone had cooled suddenly in the act of expanding. That was a common enough vista in the Zone, the telltale aftermath of a skydark firestorm hit by rain. Nuke-scaping, the wrinklies called it, although nobody but them really knew why anymore.

Reaching a deep ravine, the Rogans reduced their speed and rolled single file across the ramshackle bridge. The bridge was almost choked solid with tumbleweeds caught in corroded supports, and they had to maneuver through the obstructions carefully to avoid going into any of the holes in the predark construction. At the middle of the span, the brothers pulled weapons just a heartbeat before an old man dressed in rags rose from behind a tumbleweed barricade. His dirty hair was a wild corona of filth, and a rag was bound around the shriveled face, a wide scar bisecting the features straight across the middle. The disfigured oldster was armed with a long metal pole that had a broken bottle lashed to the tip. The jagged glass gleamed in the growing morning light.

"Hold it right there, outlanders!" the man commanded in a surprisingly powerful voice for such a scrawny frame. "If you want to cross my bridge…" Just then, he spotted the brothers. He stopped speaking and gasped, the spear shaking in his wizened hands. "What in the nuking…*it's you!*"

Never slowing the advance of their black bikes, the Rogans opened fire with their new blasters, the stuttering rapidfires tore the old man apart, blood flying everywhere as the 5.56 mm rounds drove him backward off the bridge.

"Nice to be remembered." Edward snorted, glancing over the rusty side to watch the tumbling body disappear into the thick river mists below. The run-off water from the nearby mountains had always made the bridge slightly cooler than the rest of the desert, and thus a favorite spot for folks to sit in wait for pilgrims.

"Frag that noise, and reload," John commanded, circling the hidden campsite of the deceased hermit. "We're going to need every brass ready when we hit the ville."

"Can't disagree with that." Alan chuckled.

Robert said nothing as the tires of his motorcycle rolled over the dropped spear, the glass shattering below the resilient military tires. It had been nice seeing Crazy Winston again, even if it was only for a split second. Childhood friends became enemies as adults. Such was life. The triple-stupe bastard should have known better than to aim a weapon at them. The last time they had removed only his nose; this time they took everything. Robert shook his head. Some people just never learned.

Leaving the dilapidated bridge behind, the Rogans crossed long miles of empty countryside, carefully veering past an old rad pit that didn't glow anymore, but was still deadly, and completely avoiding a low hillock bearing the graves of their parents. Let the dead bury the past. They were concentrating on the future.

With the coming of the dawn, birds were winging low across the sky, afraid to rise too high and risk being chilled by the toxic clouds. From somewhere far off came the brittle cry of a screamwing, closely followed by the guttural moan of a howler. The Rogans moved their hands closer to their longblasters at the noise, and fervently hoped the winged mutie and the groundpounder were fighting to the death over something tasty. Screamwings were triple fast, but could be chilled if a person stayed alert. Howlers, on the other hand, were nightmares, all but indescribable and insanely deadly. There were strange new muties roaming the Deathlands these days, creatures unlike anything ever seen before in memory or myth. Some people believed these odd muties had always been around, and were only now wandering into populated areas. John Rogan fervently hoped that was the case. *Because if there was something creating new muties…*

Cresting a low swell in the dusty ground, the brothers saw their halogen headlights wash across the tan wall surrounding a deserted ville. The pitiful barrier was made of adobe bricks, sun-dried blocks of mud. Each brick was about the size of a shoebox, and the wall reached nearly six feet in height, its top layer sparkling from all of the broken glass embedded into the material. The front gate was a thick wooden door, just wide enough for a person on horseback to ride through. The barrier was formidable, but swung aside at the moment, the opening flanked by crackling torches set into the adobe wall, inviting all to come inside. Softly in the distance could be heard a tinkling piano and female laughter.

"Dempster," John pronounced hatefully, slowing his bike.

The other brothers followed suit as they slowly rode through the gap in the defensive wall. There was a rocking chair for a guard, but nobody was in sight.

"Trusting souls," Edward said in disgust. "The idiots are still offering a friendly hand to everybody who passes by. What a bunch of feebs."

Dempster was pretty much as he remembered, little more than a double row of shacks surrounded by a mud wall. The last time the brothers had been here, the wall was only four feet tall, so the civies were making progress, just not a hell of a lot of it.

For some unfathomable reason, muties avoided Dempster completely, and not even stingwings would fly overhead. This made the place a natural sanctuary, and soon every biker gang and coldheart knew about Dempster. Fighting wasn't allowed inside the ville, and whenever one gang got ambitious and decided to take over the ville, everybody else combined against the usurpers. Dempster was neutral territory. Anybody inside the mud brick walls was safe from attack or revenge for old crimes.

Until today, Edward added in grim amusement.

Squinting hard, Alan grunted at the sight of a newly built guard tower rising from the center of the ville. But it was clear that there was nobody there.

"Nuking idiots," Robert groaned, annoyed and pleased at the same instant. He eased the new combo rapidfire across his lap. "This is gonna be fun."

"Shaddup," John ordered from behind his fluttering cloth mask. "Just keep your eyes peeled for the Watering Hole. That's our goal. Never mind settling old scores."

His brothers grunted in acknowledgment, but their hard gazes swept the assortment of adobe buildings looking for familiar faces.

SMOKING A CORNCOB PIPE, Daniel Winterborn was leaning against a wooden beam that supported the roof of a porch in front of the tavern. Letting the pungent smoke trickle out of his nostrils, the Apache calmly watched as the four outlanders rode their sleek machines down the street like ghosts in the night.

Damnedest thing, four outlanders on two-wheelers, and all of the wags in perfect condition! That was when he saw their collection of longblasters. Were those rapidfires? His great-grandfather had told him stories about such weapons, but he never thought to actually see one, much less four! Blood of the Earth, who the nuking hell were these men, a pack of roaming barons? As the bikers rolled by, Daniel studied the faces behind the crude masks and went cold inside. The Rogans!

Dropping the hair comb he had been carving from a piece of bone, Daniel tucked the knife into his horsehair belt. Shifting the pipe to the other side of his mouth, he swung away from the beam and stepped off the porch, heading for the horse corral across town. He had a knife, but that wouldn't mean drek against four fragging rapidfires!

Winterborn was no doomie, able to see things that hadn't happened yet, or a shaman, able to unlock the mysteries of the past, but he could smell blood on the wind. There was a graveyard outside the western wall with over a score of men and women buried under the rock and sand from failed attempts to raid the neutral ville. However, Daniel knew that there was always room for more on the last train west. And he had a bad feeling in his bones that this time he wouldn't be pitching the dirt, but catching it in the face. No, thanks.

As Daniel neared the hole in the wall, a coyote howled from a distant hilltop and abruptly stopped. Just that single clarion call to the sister moon and then unnatural quiet. The moment Daniel turned the corner of the blacksmith's shop and was out of sight of the four riders, he broke into a frantic run for the gate. To hell with his horse. Brother coyote loved to play tricks, but never lied about death. Dempster would run red tonight, and the Mother Earth would weep for all the people returning to her bosom.

NOTICING A MOVEMENT out of the corner of his vision, Alan started to reach for the revolver on his belt, yet another gift from the hated Delphi found in the cargo pods of the bikes. But as fast as he moved, the running person was gone, hopping over the adobe wall and vanishing into the rosy dawn. Had to have been Winterborn. Nobody else was smart enough to run for the hills when the Rogans came riding into town.

"There it is," Edward said, jerking his chin to the left.

Gazing through the growing sunlight, John saw the tavern and felt a brief twinge of homesickness. Located in the heart of the ville, the brick building rose three full stories and had a slate roof that defied the acid rains, plus a brass front door marred by countless ricochets until the dents resembled a deliberate pattern hammered into the metal for decoration. Iron bars covered the windows, making the tavern resemble a fortress, or a baron's home, but it was just a gaudy house. Neutral territory deep inside neutral territory. The music was louder now and gales of laughter, both male and female, reached their ears.

"Home," Robert said, his expression unreadable.

As the Rogans rolled closer, the brothers could see that armed sec men were walking on the flat roof. Faint traces of tobacco, wolfweed, stale sweat and warm beer could be smelled in the air. They flinched as a breeze carried the strong reek of urine from the public lav set off to the side.

A couple of tired-looking horses were tied to a hitching rail in front of the brick building, and a wag of some kind stood nearby. It almost looked like a pre-dark car, except that the chassis had been removed and patched canvas was stretched tight over the body of the machine.

For better mileage, John realized. Less weight meant you could go faster. Mebbe that canvas drek would keep off the acid rain, but that was about it for protection.

"Only a fool trades armor for speed," Alan said in disgust.

Bringing their bikes to a smooth halt directly in front of the door, the brothers got off and each flipped a switch, setting the alarms and antipers devices. The small on-board computers were in perfect working condition, and the bikes could protect themselves with deadly efficiently. Or so Delphi had said.

Pulling the combo blasters from their holsters, the Rogans rested the weps on their shoulders and started past the horses. Nickering softly, the nervous animals moved out of the way of the brothers. Lowering the barrels of their black-powder longblasters, the sec men on the roof watched but did nothing as the four big outlanders calmly walked onto the porch and out of sight beneath the overhang.

Sitting on the porch in a folding chair, a wrinklie softly played a harmonica. He looked up as the brothers tromped onto the porch, the rising sun behind the brothers masking their features in reddish shadows.

"Howdy," the old man said, lowering his musical instrument. "Welcome to the Watering Hole! Don't cost any jack to go in, but if you want me to watch your rides—"

Without a word, Alan thrust his hand forward and buried a knife in the man's throat. The startled oldster spread his lips as if to scream, but only a gurgling noise came out, closely followed by a crimson welling of blood.

Impatiently, Alan shoved the blade in deeper and twisted. With a gurgling shudder, the wrinklie went limp, the harmonica dropping to the dusty wooden planks of the porch.

Pulling the blade free, Alan wiped it clean on the still-warm chest of the corpse as Robert grabbed the harmonica and tucked it into a pocket. Hadn't seen one of these for some time.

"On my command," John said, working the bolt on the combo rapidfire. "And not before."

"Check." Edward grunted, then pushed open the heavy metal door with the barrel of his blaster.

Bright light and smoke poured onto the porch like peeking into a oven. Sauntering inside, John noticed the holstered blaster hidden under the vest of the dead man on the porch. So, not just a watchdog for the house, eh? He'd remember that.

Even at this early hour of the morning, the Watering Hole was full of drinking men. A old, fat man was sitting at a piano in the corner, playing and singing away. Not too badly, either. The walls were covered with predark foldouts of naked females, and sparkled with dozens of the rainbow-colored disks some folks called a CD. Nobody knew what they were for, but the disks always made nice decorations—although the scantily dressed sluts leaning over the second-floor banister were a lot prettier. Some of the gaudy sluts were smoking handrolled cigs, their bare breasts swinging in tempo to the music. John felt his blood grow warm. After so much time in the wilds of the Deathlands, that was a wonderful sight. But not why they were here today. Biz first, fun later.

As they recalled from endless childhood days of scrubbing on their hands and knees, the floor of the gaudy house was also made of red brick, the material worn smooth into a paths between the heavy tables. In the exact center of the tavern was its namesake, an artesian well. Even as a kid, John had been impressed by that. This was the only source of clean water for a hundred miles, so the locals had built a tavern around it and opened for business. Trading water for food, Dempster had managed to stay alive during the years of chaos after skydark and then the horrible Mutie Wars. The beer and gaudy sluts came later, but water was the local jack; cool, clear spring water without a trace of rads or toxins.

Just a little of our piss. John chuckled. Watching the hated customers drink from the well after riding their mother upstairs, the brothers had savored the little revenge. Flavoring the well had been their first act of rebellion, but hardly their last.

A dozen people were sitting on wooden barrels along the bar, drinking from cracked plastic cups. On the balcony directly above, a gaudy slut smoking a cheroot was looking down at the boisterous crowd. The busty woman was wearing only a loose pink gown that hung down at her sides, showing all of her worn charms. Along the left wall, a flight of wooden stairs led to the second-floor balcony. Situated at the bottom of the stairs was a young girl sitting behind a heavy wooden table. On top of the table was a ceramic bowl full of wooden markers bearing room numbers and an alcohol lantern still burning brightly in spite of the daylight shining through the dusty windows. The gaudy slut looked bored and the lantern was almost out of shine. The long night of work was nearly finished and a new day was about to begin.

Alan nudged John at the sight of the girl, and the elder Rogan grunted in reply. However, Robert and Edward were scowling at the large man sitting in the far corner. From the sheer size of the man, his heavily scarred hands and broken nose, he had to be the bouncer. When customers got rowdy, the bouncer would slam them back down in their chair or heave them out the door. No sense wasting brass on a drunk, when a good thumping was all that was really needed. The corner position gave the bouncer a full view of the entire first floor, and kept anybody from sneaking behind him to try to get upstairs for free. The bouncer was big, old and wide, with fingers as thick as sausages, a formidable enough guard even without the predark shotgun cradled in his massive hands.

Robert noticed that immediately. A pump-action. If it still worked, that would be real trouble.

Drunken men were moving throughout the gaudy house. A skinny woman with buckteeth was sitting behind a Dutch door, haggling with each customer over what they wanted and how to pay. As the Rogans watched, a teenager laid down a chicken and was sent over to the girl at the bottom of the stairs. She gave the teen a room marker, and he raced up the steps to be met by a haggard slut many times his age. Then a trapper wrapped in furs laid down a single rifle cartridge. The bucktooth woman bit the brass to check and make sure it wasn't painted wood, then sent him over to the girl. She gave the trapper a marker and he trundled up the steps to knock on the first door. It was opened by two young girls who started giggling and pulled him inside, then slammed the door shut.

"Ready?" Alan asked impatiently, his hands itching to get busy.

In stoic reply, John swung the combo rapidfire off his shoulder and clicked off the safety with a thumb.

"Hey, put down those blasters!" a raven-haired girl yelled from behind the bar.

With a smile, John pointed the wep at her and burped the M-16, the short burst of 5.56 mm rounds stitching across her chest and shattering the glass bottles on the wall behind in foamy explosions.

A drunk dropped his glass at the zipper noise of the rapidfire, another cursed, a third started to scream, and the four Rogan brothers cut loose, the stuttering streams of the predark mil lead cutting through the crowd, sending out geysers of death. Lunging out of his chair, the bouncer worked the pump-action on his scattergun just as Edward fired. The burst of incoming rounds tore the bouncer apart, knocking the scattergun from his grip. On the bar, an alcohol lantern shattered, spraying blue flame everywhere, and the posters on the wall caught fire. Going back-to-back, the Rogans kept firing, moving across the tavern and chilling everybody in sight.

A man flipped over a table for protection, but then stood with a hatchet in his hand, ready to throw. Alan shot the fellow through the flimsy piece of furniture. Shrieking, the man dropped the hatchet and fell from view, his groin gushing red across his pants. The screaming continued, but nobody paid him any attention.

Just then a door slammed open on the second floor and the naked sec man came charging out, brandishing two handcannons. Angling their chattering weps upward, Edward and Robert caught the man in cross fire, just as he trigger one of the blasters. The shot smacked the wooden bucket dangling above the well, and spring water poured forth to join the shine and blood spreading across the brick floor.

"Stop shooting! We surrender!" a bald man shouted from behind the bar, raising both of his hands. "Just stop shooting! Take whatever ya want!"

Inserting a fresh clip, Alan gave the bartender a single look and noted his hands were turned backward. To hide something in his palms? Stroking the trigger, Alan blew the fellow away with a concentrated burst to the chest. The man slammed backward into the broken bottles, dropping the hidden knife.

On the balcony, a girl threw open a door to stare down in horror at the mounting carnage. Laughing wildly, Robert shot her twice. She staggered away, clutching the tattered fleshy ruins of her naked breasts.

"Stop chilling the sluts!" John yelled, gunning down a fat man crawling on the floor.

"We only need the one!" his brother retorted.

"Need, yes! But I want at least three!"

As the brothers continued to shoot, empty brass went flying to land on the brick floor with musical tinklings. The madam of the tavern suddenly popped up from behind the Dutch door with a loaded crossbow. She fired and Alan dodged, the arrow scoring a bloody furrow along his cheek. Bitch!

Snarling in rage, Edward shot the madam once in the belly. Losing the weapon, the screaming woman grabbed her guts and doubled over, then Edward shot her in the forehead, blowing out her existence in a ghastly spray of bones, blood and brains.

Suddenly the bronze front door was slammed open and there stood two armed sec men holding black-powder longblasters.

"Freeze, this is neutral ground!" one of them bellowed. "Surrender, or die!"

Pivoting at the waist, John grabbed the ammo clip extending under the combo rapidfire and pulled the trigger on the 40 mm gren launcher set under the M-16 barrel. Even as the sec men brought up their longblasters, the M-203 roared and the predark charge of steel fléchettes tore them into bloody hamburger. The shattered longblasters fired randomly as their chilled owners fell lifeless to the porch, no longer recognizable as human beings.

At the bottom of the stairs, the girl flipped over the battered table and took refuge behind the heavy piece of furniture. The air of the tavern was thick with blastersmoke, and screams, along with the unmistakable stench of chilled people. The horrible reek made her gag and she tried not to retch. Escape was her only hope. But the front door was impossible to reach, as were the stairs. She'd have to cross open floor to reach either, and that meant instant death in this firefight. What should she do?

A terrible silence unexpectedly filled the bar as the rapidfires stopped shooting. Trying to control her breathing, the cringing girl wondered if the invaders had run out of brass when the table was shoved aside and there stood two of the coldhearts, grinning down at her like muties discovering a newborn. Then recognition hit and she gasped out loud.

"You!" she cried, raising an arm for protection.

"Hi, Lily." John chuckled as Robert slammed the stock of his rapidfire directly into her face.

The girl went reeling, the pain making her blind. Then a terrible warmth spread through her body and the girl felt herself falling for the floor, but never hit it. Lily Rogan merely kept going, tumbling into a bottomless void. Her last conscious thought was a desperate prayer for death to escape the cold revenge of her brothers.

AFTER A QUICK DINNER of MRE packs, Ryan and the companions divided up into teams. As bachelors, Doc and Jak took the first watch, and worked out a simple sweep of the redoubt to watch for any more hunting probes or another of those jelly guardians.

Meanwhile the others hit the showers and went to bed. The following day was going to be busy, and tired minds made mistakes. A single slip in the coming fight could get them all chilled, so in spite of the urgency to leave, a few hours of sleep had been deemed necessary.

The big showers in the barracks had only delivered rusty water, no matter how long the companions allowed them to run. So they checked the private stalls in the officer's quarters and found two that delivered clean water. It wasn't very hot, but they were used to a lot worse, and at least it was clean.

Krysty had insisted that Ryan go first, and he hadn't put up too much of a struggle. Soaking for a long time in the shower, Ryan placed his throbbing hands under a stream of cold until his teeth started to chatter. Turning off the shower, Ryan awkwardly wrapped a towel around himself and padded over to the bedroom he had chosen. The mattress wasn't in very good shape, by after laying a bedroll on top, it was comfortable enough.

Following Mildred's orders, he took some aspirin and then sat at the desk to do some work. Clumsily taking loose 9 mm brass from a U.S. Army ammo box, he inserted them into the empty clips for the MP-5 and the SIG-Sauer. Thankfully, both weps took the same size brass. When a clip was full, Ryan would place it aside, then start on the next from the waiting stack.

Eventually, he was done. Now, Ryan carefully applied fresh meds to his red hands, then slid on a pair of calfskin gloves he had found in a foot locker. As a test, he made a fist with his right hand and punched his open left palm. Then did it the other way. The blows stung, but the pain was barely there. Good. That meant he could handle a blaster without any problems.

A shadow appeared in the doorway, and Ryan brought up the SIG-Sauer without conscious thought before realizing it was Krysty.

"Hey," he said by way of greeting, clicking back on the safety and laying the blaster on the table. "Was there still any warm water?"

"Hey, yourself, lover." Krysty smiled, padding barefoot into the room, a towel held to her chest with a bare arm. "And yes, there was plenty of hot water."

"Really? I guess the bastard pipes were just waiting for me to leave before they decide to work," Ryan said, giving a rare chuckle.

"Seems likely," Krysty said softly, placing a bare foot on a chair. She removed the towel and started drying her legs, slowly working her way upward.

"Dishwasher works in the galley, too," Ryan said, his heart starting to pound at the delicious sight. He watched her every movement. "So Doc finally got a chance to thoroughly clean the hogleg."

Raising her head, Krysty laughed at that. "I remember the first time I saw him tuck the LeMat into a dishwasher and turn on the machine, I thought he'd gone insane."

But Ryan didn't reply, his eyes feasting on the statuesque beauty standing naked in the subdued light of the mil lamp. There were no scars on her skin; it was smooth and perfect. Briefly he recalled the first time he'd seen her in that burning barn, and once more felt the exact same electric punch to his guts he had on that fateful day.

"Been a long time since we had any privacy, hasn't it, lover?" Krysty whispered, moving the towel across her taut belly and then drying under her full breasts.

"Too bastard long," Ryan replied huskily, gingerly flexing his gloved hands. "Almost forget what you looked like this way."

"Then we better refresh your memory." The woman dropped the towel. Stepping away from the chair, Krysty held out both arms in an unmistakable invitation.

Kicking back his chair, Ryan strode around the table and took Krysty in his arms, pulling her close. For a long moment they simply stood there, savoring the delicious feel of skin against skin. Then Ryan took her by the chin and tilted her face to meet his. They kissed, tenderly at first, then with growing passion as the physical need for each other washed away the events of the day, and soon there was only the here and now of their intimacy.

Moaning in pleasure, Krysty moved her soft hands along the rock-hard body of the man, touching every scar. So many battles, so much pain.

Kissing her velvet throat, Ryan slid his gloves down to cup her buttocks, then jerked them away. Krysty could feel his passion ebbing and took his gloves in her hands to place them on her breasts.

"Yours," she whispered. "I am yours, forever."

Ryan looked into her eyes, asking a silent question. She answered by leaning closer and kissing him passionately, her tongue darting into his mouth, her hands caressing his manhood until he was firm and ready.

Scooping her up in his strong arms, Ryan walked Krysty to the bed and put her down gently. He took her by the hips, trying to be tender as he pushed between her knees and slid into the electric wetness of her moist folds. But her hips thrust forward, driving herself onto him, so he responded with increased urgency. Their sweaty bodies rocked back and forth, soon finding the rhythm eternal, until they were one, a single groaning entity. Not a word was spoken. None was needed.

As Ryan plunged deep inside, Krysty laced her fingers behind his muscular neck, her living hair reaching out to brush his face as the two lost themselves in the wondrous pleasures of the night.

Slowly the long night passed. Secrets were shared, fantasies fulfilled. All too soon dawn would come and the work would begin. But for now, at this time, there was only each other and a precious few moments of joy to savor, a private celebration of life primordial from deep within the burning heart of the savage Deathlands.

Chapter Eight

After everybody was washed and fed in the morning, the companions got to work. A few hours later, they were ready.

Getting into a Hummer, Ryan turned the engine on and revved it a few times until it was running smoothly. Shifting into gear, he started driving along the zigzag tunnel that led to the exit. The rest of the companions walked closely behind the wag, their arms loaded with supplies. The rear of the Hummer was packed solid and there wasn't room for a spare brass cartridge.

Reaching the end of the tunnel, Ryan got out and helped J.B. tie a heavy rope to the rear of the wag.

"Sure hope that holds," Doc rumbled, lighting the oily rag tied around the neck of a glass bottle filled with fuel and soap flakes.

"It'll hold," Ryan stated, leaning into the Hummer. As he wedged a short stick between the front seat and the gas pedal, the engine roared into overdrive, the needle on the dashboard almost going into the red. Once the engine settled down a bit, Ryan pressed down hard on the brake with a gloved hand and shifted it into gear. The wag trembled but didn't move.

"Everybody ready?" Ryan asked, trying not to let the pain from his hand show in his voice.

"Let her rip," Krysty said, standing near the keypad.

Gratefully, Ryan let go of the brake and the wag lurched forward only to stop again as the thick rope attached from the rear stanchion became tight. The other end was anchored to the front of the LAV, but going around so many sharp corners, the companions had been worried the old rope might not be able to stand up to the job. Stretched as tight as a guitar string, the thick rope quivered from the jerking urges of the trapped Hummer, but showed no sign of fraying or giving way.

"Hit it, lover," Ryan growled, pulling the SIG-Sauer from his belt.

Moving quickly, Krysty punched in the code, pressed the lever and the blast door started to slide aside.

"Now!" Ryan shouted, and the others hurtled a barrage of Molotov cocktails at the black metal portal. The bottles crashed on the floor to form a crackling pool of flames that stretched from side to side.

As the tunnel came into view, at first Ryan thought it was empty. Then something black peeled away from the ceiling to drop into the water and rise horribly, the twinkling skeleton inside the translucent creature flexing and shifting position as it began to move toward the redoubt. Then it paused, finally sensing the presence of the flames.

Just then, the blast door boomed as it opened completely, and the black guardian came closer, rising tall as if to attack the group of people standing behind the small puddle of burning fuel. But even as the portal stopped moving, Krysty hurriedly punched in the code and the door started to close once more.

"Do it!" Ryan said.

With a slash of a knife, Jak cut the rope and the straining Hummer lurched forward. Unfortunately the timing was off by a hair and the blast door hit the Hummer just as it charged through the fire. The wag rebounded from the impact and slammed against the jamb, the pool of flames licking upward directly beneath the armored chassis.

On impulse, Ryan took a half step toward the Hummer, unable to take his eyes off its stacked fuel cans and satchel charges filling the rear cargo area. If those went off inside the tunnel, the companions would be obliterated.

Then in a squeal of rubber, the studded tires of the Hummer dug in and the wag shot outside. Instantly the guardian dropped on the Hummer, covering the windshield and reaching in through the sides with ropy pseudopods of gelatinous ooze. Then the moving blast door took it from their sight.

The opening was down to a mere crack, but J.B. still waited until the very last tick before flipping the detonator switch in his grip. In a titanic blast, the C-4 plas, M-2 blocks and condensed fuel ignited into a strident blast that merged with the hollow boom of the nuke-proof door as it solidly closed.

Allowing themselves to breathe again, everybody strained to hear what was happening on the other side of the portal. But there was only silence, which was hardly surprising. Built to withstand a near-direct hit from a thermo nuke, there was nothing known to exist that could even scratch the material.

"Think that did it?" Krysty asked, hesitantly reaching out to touch the portal. The black metal was cool and smooth, giving no indication of what was happening on the other side.

"Fragging well hope so," Ryan shot back sourly. "But we'll have more Molotovs ready the next time we open that door."

"Tunnel could collapse," Jak said, hunching his shoulders. For the briefest moment, the razor blades hidden among the feathers and other camou on his jacket twinkled in the overhead halogen lights. "Might be trapped worse than before."

"I know explosives," J.B. said firmly, straightening his fedora. "The tunnel will hold. Trust me."

"John?" Mildred said, putting a wealth of questions to the single word.

"It'll hold, Millie," he answered confidently.

"Let's find out," Ryan growled, holstering the blaster and starting back down the tunnel.

Returning to the garage, Ryan studied their chosen war wag with satisfaction. Even in the predark days, the LAV-25 had been a mighty machine. These days, it was all but unstoppable. The Light Armored Vehicle was a rolling powerhouse of steel and mil tech.

Eight great wheels supported a multiton chassis, the tires bulletproof even at point-blank range. The independent suspension allowed the juggernaut to cross the most rugged terrain imaginable with little or no reduction in speed. The hull was waterproof up to depths of five feet, and would float after that depth. Two small propellers in the rear could propel it through water at a speed of nearly 30 mph under ideal conditions, but it generally moved a lot slower than that. The belly was armored against landmines, the front window was made of bullet-resistant Armorlite plastic, and the louvered gunports could be closed tight enough for the LAV to be gas-bomb proof. There was even a heavy-duty winch on the front to assist the wag to traverse steep hills or to pull itself out of a swamp. The companions would have used that to rein in the Hummer, but the cable couldn't be cut quickly and timing had been of the essence.

Designed for a crew of six, plus two officers and a driver, the LAV had more than enough room for the six companions, plus numerous boxes of supplies from the Deep Storage Locker. Blasters, ammo, grens, food, bed rolls, medical supplies; the wealth of the ancient world filled the deck, secured under camou netting or strapped down into empty jumpseats set along the metal walls.

Watching Jak pour yet another canister of condensed fuel into the machine, Ryan had to privately admit that although the LAV was impressive, it was far from being perfect. All of the fancy electronic gear was useless, zapped by the EMP of the nuke storms or chilled by the long decades. The smoke generators were clogged solid with grease, and the control circuits for the 25 mm minigun were fried, the deadly rapid-fire was chilled.

But those were minor considerations in comparison to the incredible rate that colossal Detroit engines consumed fuel. Even after the earlier fight with the guardian, the tanks of the redoubt registered half full, which meant there was enough condensed fuel for a hundred trucks working for ten years. Juice enough for an army on the move. However, the huge tanks of the LAV could only hold so much, and Ryan had grudgingly allowed spare canisters of juice to be attached to the wag's armored back end. Those would be a prime target for any coldhearts they encountered. A single round into one of the gas cans and the LAV would be covered with flames. The wag was supposed to be fireproof, but a single crack in the armored hull, or in the louvered gunports, and the companions would burn alive. If the jelly was still alive outside, Ryan had decided that running away would be the best plan. How fast could the damn thing roll, anyway? Faster than a running person; that only made sense. What good was a guard that coldhearts could outrace? But faster than a wag? No nuking way.

"Tank full," Jak announced, screwing the cap back on to the ten-gallon container. "What do?"

"Set it aside. We're carrying enough as it is," Ryan stated truthfully.

Nodding in agreement, the teenager carried the sloshing container to the fuel pumps and put it out of the way. When Jak had first joined the companions and learned about the incredible redoubts, he could barely believe the tales of condensed fuel. The stuff looked and worked like regular juice, what Mildred called gasoline. Yet the fuel refused to evaporate, and an open cup of the stuff would still be there a month later, while gas would evaporate and be gone in less than a day. The mat-trans were useful, but it was the condensed fuel that truly impressed the teen. It was perfect for regular engines, or diesel engines, which even Mildred couldn't explain, and nothing was better in a Molotov cocktail. Just amazing stuff. Condensed fuel was even better than the nuke batteries, in his opinion.

"One last check," Krysty shouted to the others, cradling the MP-5 rapidfire in her arms. All the while they had been working, the companions kept a careful watch for any suspicious movements in the redoubt. They knew from experience that a Cerebus cloud could gain access to a redoubt, so if the black jelly was another guardian, then it could also get inside.

In an effort to counter that, Doc and Jak had stacked a dozen full cans of fuel near the mouth of the access tunnel and disabled the fire-suppressant system in the ceiling. If the blob appeared, a single gun shot in the cans would engulf the thing in flames. Unless they missed or there were two of them...

Meanwhile, J.B. had tried to attach the Vulcan minigun from the middle level of the redoubt to the top of the LAV, but Ryan had done too good a job of ripping out its control circuitry. Most of the normal mechanical controls were missing, and after several disastrous false starts, J.B. had finally admitted defeat. It was a rare occurrence when the Armorer couldn't master a wep, and he took the news in ill humor.

Thankfully, the LAV wasn't completely unarmed. Aside from the rapidfires and grens of the companions, Jak and Doc had skillfully wired several Claymore antipers mines to the angled sides of the wag. Anything coming within thirty feet of the LAV would be blown in two by the stainless-steel ball bearings and C-4 plas packed into each Claymore.

"That's it for me," Mildred announced, swinging a bag of trade goods into the rear of the transport.

The physician had carefully gone through the vault and chosen a selection of items that couldn't be used against them in a battle, but that would be priceless at any ville: aluminum mess kits, plastic combs, pocket mirrors, seed corn, Swiss Army knives and such. Those were trinkets for the civilians. The nobles at a ville would get U.S. Army boots, live brass and revolvers. However, nobody got a rapidfire, or grens.

Already inside the LAV, Doc took the bag and stuffed it into a hammock rigged for carrying the more delicate of the cargo. The useless items such as the radar, radio and such had been removed to make extra space. And every little bit helped. A couple of years earlier in another armored wag they nicknamed *Leviathan*, the companions had filled a trailer and packed it full of supplies to drag along behind. They lost the trailer on the first day, and the resulting blast of the detonating spare ammo came perilously close to ending their lives. Since then, everything went inside a wag or was left behind. With the exception of those all-important gas cans, which would be disposed of quickly if necessary.

Taking a jumpseat set along the wall, Doc gave a grunt of discontentment. Oddly enough, a few months back, they had encountered *Leviathan* again, but this time it wasn't under their control and the resulting firefight had been hellishly fierce. The companions had won, but only due to the direct assistance of Kate, a trader. Some people thought that the woman was the original Trader, the legendary master of the Deathlands, but the companions knew the truth.

There were so many wheels within wheels, Doc mused, wiping off his hands. The Deathlands was filled with more mysteries than there were ways to die.

"What do you think about calling this tin can *Leviathan Two?*" Mildred asked with a smile, climbing into the transport.

Stoically, Doc raised both bushy eyebrows. "Really now, madam!"

"Okay, okay! It was just a thought."

Outside in the garage, Ryan did a last walk around the place, checking things over. There was no reason to think that once they departed the redoubt they couldn't get right back inside. Even if there was another of the jelly muties hiding in the water. But he liked to be prepared. What was it the Trader had liked to say? To achieve a victory, plan for failure. Smart words.

"Looking for something?" J.B. asked, resting a nuke lamp on top of the hood of a civie station wagon.

"No, just doing a double check," Ryan answered gruffly. Then he motioned at the nuke lamp. "How many did you make?"

"Three," J.B. replied with pride, lifting the heavy device. "There were a lot more nuke batteries and headlights, but I couldn't find enough of the right kind of wire to retard the voltage from blowing the bulbs. But three will be enough."

In spite of the fact that the companions had been traveling through the mat-trans system for years, it was only a few months ago that J.B. came up with the brilliant invention of the nuke lamp. Candles were cheap, but blew out easily and never gave off much light. Road flares smoked and smelled awful, and also burned out quickly. Most flashlights required batteries that hadn't been manufactured in a hundred years, and survivalist flashlights like Mildred's were incredibly rare. Then it occurred to the Armorer that all of the mil wags in a redoubt used a nuke battery to start the engines. The sealed powerpacks seemed to last forever and put out enough voltage to crank over even a tank engine. So taking some wiring from a civie car, and doing some fancy soldering, J.B. soon built a nuke lamp, a nuke battery with a predark headlight hardwired into place. The device gave off a blinding beam of white light, especially if a halogen lamp was used, and never ran out of power. Of course, the nuke lamps were much too heavy to carry in a backpack, occasionally short-circuited and always died if they fell into water, but they were still better than anything else known.

"Whatever else, at least we won't be in darkness anymore," Krysty said, coming closer. She lifted one of the nuke lamps in her free hand and thumbed the switch on top. The headlight gave an audible click, and from the headlight a blue-white light beam shot out that cut across the garage like a laser.

"Gaia, we certainly could have used these when we were underground in Tennessee," she commented, moving the beam along the far wall.

"Could have used a nuke in Tennie," Ryan corrected, picking up the third nuke lamp. "All right, looks like we're ready as we'll ever be. Let's get moving."

As the three companions went to the rear door of the LAV, Mildred and Doc helped them in by taking the nuke lamps and tucking the devices under the jumpseats. Jak stayed outside the wag, his MP-5 rapidfire resting on a shoulder. The teen had decided to be the door man for this run. Where there was one guardian, there could be more. Hopefully, the exploding Hummer had killed the jelly. But if half of it could still fight, then mebbe small pieces could, too. He had seen a lot of strange things over the years, and most of them had tried to ace him. When in doubt, always assume the worst.

Maneuvering through the jumble of supplies to reach the front of the wag, Ryan checked to make sure both gren bins on the walls were full, then eased himself into the driver's seat. Taking the navigator seat on the opposite side, Krysty flipped a few switches and started the electrical system. The internal lights pulsed a few times, then came on in a subdued glow, and ventilation fans began to softly whir.

Checking a rearview mirror, Ryan waited for J.B. to close and latch the rear doors before starting the engine. The entire vehicle shook slightly as the four nuke batteries under the corrugated floor surged with power and turned over the massive 275-horsepower Detroit diesel. Instantly the indicators on the dashboard came to life, the meters swinging promptly into the green zones for electrical power, fuel, oil, hydraulics and engine temp.

Turning a few dials, Krysty killed the flashing red indicators showing that there was trouble with the missing radar and radio equipment. They dimmed to a dull glow, but the strobing was still noticeable, so she placed a strip of duct tape over the lights to mask them from sight. Busting the bulbs would have been easier, but the woman hated to smash anything so incredibly old. Besides, the spare bulbs might come in handy someday.

Shifting the transmission into low gear, Ryan started to roll forward and entered the tunnel, with Jak walking close behind. Reaching the blast door, Ryan eased to a halt, the brakes sighing in response.

Standing at the keypad, Jak exchanged a glance with the big warrior behind the bulletproof windshield, then tapped in the exit code and pressed the lever. As the blast door started to ponderously move aside, Jak walked quickly to the rear of the LAV where J.B. already had one of the armored hatches open and waiting. The teen quickly climbed inside and shut the hatch tight, making sure the lock was engaged.

As the huge black exit door slowly began to open, the companions waited with baited breath for any sign of the guardian or its spawn. But the watery tunnel appeared to be devoid of life. The charred wreckage of the Hummer stood off to the left, the nearby array of bricks cracked and discolored.

"Roof looks solid," Ryan noted, turning on the headlights.

Rolling to the very edge of the floor of the redoubt, Ryan studied the interior of the tunnel as the blast door completed its ponderous journey and boomed into the wall.

"Hold on tight," Ryan advised his friends, shifting into gear.

Everybody grabbed for the straps hanging off the walls, as the one-eyed man switched on the eight-wheel drive and the big wag nosed into the tunnel. As the front tires cleared the floor, the prow of the LAV dipped downward and then the front of the transport sharply dropped into the water with a tremendous splash. Thrown forward, the companions almost lost their seats. The rear of the LAV moved off the floor and also dropped into the flooded tunnel. Loose items went flying, and a couple of grens bounced out of open bins on the walls to roll freely on the floor.

As the companions unbuckled their seat belts and scrambled to reclaim the explos charges, Ryan checked to make sure the internal seals were holding and no moisture was seeping into the wag. The dark waters rose to just below the window level. If the LAV flooded, they would probably have to use the top hatch to get out. But the seals registered tight and there was no sign of leakage.

"So far, so good," Krysty muttered, switching on the wiper blades to clear the dripping windows. The slightly blurry headlights of the vehicle extended far along the tunnel until the sheer distance rendered them useless. Big tunnel! Checking out the side window, Krysty saw that the nearby brick walls were dripping from the spray, and a choppy surface was still rippling with waves from their sudden immersion.

Glancing over a shoulder, Ryan saw the others return the grens to the wall bins. J.B. used some of the duct tape to cover the open tops. Smart move.

"All clear," J.B. reported, sitting again and buckling on his seat belt. "But it's a good thing we taped the handles on the grens. One of the arming pins came free and if I hadn't shoved it back in less than eight seconds…" He spread his hands wide in the imitation of a detonation.

Brushing back one of her beaded plaits, Mildred shivered at the thought of the charge going off inside the metal vehicle. There wouldn't have been enough of them remaining to mop up with a sponge from the explosive compression, and then the halo of shrapnel would have ricocheted off the armored walls for minutes. Which was a lot longer than it would have been necessary to reduce whatever was left of them into mincemeat.

"Spam in a can," Mildred stated, remembering a phrase she had heard once in a old B&W war movie. It was a hell of a grisly image.

Closing her eyes, Krysty whispered a little prayer to Gaia in thanks, Doc looked queasy from the implied results and Jak popped a stick of chewing gum into his mouth and began contently chewing.

"Just hope it doesn't happen again," Ryan growled, shifting into gear once more.

"Better not." Mildred sighed, leaning back in her seat. Five minutes out of the redoubt and they almost blew themselves up. Why didn't she have gray hair yet?

Tapping the sonar screen, Krysty got no response. But even if the belly unit had still been working, that drop could have broken it. The LAV was tough, but not indestructible.

Bobbing slightly in the dark water, the wag started forward, the eight huge wheels sending out a spray behind them. Switching on the propellers, Ryan felt the transport lurch and then begin to move faster and smoother, the rpm of the engine steady rising as the temperature started increasing. Nuking hell, something was wrong with one of the air intakes. Damn engine was overheating already! Cutting off the propellers, Ryan saw the temperature start to go back down, and settled in for a bumpy ride using just the eight tires.

"What do you think we'll find at the end, lover?" Krysty asked, rigging the rapidfire to hang around her neck.

"Hopefully a way out," Ryan answered as the wag splashed along the tunnel.

"And if not?"

"Then we make one. We got enough plas to crack the moon."

"True enough," the woman agreed, and settled in to watch the surface of the water for any suspicious movements.

For almost an hour the LAV rolled and floated along the flooded tunnel, the headlights never revealing anything but the endless brick walls. Once, the water surface rose to a dangerous level as the machine dipped into a depression of some kind. Braking to a halt, Ryan waited for the waves to calm until the submerged headlights revealed they were in what resembled a blast crater, or a pothole, about ten yards wide.

Then the LAV floated slowly to the surface once more, and they kept going. Advancing cautiously, Ryan held his breath, waiting for the water to rush in through the gunports, when the front tires grabbed on to the floor of the tunnel and the LAV lifted out of the hollow back to a safe position. Lowering their speed, Ryan breathed a sigh of relief, then the LAV tilted slightly to the left.

"We aren't rolling," Krysty said in shock, looking at the dashboard controls. The blinking indicators threw a rainbow across her worried features. "So how can we—"

There came the sound of a muffled crack from under the heavy machine, and the right side of the LAV listed, the choppy water rising to slosh against the windows.

"The floor is crumbling!" Ryan cursed, stomping on the gas pedal. "Fireblast, we're too heavy! Gotta get clear of this crater! Hold on!"

The Detroit power plant roared with power and the LAV violently lurched forward to miraculously right itself. But then from behind came a great bellow as a huge air bubble broke the surface, closely followed by a splintering sound that rapidly rose in volume.

Clenching the steering yoke tightly, Ryan revved the engine to the max. Whether or not the blast from the Hummer had weakened the floor of the tunnel, or if was merely the weight of the LAV, it seemed clear that the predark tunnel was crumbling apart, and triple fast. Ryan knew that their one hope was to get clear of the weakened area before the sheer tonnage of the war wag started a chain reaction of destruction. The LAV could float, but not fly, and with the water gone, they would drop along with the rest of the debris into whatever lay below.

Suddenly the speedometer shook and Ryan saw that the wag was slowing. But the engine was at full power!

"Keep moving!" Krysty cried, staring in horror out the side window. "Don't stop for anything!"

That's when Ryan saw that the water level outside

was dropping fast, moving toward the struggling machine, the current battering them to a virtual standstill. Shitfire, the blast crater had to have weakened the concrete bed and their weight had finished the job. The entire tunnel was collapsing!

A falling brick bounced off the hood and then something crashed onto the roof. A building wave of water swamped the machine, shoving it backward in spite of the eight desperately spinning tires. More bricks fell in a sledgehammer cacophony, and Ryan fought to keep the wag traveling straight. If the LAV turned sideways, they would be helpless.

Reaching over to the controls, Krysty turned on the propellers, and the LAV surged forward again, gaining precious yards.

If we can just outlast the flood, we'll be fine, Ryan grimly thought, battling to get more speed from the lumbering diesel. Come on, you nuking piece of tin shit. Move!

But the backwash kept increasing in volume and force until it was more than the war wag could handle. Slowly, the LAV was forced into the crater until the rear dipped as the back wheels went over the rim. Then the next pair of tires followed, and the next. The sound of the water was rising until it sounded like an ocean whirlpool, or a waterfall, the noise echoing along the brick tunnel until reaching deafening levels.

"Fire the rear Claymores!" J.B. shouted over the roar of the rushing torrent. "All of 'em! Mebbe that'll shove us forward!"

The idea was crazy, but with no other choice Ryan decided to take the gamble and reached for the arming switch. But before he could, there came a crash of masonry and the LAV flipped over sideways as a section of the weakening brickwork dropped way completely. Everybody was shoved hard against their safety belts, and loose items went tumbling.

Now at the mercy of the rampaging flood, the wag slid directly into the hole and turned over again, leaving the companions upside down.

As the companions desperately grabbed their seat belts tightly, they were brutally pelted by grens and food packs from every direction. Throwing back his head, Jak cried out and went limp in his seat, blood on his face. Something slammed into the side of the LAV, and a tire loudly exploded. There came another strident collision, and the bulletproof front window shattered, the explosion of shards cutting both Ryan and Krysty. Moss-covered bricks and muddy water poured into the wag, smothering the companions, sloshing to the rear. A headlight smashed, casting the interior into darkness. Somebody screamed. Another person cursed. Then the world seemed to completely drop away, and the armored wag began to wildly bounce down a series of widening cracks, plummeting into a rocky darkness that seemed to have no end.

Chapter Nine

With both of her hands tied behind her back, Lily Rogan came awake fighting for breath. Something kept punching her in the belly, making it almost impossible to drag in air.

Forcing open her tearing eyes, the girl saw only rushing ground in front of her face and just for a moment thought that she was falling. Then Lily realized that she was actually moving sideways above the soil.

This was a bike! she thought in alarm. I'm strapped to the rear of a racing two-wheeler! So why was there no sound coming from the big machines?

Suddenly, foulness seemed to well inside the woman. Her brothers were using predark tech? Slavery, chilling, rape…these were things she could accept. That was just the way of the Deathlands. But using tech was unforgivable. Lily dimly remembered hearing stories from her elders how science had brought down the nuke storm of skydark and destroyed the world. Afterward, howling mobs of civies had chased down every traitorous whitecoat that could be found and brutally nailed them to crosses, then set fire to the dirty libraries and labs. But now her brothers were using tech? It was beyond belief. Clearly, they had finally gone insane.

The bike hit a bump, slamming the girl against the fender. In raw horror, Lily focused on the spinning tire only inches away, a cold dread filling her veins at the thought of her hair getting caught in the spokes. If her flailing hair became entangled in the wheel, her face would be pulled into the wheel and quickly removed. Or worse, the hair would rip off her scalp and she would quickly die of blood loss. But not slowly. She once saw a person die that way when a stickie attacked them from behind. It had taken the screeching man a long hour to finally buy the farm.

Twisting her head to the side, Lily found that she could keep her flying hair away from the deadly spokes of the wheel. It also was easier to take a breath. Straining against her bonds, the bruised girl took in ragged breaths until the last of the fog left her beleaguered mind.

Trying to rock to the motion of the jouncing bike, Lily fought to maintain her balance and stay alive. If her bonds loosened, she would fall under the two-wheeler and be crushed to death. Lashed into this position, a prisoner had to fight to stay alive, with no chance to think about escape. She was trapped, bound and helpless. Captured alive by her crazy brothers. Dirty tech-lovers.

Slowly the land below Lily changed from sand to grass. Were they heading into the forest? But that was full of muties! A dip in the ground rammed the fender into her aching torso, slamming her against the cargo pod. At first she flinched from the contact, but soon understood that the cargo pod was all that was keeping her on the fender, and finally allowed herself to lean against it fully.

Unknown amounts of time passed. Starving, queasy, bruised and barely able to breathe, Lily was starting to hallucinate about her childhood. With the death of her father, her slut of a woman had gone to work at the local gaudy house with obvious delight. Try as she might, Lily simply couldn't understand that, but some women seemed to love being treated like an animal. It was beyond comprehension. And with her growing physical beauty, the young girl was doomed to the same fate. It was only everyone's fear of her four mad brothers that kept her out of the life. No man alive would risk the terrible wrath of the Rogan boys by daring to touch their little sister.

Suddenly the bike banked sharply and mercifully began to slow. Soon the brakes squealed and her torment stopped as the machine came to a complete halt.

Craning up her head, Lily dragged in great lungfuls of air, and waited for the world to stop spinning from the riotous ride. There was some sort of sharp stink coming off the engine, not the reek of shine, or the weird smell of predark juice, or anything else that she could identify. It almost smelled like wet dirt after lightning had struck the ground. Did the wag use lighting as fuel? Was that possible? What disgusting tech was being used to befoul the world now?

Ever so slowly, the black spots faded from her sight and Lily felt her heart cease to pound. That was when the pain returned to her temple and she remembered the slaughter at the Watering Hole. Friends and customers torn into pieces by the fancy rapidfires held by her brothers. Slack faces looking into eternity from every table, blood flowing like the tears of the world. Forcing away those useless thoughts, Lily raised her head to hesitantly look around. Let the dead bury the dead. Her task was to stay alive and not join them.

The other three bikes were parked nearby, the riders out of sight. The ground was covered with green grass and there were trees forming a sort of wall around the clearing. Off to the side was a large boulder with a small waterfall splashing out of the side to form a pond. Could that be natural? she pondered. Probably not. More nuke-sucking tech. She could feel it in her bones. This was a place of foulness worse than any rad pit.

The muddy bank was thick with reeds and flowers. There were some insects flying about the plants, and a frog gave a deep-throated ribbet. Past the boulder, there seemed to be some sort of a concrete building, but Lily couldn't see that far behind, the cargo pods of the two-wheelers blocking the way. Was this their spread?

As Lily watched, two of her brothers strode into view, those fancy rapidfires strapped across their backs. Now, Lily noticed there was a gap in the trees and the two men moved some cut bushes to cover the opening, then lashed wire between two trees to hold the uprooted shrubbery in place. It really didn't seem like much of a gate, and she doubted that it would stop a howler or a stickie. Then Lily blinked at the brutal realization that the barrier wasn't mean to keep folks out, but to keep captives in.

Just then a shadow cut off the sun, and she looked up to see only a dark outline.

"Okay, get off," John commanded.

"I can't," she croaked, wiggling slightly. "My hands..."

With a guttural laugh, John slashed out with a knife and the rawhide strips binding her wrists easily parted. Completely helpless, Lily slid off the fender and hit the ground sprawling, her legs splaying wide, the skirt hitching up to her waist exposing her lack of underwear.

"Son of a bitch," Robert said, wiping his neck with a red cloth. "The little bitch is open for biz!"

Lily quickly lowered her skirt and closed her trembling knees. She struggled into a submissive kneeling position, but kept her face turned down, knowing the only way out of this was total obedience. Death would set her free, but the path to that escape was filled with more pain than she could accept. The price was too high to pay.

A few yards away, the other sluts from the gaudy house were clustered together, weeping and holding one another for protection. Shelly, Elisa, Lara. Their faces were streaked with road dust, their hair sticking out in wild disarray, their clothing ripped and torn, the combination giving them an almost feral look. Shelly and Elisa were fully clothed, but Lara was wearing only a thin cotton dress made from an old bedsheet. Most of the buttons had been ripped away to partially expose her pink-tipped breasts, and it was abundantly clear that she was wearing nothing underneath the thin material. Her dark eyes full of terror, Lara was also bleeding from the wrists where she had clearly tried to chew her way loose.

That had been foolish, Lily thought, rubbing her own wrists. If she had gotten free during the ride here, what then? Fall off the bike and get chilled?

Sheathing his knife, John grabbed Lily by the hair and pulled her up to face the sun. Noon? No, it was afternoon, she realized, almost evening. Wherever this was, it was very far from Dempster. No hope of the ville sec men coming to rescue her, then. Even if any of them were still alive.

Blinking against the pain, Lily tried to keep a neutral expression. Obey. Obey their every command and live. She knew there was no other choice. Death wouldn't be offered to her as an option.

"Bah, little sister is too groggy to party," John declared, releasing his grip. "Too damn ugly, too. Must be part mutie, I bet."

Lily said nothing, accepting the insult.

"Okay, bitch, get moving and start cooking dinner." John laughed, wiping a hand on his shirt as if she were diseased. "Meanwhile, we are gonna go ride your friends for a while."

"Yes, sir," Lily muttered, rising stiffly to her bare

feet. Friends? Those are no friends of mine, she thought bitterly, remembering how badly she was treated at Dempster by the madam and the others. Once her brothers had left the ville, everybody in town had taken their revenge on her for their actions.

"At least Lily knows her proper place."

"What about the others?" Alan asked, pulling a knife from his sleeve and testing the edge on a thumb.

"Their place is bent over a table," Robert croaked, fingering the jagged scar on his throat.

"Nuking right it is!" Edward growled. Going over to the women, he grabbed the one in the ripped dress and hauled her erect, the rest of the dress coming off in the process.

Shivering more in fear than from the cold, Lara tried to smile at the big man, but his expression only made her flinch in horror. Laughing at her reaction, Edward started to run his hands over her body, while the rest of the brothers went to the other sluts and brutally stripped off their clothing, slapping the girls when they didn't move fast enough to comply with their unspoken commands.

"Too bad we couldn't haul along one more," John said, clearly enjoying himself. "But beggars can't be choosers, eh, brothers?"

The three Rogans raucously agreed and hauled the now screaming women across the grass and into the concrete building.

As the iron door closed with a solid boom, Lily cast a furtive glance at the row of sleek motorcycles, but raw fear put an end to her thoughts about jacking a ride. What should she do? What could she do? The obvious answer was get busy cooking.

Shuffling to the fire, Lily found wood and a bucket of water, along with cans of food such as she had never seen. She couldn't read the words, but the pictures were clear enough. One showed what looked like beef stew, and another can illustrated whole white potatoes, plus coffee, sugar… This was chow for a baron. A fortune in predark food. Where had they gotten such things? Thank goodness no tech was involved here.

Building a blaze, Lily got some water boiling for coffee, and started the stew simmering, stirring the food with a green stick after peeling off the bark. Concentrating on the task at hand, Lily did her best to ignore the sounds of pain and laughter coming from inside the concrete building. Better them than me, she thought. She had heard about the perverted appetites of her brothers, and there was no doubt what was happening to the three women behind the closed iron door.

Going to fetch some water from the pool, Lily passed near one of the machines, and it gave a mechanical whoop, the headlights flashing wildly. What the hell?

Almost instantly, the door to the building was thrown open and John stepped into view. He was stark naked and clearly interrupted in the middle of having sex, but there was also a ready blaster held in his hand. A single glance from the furious man sent Lily scurrying back to the cook fire.

"Mind your place, bitch," John snarled menacingly,

clicking back the hammer of the massive wheelgun. "Or else you'll be next!"

Dumbly, she nodded in submission. After a few moments he closed the door with a bang.

As the day wore on, Lily stole a few spoons of the stew to ease her stabs of hunger. When evening arrived, she did her best to keep the stew and coffee from burning. Her brothers would want lots to eat when they were done. Hopefully they wouldn't have her for dessert. Hunching her shoulders, Lily grabbed a fistful of warm ashes and rubbed it into her hair, then smeared dirt across her pretty features. Then bit a lip and smeared the blood about. The less attractive she looked, the better.

Eventually night came and the usual storm clouds covered the stars. With the moon behind a flat-top mesa on the horizon, the wooden glen was blanketed in darkness, the only source of light coming from the campfire, and some twinkling red dots on the curved dashboards of the sleek ebony wags.

Hoarding the small supply of wood, Lily banked the flames and did her best to nurse the blaze along, adding water to the stew when needed, and finally throwing away the old coffee to make a new batch. There was more than enough, so they shouldn't miss a handful wasted. Or would they?

Almost dropping the bucket, Lily jerked at the sounds of three blaster shots. Then the door to the blockhouse swung open and the four men walked out of the building. John was holstering a blaster, and there was no sign of the kidnapped gaudy sluts.

"Now we're gonna have a little chat with you about trying to jack a bike," Edward said, pulling off his belt, starting to wrap it around a scarred fist.

Backing away from the crackling fire, Lily pressed her face into her hand and began to weep, knowing the night of pain was only just beginning.

RUNNING, RUNNING endlessly. Ryan was running through the predark ruins of some nameless city. The one-eyed youth was down to the last arrow in his crossbow and the black-powder Colt blaster in his holster was empty. Fireblast, there had been so many of the muties he thought the fighting would never end! Now he was alone, lost in a strange city, cut off from the colonel, and bleeding from the wound in his aching side.

Stopping on a corner, Ryan glanced down all four streets of the intersection to make sure the area was clear. Then he gingerly removed the shirt, the cloth sticking to his skin from the layers of dried blood. That bullwhip had cut him deep, but the youth had managed to chill the mutie master before the cold-hearts arrived and changed the tide of battle. Why the nuking hell would anybody fight on the side of the stickies? Made no damn sense at all.

Pulling out his Bowie knife, Ryan carefully cut the shirt into long strips and bound the wound as best he could. He knew some shine would help, both to fight infection and for the pain. But his canteen was empty. Mebbe he could find a tavern or liquor store in the ruins.

Glancing hopefully about, he saw a building that stood out from all of the others. Damnedest thing, the exterior was just as badly damaged as all of the others, cracked with age, and with hundreds of ancient pockmarks, blaster holes from the rioting after skydark. But it was clean of any ivy or dirt on the windows. Walking closer, Ryan stared at the building, and shivered from the oddest feeling that somebody was staring back at him from inside. Was the place inhabited? If so, mebbe he could trade for some food or black powder.

However, the front of the building was covered with a steel grating, as impenetrable as the Border ville gate. But on the side of the store was a small set of brick stairs that lead to a green metal door. A door on the second floor? That was odd.

As he climbed the steps, Ryan saw there was some sort of a symbol etched into the metal. Not just scratched into the paint, but actually carved into the steel itself and then painted over as if to hide its existence. A circle, surrounded by an oval with a small star set off to one side—

WITH A GASP, Ryan sat up and banged his head on something hard. Spitting curses, he massaged the cut and tried to look around, but everything was pitch-black, and the world seemed off kilter. The dream. He had been having that dream again. The empty desert ville, the door on the second floor and that weird symbol of circles and a star. It had to have been years since the last time he suffered through the triple-damn thing. Then everything came rushing back and Ryan realized that he was still buckled into the driving seat of the LAV.

Fireblast, they had to be underground! There was dampness on his shirt. He checked himself over for wounds, but it was only mud from their descent. Had they actually survived the fall? Incredible. Thankfully, they didn't seem to be falling anymore, but there was still the background sound of running water.

Trying to shift about in the driving seat, Ryan felt something crawl across his face and swatted at his cheek. Nothing there. It took the groggy man a few seconds to realize there was dirt falling on him. But how…oh yeah, the windshield had been broken.

Trying to listen past the splashing water, Ryan dimly heard labored breathing. Okay, some of others had to also be alive. Good. However, they were probably hurt, and any one of them could have been aced in the landslide. *Krysty.*

Trying not to think about that, Ryan struggled to get out of the tilted seat, and found that the Steyr had somehow become tangled with the steering yoke. Trapped by his own longblaster! Forcing his hands to reach behind his shoulders, the Deathlands warrior finally reached the strap and clumsily got the buckle released. The Steyr promptly came loose and started to slip out the broken window. Damn! Ryan made a desperate grab for the wep, but it sailed free and disappeared into the darkness. He began to curse again when the weapon clattered onto something hard and there was an answering echo.

The wag had to be in some kind of a cavern or underground passage, Ryan guessed. There was no way of telling at the moment, and he had much more pressing problems at the moment.

Fumbling his hands along the dashboard, Ryan found the controls for the interior lights and flipped the switches, but there was no response. Either the tubes were busted or the wiring was ripped. If the nuke batteries had broken open, then the whole chassis would have been electrified and everybody chilled.

Rummaging in his jacket pocket, Ryan found his butane lighter and pulled it free, then paused to sniff. Okay, the air was clear of gas fumes. No chance of roasting themselves alive from a fuel spill. Satisfied, he thumbed the butane lighter alive, the tiny flame a welcome sight. Turning the wheel to the stop, Ryan made the blue flame grow inches high, casting a moonlight glow around the interior of the angled wag.

With her thick hair hanging limply across her face, Krysty was slumped over in the navigator seat, an arm sticking out the smashed side window. Reaching out slowly, Ryan gingerly touched her exposed throat and sighed in relief when he felt a strong pulse. She was just unconscious.

"Anybody alive?" Ryan asked over the noise of the

rushing water. His voice was low and guttural, sounding like something that had just crawled out of a grave. Blind norad, he could use a drink of water.

Groans and mutters answered from the darkness below.

Extinguishing the lighter, Ryan tucked it away, knowing this next action would require both hands. Fighting his way free from the seat, Ryan found the footing tricky on the slanted floor, and as he moved, the armored wag shifted position slightly. Shitfire, the ground had to still be settling. Or else they were simply on a slope and about to plunge into an abyss again. There was a towline and winch on the front of the APC that might stop the wag. If he could get outside without starting an avalanche, and if he could find something to attach the line to... He'd have to take it easy or else he might send them all straight to the bottom of who knew what? It was a nuking miracle they were still sucking air, and he damn well knew for a fact the universe never gave you two miracles in a row.

"Dark night, my head... Millie, you okay?" J.B. asked from the blackness.

"B-been better," Mildred panted, fingers checking over her body for any damage. No bones seemed broken, and there was no feeling of numbness to indicate a major trauma. That was good news.

"Where are you?" J.B. asked, and there came a clatter of objects falling over. "Damn!"

Reaching out for the man, Mildred encountered only air until touching his glasses. He grunted in surprise, then took her hand and gave it a reassuring squeeze. The two shared a private moment in the Stygian blackness, each celebrating that the other was still alive. Then the couple was interrupted by the scratching of the metal striker and the hissing flame of a butane lighter held by Ryan. The one-eyed man's face was grim in the flickering light. The two shared a nod, acknowledging their amazing luck.

Now looking around, Mildred could see that the LAV was tilted backward and canted slightly to the left. Ammo boxes and fuel cans were tumbled together, muddy shards of bulletproof glass lying everywhere and reflecting a rainbow of colors. There was the sound of water nearby, along with the rustling noise of crumbling dirt, occasionally punctuated by the dull thud of a falling object. Probably a brick or loose stone. They were underground!

"What happened?" Mildred asked, swallowing hard. The armored personnel carrier wasn't on an even keel, and her stomach was very unhappy about the unorthodox position.

"We survived," Ryan answered humorlessly, one hand holding on to the rim of a gren bin, the gray duct tape bulging from the pile of mil spheres inside.

Unexpectedly, there came a long string of biting vulgarities, and Ryan allowed himself a rare smile at the realization it was from the usual demur Doc.

"That's pretty good, Doc." J.B. chuckled. "Never heard that last one before. A camel, you say?"

"Indeed, it was a particular favorite of my old host,

Cort Strasser," Doc rumbled, pushing a bedroll off his chest. "Especially when he was torturing me…" The scholar broke into a ragged cough before continuing. "And what is our current status, my dear Ryan? Are we buried alive?"

"Can't tell yet. I'll let you know," Ryan replied, then stopped at the sight of Jak. The teenager was slumped over in his jumpseat, blood matted in his white hair.

"Millie, Jak's hurt!" J.B. cried.

"So I see. Get me out of this," Mildred demanded, struggling with the seat belt. "The goddamn buckle is jammed, or something!"

Drawing his panga, Ryan cut the physician loose and she crawled like a crab across the piles of jumbled supplies to reach the still teen.

Curiously, Ryan stared at the shiny length of the curved blade. Panga? Didn't he just have the Bowie? No, wait that was just the dream. Damn thing felt so real sometimes he got confused when he awoke, not sure which was real, and which was the dream. He sheathed the blade. Old battle didn't matter. The Mutie Wars had been over for decades.

Easing out of his jumpseat, J.B. immediately lost his hat, the fedora fluttering down to land on the closed rear door amid a surplus of random items. Muttering under his breath, J.B. grabbed the hammock and hauled himself in the other direction, pawing through the cartons, boxes and bags.

Removing the tunnel brick that was lying on Jak's shoulder, Mildred gently probed the scalp wound with her fingertips and found no serious damage. A couple of stitches should fix the teenager just fine. Unless he had a concussion, but there was nothing she could do about that. CAT scans and X-rays were as long gone as delivery pizza and cable TV.

Looking around in the dim light, Mildred found her med kit and got to work. Sitting nearby, Doc flicked his own butane lighter into life to aid with the medical administrations, and soon the teen exhaled sharply and sat bolt upright.

"Shit," Jak drawled. "Get nuked?"

"Close enough. The tunnel collapsed," Mildred told him, threading a new length of fishing line into the upholstery needle. "Now be still. I'm not done with the stitching. You have a nasty scalp wound."

"Know that," Jak answered sullenly, looking away from the curved length of needle-sharp steel in her hand. He glanced about, his red eyes going wide. "How wag?"

"We don't know yet. But Ryan is going to do a recce."

"Good. Ouch!"

"I said to sit still!"

From the front of the wag there came a low groan and then a third butane flame appeared brightening the interior of the war wag considerably.

"Hi, lover," Krysty whispered, her hair flexing weakly around the pale face.

Impulsively, Ryan extended an arm, but the woman was out of reach. "You okay?" he asked, concern deepening his voice.

"Just fine." She smiled weakly. "Mother Gaia must have been with us today."

"Not all of the bastard time, she wasn't," Ryan replied, slipping slightly on the floor. "Just at the end."

"Where it counted the most."

He turned off his lighter. "If you say so."

Finding a canteen, Ryan took a long drink, then passed it to the others. By the time it came back, the container was empty, but everybody stopped coughing. Good enough for now.

Bracing his boot against the gunport, Ryan awkwardly walked down the inside of the wag, stepping from gunnery chair to the fuel can, to a cardboard box full of MRE packs, then landing solidly on the closed rear door.

Waiting for any movement from the wag, Ryan relaxed a bit when nothing happened, then kicked off the latch. As the hatch swung free, loose items began to rain out, clattering down onto what sounded like bare stones, but then there came a couple of watery splashes.

"Here," Doc said, holding out his ebony stick.

Accepting the sheathed sword, Ryan wedged it into place as a prop to hold the hatch open, and shook the stick a few times to make sure the lid wouldn't slam back down onto somebody's hand or head. That much steel would remove fingers faster than an angry baron.

"Aw, mutie shit," J.B. cursed in the red light of the two hissing butane lighters. "The nuke lamp is dead."

"All three of them?" Ryan demanded irritably, shifting his balance as the LAV changed position slightly.

"Just a minute."

But it was a lot quicker than that when a searing beam of electric brilliance split the darkness. Temporarily blinded, the companions cried out in pained response and covered their eyes. The interior of the war wag was now illuminated brighter than daylight as the white beam reflected off the sea-foam-green ceiling and walls in a crazy quilt pattern.

"Sure wish I had a rheostat for this baby," J.B. said, turning the column of light to shine on the nonreflective surface of a canvas duffel bag. "Be nice to dial up the level of light wanted."

"Better if ground not collapse," Jak said gruffly, adjusting the bloody bandage tied around his head. "Wish that, instead."

"Yeah, yeah. Look, you gonna die, or what?"

"Not today."

"Good. Then lend a hand moving some of this stuff."

Straddling the open doorway, Ryan raised a hand to shield his eye from the glare of the nuke lamp as J.B. moved the beam across the wag to finally angle it downward. In the shockingly white beam, Ryan could finally see what was below them. Stones and dirt, the dank earth dotted with canteens and ammo boxes. The splashing sound was louder now, but nothing was in sight. Was the noise another echo? He knew that sounds did strange things under the ground.

Bracing himself, the big man stepped off the wag and fell the few feet to the ground. He landed on the balls of his feet in a crouch, instinctively braced for the soil to give away again and start another slide. But the ground held, and Ryan slowly stood to pull the SIG-Sauer from its holster.

Looking carefully around, Ryan observed that the LAV was resting inside a pile of dirt on a ledge next to a rushing river that disappeared into darkness. That was when he noticed droplets sprinkling from above like a gentle rain.

Advancing warily to the rim of the ledge, Ryan saw smashed bricks and pieces of broken concrete mixed among the stones. When the tunnel collapsed, the debris filled in the hole made by the cave-in, landslide, whatever you call it. Great. There was no telling how deep they were, and there was no nuking way they were going to be able to dig through that mess without bringing down the rest of the cavern.

"We landed on a rock shelf in a river chasm," Ryan announced, holstering the blaster. "Doesn't seem very stable."

"An underground river?" Mildred shouted back.

"Looks like, yeah."

Just then a bedroll came tumbling out of the tilted wag, followed by a fedora and an MP-5 rapidfire. The blaster hit a stone, making a metallic clatter, the sound repeating off the rocky passageway of the river for a very long time. A boot dangled from the bottom of the war wag, and then J.B. hit the ground.

"Okay, lower away," the Armorer said, looking upward.

There came some mutterings from inside the LAV, then the nuke lamp began to descend as if by magic. It was only when the device got close that Ryan could see the length of rope tied around the handle.

As the lamp slowly rotated on the end of the rope, the white beam swept through the darkness, clearly showing the details of the ledge and the river chasm.

"The water must have undercut the exit tunnel of the redoubt," J.B. said, going to the edge of the shelf. In the light of the nuke lamp, the two men could spot stalagmites and stalactites in the passageway.

"This has been here for years, decades," Ryan reluctantly agreed, adjusting the patch over the ruin of his left eye.

"Mebbe this was the home of the guardian," J.B. said as a question.

Ryan shrugged. But then he tensed as a rat swam by, and he drew his blaster once more. Working the arming bolt, J.B. swung around his Uzi and together they tracked its passage until the animal was gone. No sense wasting ammo just because they had extra. That was feeb thinking.

"That wasn't an albino," Ryan said, thoughtfully chewing a lip. "So there must be some kind of avenue to the surface."

Starting to reply, J.B. broke into a grin and grabbed his fedora off the ground. "Rats are a lot smaller than us," he reminded his friend, beating the hat against a leg to get it clean. "There might just be a crack, or old predark pipes."

"Then we dig," Ryan stated. "Or swim."

J.B. put the fedora back into place, saying, "Digging sounds good to me."

With a dull thud, the heavy nuke lamp landed.

Taking out the panga again, Ryan cut the device free and shone the beam about for a recce. The landslide was extensive, stretching for hundreds of feet in both direction of the riverway. Wetting a finger, Ryan raised it, but couldn't feel any passage of air. They might be in a closed chasm, the air trapped here since before skydark.

"Ace those lighters!" Ryan snapped. "No more flames until we're sure of the air supply."

Even as the two flames disappeared inside the war wag, something large dropped through the hatch to land next to Ryan.

Uncoiling like a jungle cat, Krysty slowly stood, her hands moving clumsily along the new rapidfire.

"Hey, lover." She smiled, then scrunched her face, puckered and spit to the side. A bloody tooth hit the ground. Gaia! Well, at least she didn't have to wait for the pliers anymore.

"You okay?" Ryan asked, glancing at the object on the dirt.

"Much better, actually," Krysty replied, wiping some blood off her full lips.

Walking closer to the vehicle, the woman checked the sides of the wag, then underneath. "Any hope of getting this free?" she asked, massaging her cheek to ease the discomfort. The pain was already fading.

"No way we're getting this bastard loose," J.B. said unhappily, pointing into the shadows. "See there? The transmission is busted apart, three of the axles are broken, all four of the tires on the right side are flat…" He grimaced. "Good thing the wag is armored top and bottom against landmines. That was what saved our asses."

"If indeed, we are saved, old friend," Doc rumbled from above. There came a rustle of cloth from inside the wag and a backpack landed with a thump.

Setting the nuke lamp a safe distance from the edge of the ledge, Ryan and the others started ferrying the backpacks and assorted boxes away from the LAV, food packs, ammo boxes, other supplies. During the process, Krysty started taking small sips from her canteen at regular intervals, and spitting red-tinted water into the river. After about a hour, she stopped doing it and began to hesitantly smile again.

"Can't see a thing, dear lady," Doc rumbled politely, hauling a rolled-up tent to the side pile.

Straightening her back, Krysty grinned. "It was a back molar," she explained. "But thanks."

"No hard foods for a few days," Mildred advised, setting down a metal box full of C-4 blocks. "And add a little salt to the water you're using to rinse with until the bleeding stops."

"It has stopped," Krysty said, using a finger to pull back her cheek and expose the rear row of teeth. "The hole is already closed. See?"

"Well, so it has," Mildred observed, sounding impressed. Damn, Krysty healed fast! "Just lay off the beef jerky for a while to play it safe. Okay?"

"Sure. No prob."

In short order, the LAV was empty, and the others descended. Obviously woozy from his head injury, Jak needed a little help from Mildred, and he gratefully sat once they reached the shelf.

"River," the teenager said, tilting his head. "Mighty close. Any gators?"

"Just a rat so far," Ryan answered.

Frowning, Jak pulled his Colt and checked the weapon. "Good," he said softly, but kept the wep in his hand.

In the harsh beam of the nuke lamp, the companions took stock of their supplies. There was plenty of food and water, and enough blasters and brass to take down a baron. In fact, there was way too much for them to carry, even though a lot of things had been smashed in the landslide. Several cans of fuel had jarred open, the ground directly below the LAV soaked dark with the explosive fluid. Ryan scowled at the sight. The damn stuff didn't evaporate so there was almost no smell. If they had jumped from the LAV with a lighter going, the whole ledge might have gone up, the flames rising directly into the wag like a chimney. He tried not to shiver. They would have been fried alive, with nowhere to run. That was close. Too damn close.

An entire box of MREs was found soaked in the

river, the envelopes intact, and floating downriver out of reach like fat silver islands. Two bedrolls were missing, and a couple of the spare bolt-action BAR longblasters were damaged, their barrels bent out of alignment where something heavy had slammed onto them. The curve wasn't much, but the longblasters were rendered completely useless.

"Save the brass," Ryan advised sagely. He darted forward and stood with the Steyr longblaster in his hands. He gave the weapon a cursory inspection, then grudgingly slung it over a shoulder. It seemed okay. But it would be wise to depend on the 9 mm SIG-Sauer until he was able to field strip the Steyr to make sure it was undamaged. There were a lot of ways to leave this world, and the dumbest was to get blown open by your own wep because the barrel was clogged with dirt.

"What do we do now, my dear Ryan?" Doc asked, tucking his ebony stick into his belt like a Medieval sword.

"We have to travel by the river," Ryan said slowly, brushing back his filthy hair. "There's no other path."

"We can make a raft from the remaining four tires," J.B. stated. "Did it before that time in the Darks."

"Had wood then," Jak countered.

"So we make do. You wanna swim?"

The teenager looked at the murky river a few yards below them. The surface was stained with swirling colors from the spilled fuel, and jagged rocks rose from the water like the teeth of a submerged beast. "Shit no," he stated simply.

"I just hope this leads to the surface and doesn't go deeper underground," Mildred said with a worried tone. "I want to be buried after I die, not vice versa."

Sorting out the items needed, the companions got to work. Getting the tires loose required some serious digging, but eventually the task was accomplished. J.B. and Jak used most of the nylon rope to lash the tires together as strongly as possible, with Doc adding the empty fuel cans underneath for a little extra buoyancy. A sheet of canvas was stretched over the collection and a camou net was cut into squares to hold down their supplies.

Opening a few MRE packs, the companions had a fast meal and made some hard decisions. They took most of the ammo that fit their blasters, one canteen of water each, six MREs each, and all of the grens they could carry.

"What do we do with the rest?" Krysty asked, nudging a pile of Claymore mines and two rocket launchers. Those had been the prize of the redoubt. Any baron alive would trade everything he owned for just one of the launchers.

"Leave it all," Ryan said, shifting his backpack.

Lashing the netting around the loose items, they tied the piles to the raft, trying to balance it by sheer guesswork. Stopping for a brief break, the companions then lashed the raft to the front winch. J.B. wired a nuke lamp to the electric motor, then lowered the raft over the side of the ledge and into the river. It landed with a splash, and bobbed around for a few moments before leveling out.

Knotting an extra rope at his waist, Ryan rappelled to the raft, then released the knot so that the nylon length could be drawn up again. By the time Krysty descended, he was already lashed to a pile of supplies with a piece of seat belt. While Krysty did the same, J.B. joined them with the rebuilt nuke lamp, and soon everybody was on board.

"Hate to see go," Jak said, rubbing the bandage on his head.

"Just another wag," J.B. countered, folding his hat and tucking it away inside his leather jacket for safe-keeping.

"Meant the redoubt, Blaster Base One." Jak snorted, looking upward at the roof of the underground passageway. In his imagination, he saw through the umpteen tons of rock and steel separating them from the treasures of the redoubt.

"Say again?" Mildred asked with a frown.

Jak shrugged. "Thinking we make that home. Every ville needs name, so call Blaster Base One."

"Sure as hell had enough weps and brass to earn the title," J.B. said in tired amusement. Then he stopped talking as something lashed about just below the mottled surface of the river. When the motion stopped, there was only the fading contrail of a snake or eel. Or a lot of worms. There was no sign of the rat from before, but its absence did nothing to brighten his mood.

"Stay sharp," J.B. said in warning, resting a hand on his Uzi machine pistol. "We may have company."

"Gator?" Jak asked, pulling his blaster.

"You tell me."

The teen grunted in reply.

"Glad we have the raft," Krysty muttered, her hair tightening protectively around her face as she tightened the rope about her middle.

"Indeed, dear lady, I have smelled worse," Doc said, wrinkling his nose. "But not by much."

"Never been to Atlantic City, have you?" Mildred chuckled, then froze at the faint sound of something rustling in the darkness.

"Is the LAV sliding loose?" Krysty asked in a worried tone, lifting the nuke lamp to play the beam around. Only small pieces of the LAV were visible from this angle, but the pieces of the shattered windshield reflected the light like a million tiny stars.

No, wait a second, those weren't pieces of glass, but eyes! Ryan realized.

"Rats!" the one-eyed man cursed, drawing his blaster to start shooting at the vermin. A furry body exploded after being struck by the 9 mm Parabellum round, but the rest of the horde poured over the edge and down the embankment, streaming for the bobbing raft and its occupants.

Chapter Ten

High in the sky, the vulture circled the corpse lying sprawled on the desert ground. Distant thunder rumbled in the fiery orange clouds above as the winged predator came closer and closer to the mound of decaying flesh. Always watchful of potential enemies, the bird looked at the rocks and cactus near the food, but saw nothing unusual. The area was clear. It could freely claim the prize. The food was there for the taking!

Swooping sharply, the vulture landed on the pile of skin and organs, and plunged in its beak to tear loose a stinking gobbet of organ meat.

Deadly silent, the wave of stickies rose from the loose sand and swarmed over the startled bird to lash out with their disfigured hands. Suckers ripped off its wings and the vulture shrieked in agony, blood pumping from the ghastly wounds. Then a tall stickie bit completely through the bird's feathered neck, crimson spurting from the ragged stump. Its inhuman face smeared with gore, the triumphant stickie stumbled away with the morsel of living flesh. The eyes of the tormented bird rolled in unimaginable pain as the rest of the stickies grabbed hold of its body and tore off gobbets of flesh. The chunks adhering to the sucker-covered hands as if welded into place. The vulture called out once in unimaginable agony, then death came quickly.

Lumbering forward, the largest stickie beat the others away, then spread the least tasty of the organs around the area, trying clumsily to make the mound of assorted parts vaguely look like a single animal once more. The chief stickie started to leave, when a thought rose from deep within its primitive mind. The misshapen humanoid paused, unsure of what to do, afraid and confused. Then it hesitantly returned to the artificial corpse and took a handful of loose feathers. Slowly, the stickie started to walk around the pile of flesh, wiping away the footprints of the family. When finished, it realized in shock that its own footprints were visible. Turning clumsily, it started to walk backward to erase all traces of the feeding.

Retreating into the rocks, the stickie cast away the gory feathers and curled itself into a ball, trying to go as small and still as possible. It felt a sort of electric tingle in its chest, very similar to the rush of pleasure it received while mating. More food would come. If the family left just a little bit of chewy food out, the winged things would descended from the sky to eat, and the family would have tender food again and again. Leave a little, get more. A cycle of food. Endless food. Full bellies! The babies wouldn't cry, the females would no longer be sickly, and the young males would grow tall and strong, layers of thick muscles covering their normal skinny bodies. But no male was larger than him! He got all of the females first, and killed without pause any male that dared to challenge his rule!

With a start, the chief stickie became alert. There was an odd noise. Not the wind, nor the rain, or anything else it knew. A sort of hum like a bee. It was… pleasant, compelling, like the siren song of the hot wind, the fiery hot wind that tore things apart. The hot wind always meant fresh meat on the ground. Most blessed was the loud hot wind, the red dancer that gave of food!

SITTING INSIDE HIS mobile command post, Delphi watched as the ragged bunch of stickies shuffled out of the rocks and started hesitantly toward his vehicle.

Rising from the chair, he reached up to take a small rectangular box from a clip on the ceiling where it had been recharging, then strode quickly to the armored door. The portal cycled open at his approach, then closed as he stepped through.

From the top of the hill, Delphi could see the trap of rotting meat below, and as the stickies got closer, he smiled at the bloody streaks on their faces and hands.

"Ah, very good, my children," he whispered. "Excellent, in fact. I am most pleased."

Hooting wildly at the words, the mob of stickies rushed forward, waving their sucker-covered hands and arms in an orchestrated attack pattern, several of the smaller muties breaking loose to try for a flanking maneuver.

"Superb!" Delphi chortled. Then, calmly lifting the box, he pressed a button with his thumb and a golden ray extended to wash over the charging muties.

They stopped instantly and began to shake all over. An older stickie rolled her eyes and dropped dead. Two others fell to their knees, trembling uncontrollably. But four of the larger males and two females yet stood, their almost-human faces staring quizzically into the golden beam of light.

"Yes, hear the message in your heads," Delphi whispered, touching another control, boosting the signal. "Listen to the song inside your minds, my lost children, my pretty ones."

There was no reaction from two of the creatures, but the largest male waddled closer and looked down at the loose rocks on the ground. Then he stared back into the throbbing light, and back down again at the rock.

"Yes, that's it," Delphi urged gently, raising the power on the cybernetic machine. "Hear the song. Listen to the music. Learn, think! Learn how to think!"

Confused and frightened, the big stickie was breathing with difficulty, odd expressions moving across its slack features.

Satisfied for the moment, Delphi released the inducer and used a different setting to send a soft green glow over the muties. They all began to coo in pleasure, and most of them crouched a little in sublimation to him in a crude bow.

His eyes shimmering, Delphi smiled coldly at the gesture. Yes, they remember me and are learning much faster than anybody could have ever dreamed, not even TITAN or the administrators of Operation Chronos. Bioweps were toys in comparison to the staggering possibilities of the stickies. And soon, my little ones would be ready to claim their heritage.

WHIPPING OUT HIS SWORD, Doc slashed the anchoring rope and the raft floated away from the bank. Crouching, Krysty and Mildred unleashed their rapidfires to rake the stony ledge with 9 mm rounds. Unstoppable, the rats dived into the water and swam after the companions like a boiling wave of hatred. Caught on the lazy current, the lumpy raft drifted into the middle of the river, the sizzling beams of the two nuke lamps stretching far ahead into the subterranean river passage. Bits and pieces of predark material showed below the surface of the running water, and pale roots carpeted the ceiling among the dripping stalactites.

Roots! We're close to the surface, Krysty realized, firing a short burst from her rapidfire. Certainly no more than a hundred feet underground.

"Little bastards smell blood!" J.B. growled, adding a burst from the Uzi. The machine pistol chattered away as he moved it in a fast figure-eight pattern. Furry bodies exploded, but more replaced them.

"Yeah, our blood!" Ryan added, dropping a clip

The Gold Eagle Reader Service™ — Here's how it works:

Accepting your 2 free books and gift places you under no obligation to buy anything. You may keep the books and gift and return the shipping statement marked "cancel." If you do not cancel, about a month later we'll send you 6 additional books and bill you just $29.94* — that's a savings of 10% off the cover price of all 6 books! And there's no extra charge for shipping! You may cancel at any time, but if you choose to continue, every other month we'll send you 6 more books, which you may either purchase at the discount price or return to us and cancel your subscription.

*Terms and prices subject to change without notice. Sales tax applicable in N.Y. Canadian residents will be charged applicable provincial taxes and GST. Credit or debit balances in a customer's account(s) may be offset by any other outstanding balance owed by or to the customer.

If offer card is missing write to: Gold Eagle Reader Service, 3010 Walden Ave., P.O. Box 1867, Buffalo NY 14240-1867

NO POSTAGE
NECESSARY
IF MAILED
IN THE
UNITED STATES

BUSINESS REPLY MAIL

FIRST-CLASS MAIL   PERMIT NO. 717-003   BUFFALO, NY

POSTAGE WILL BE PAID BY ADDRESSEE

GOLD EAGLE READER SERVICE
3010 WALDEN AVE
PO BOX 1867
BUFFALO NY 14240-9952

Get FREE BOOKS and a FREE GIFT when you play the...

LAS VEGAS GAME

Just scratch off the gold box with a coin. Then check below to see the gifts you get!

YES! I have scratched off the gold box. Please send me my **2 FREE BOOKS** and **gift for which I qualify.** I understand that I am under no obligation to purchase any books as explained on the back of this card.

▼ DETACH AND MAIL CARD TODAY! ▼

366 ADL EEXG　　　　　　　　　　　　　　**166 ADL EEW4**
　　　　　　　　　　　　　　　　　　　　　　(GE-LV-06)

FIRST NAME　　　　　　　　　LAST NAME

ADDRESS

APT.#　　　　　CITY

STATE/PROV.　　　ZIP/POSTAL CODE

7	7	7	Worth TWO FREE BOOKS plus a BONUS Mystery Gift!
🍒	🍒	🍒	Worth TWO FREE BOOKS!
🔔	🔔	♣	TRY AGAIN!

Offer limited to one per household and not valid to current Gold Eagle® subscribers. All orders subject to approval. Please allow 4 to 6 weeks for delivery.

from the SIG-Sauer and reloading. Krysty's tooth. Jak's wound. *Fireblast,* every hungry thing down here was going to be coming after them soon, Ryan realized. Mebbe even another jelly guardian.

A fat rat jumped from the river onto the raft and Doc whacked off its snarling head with his sword.

"En garde!" he snarled, and stabbed the silvery blade into the water again and again, scoring a chill each time. But there were always more rats to replace the dead.

Moving away from the landslide, Ryan watched as the LAV disappeared from view, and made a battlefield decision. Leaning dangerously over a stack of supplies held in place by netting, Ryan pumped an entire clip into the ledge. Dropping the spent clip into the river, he slammed in another and started shooting again. The rounds were ricocheting off the armored hull of the war wag, throwing off bright sparks. Finally he got the desired results when the damp ground whoofed in flames from the spilled fuel.

"Mother of God, are you insane?" Mildred demanded, working the bolt on her rapidfire to clear a jammed round. The bent cartridge came free and sailed away to bounce off a rat in the water and splash out of sight.

"We'll find out soon enough," Ryan snapped as the dancing light of the growing conflagration rapidly grew. The rats screamed at the appearance of the fire, and were caught by the flames, their cries becoming high-pitched shrieks painful to hear.

The noise seemed to drive the other rats crazy. Grimly, Jak peppered the ceiling with his MP-5 and Doc slashed at anything that moved in the river while the others quickly reloaded.

Standing amid the stacks, Mildred and J.B. racked the disappearing shoreline with their rapidfires, while Krysty concentrated in the rats already swimming their way. The cacophony was nearly deafening in the narrowing confines of the tunnel, especially when it was punctuated by heady zips from the 9 mm Uzi. The Heckler & Koch MP-5 submachine gun, and the Uzi machine pistols used the same 9 mm ammo, but the Uzi was noticeably louder.

Holstering the SIG-Sauer, Ryan took the S&W M-4000 scattergun from J.B. and racked the pump to blow a hellstorm of double-aught lead at the rats scurrying along the moist earth walls. The blast aced a dozen of the rodents and made a large section of the sodden dirt collapse with a sucking sound, sending out waves of muck that almost swamped the homie raft.

Dropping from above, a sleek rodent landed on a pile of netting and rose on its hind paws as if choosing who to attack first. Thunder erupted as Doc unleashed the Ruger .44 wheelgun, the flame from the barrel reaching out to engulf the body of the animal. Literally blown to pieces, the shattered corpse sprayed outward and fell upon its chittering brethren.

Just then, the natural curve of the river took the chasm out of sight.

"Dark night, it didn't work!" J.B. cursed, fumbling in his munitions bag.

Pulling out a military canister, the Armorer yanked the pin, ripped off the safety tape, flipped away the handle and threw the bomb as hard as possible. The canister just missed a stalagmite and hit the slick mud just above the water level and stayed there.

"Cover your ears!" Ryan bellowed, placing both of his palms flat to his head. "We've got about four seconds—" But that was as far as he got before a harsh yellow light flashed from around the turn, and the whole tunnel shook violently. Nuking hell, that wasn't the gren. The LAV had finally detonated!

The surface of the water danced, and the rats started screaming as writhing tongues of flame extended through the air. A stalactite dropped from the ceiling and stabbed into the river like an executioner's ax, just missing the raft by the thickness of a prayer. Rats fell stunned from the walls, and that was when the thrown canister of willie pete cut loose. The charge of white phosphorus blazed with searing light, then rapidly expanded outward in a burning death cloud, and actually seem to force back the titanic explosion from the burning LAV for just a second. Then the irresistible force mastered the immovable object and the companions were buffeted by the chaotic shock waves of the conflicting explosive forces.

Flying rocks and rats pelted the companions on the raft as the nonstop sound of blasters rattled from the unseen wreckage of the war wag as the vast stores of ammo cooked off from the intense heat. A strident blast announced a Claymore had triggered, then four more detonations closely followed in quick succession, the noises overlapping. There followed an earthy groan, and the popcorn-like sound of splintering stone.

"Cave-in!" Ryan warned, not sure that anybody could hear him in the tumultuous bombardment.

Now the one-eyed man feared that he had gone too far in trying to ace the horde of rats as pieces of the ceiling began to drop away—stones, bricks and blobs of mud. Mildred lost her grip on the MP-5, the rapid-fire sailing away into the darkness before she grabbed the canvas strap and reclaimed the blaster.

Keyed to battle pitch, Ryan jerked to the side as a brick scraped down along the side of his arm. Doc staggered as another slammed into his backpack, and Jak had his Colt Python knocked from his grasp. The silvery weapon went tumbling toward the water and bounced off a shiny stalagmite. In foolhardy bravado, Jak lurched forward, nearly going off the shaking raft to catch the blaster while it was still in midair. Pulling it back, he exhaled, then frowned and flipped over the blaster to start shooting at the churning river.

A moment later a dead-white alligator rose from the depths and snapped at the teenager even as he fired again and again into the open maw.

"Gator!" Mildred yelled, burping the MP-5 until the clip was empty. Quick-drawing her ZKR, she fired directly into the red eyes of the albino monster. Clear fluids erupted from both hits, and the reptile reared backward to roll sideways below the waves.

"Thank Gaia, that was no Frankenstein." Krysty

sighed in relief, referring to a mutie alligator they had once fought. That damned thing had been all but bullet-proof.

"Agreed," Mildred replied, reloading her weapons with trembling hands.

Filthy water heaved up from the other side of the little raft as a second alligator appeared to sink its shockingly white teeth into one of the tires. Ferociously, the gator shook the entire raft. Two of the lashings came free, a net ripped and loose items began cascading overboard. Spinning, Doc added the booming firepower of the Ruger and the LeMat in a double assault, closely followed by Mildred and Krysty stitching the gator with fat 9 mm rounds. Blood showed from every hit, and the reptile bawled loudly as it rolled to get away from the stinging pain and slip back under the waves.

Moving fast, J.B. grabbed the netting and tried to recover a MRE pack, but jerked his hand back just in time as the first gator rose from the murky depths, its ruby-red eyes staring directly into his own filled with malevolent intelligence.

"Triple-damn gators are everywhere!" Ryan growled, thumbing a fresh cartridge into the belly of the scatter-gun, when something landed on his back and started crawling into his hair. Nuking hell, a rat! Reaching behind, Ryan grabbed the animal biting at his ear and squeezed with every ounce of strength he possessed. There was a horrid squeak, and the furry thing went still, unspeakable fluids dripping between his fingers.

Pulling the corpse loose from the tangle of black hair, Ryan gave the rat an extra crush just to make sure before flinging it away. The pulped form hit the water with a splash. A few moments, other rats converged on the corpse, and Ryan gave them three fast rounds of 12-gauge buckshot from the scattergun.

A scrawny rat landed next to Jak while he was reloading, and he stomped it flat before kicking the rodent overboard. Closing the Colt with a snap, Jak then shot two more rats climbing out of the water onto the raft, and then put four rounds into a pale gator peeking out of the choppy waves. The gator glowed like a rad-blast ghost in the bright beam of the nuke lamp.

Tying the netting closed with a piece of explosive prima cord from his munitions bag, J.B. turned and pulled out an implo gren, only to shove it back in again and try twice more before finding what he wanted. Not a spherical gren, but a pair of squat canisters. Bingo, as Millie liked to say. Priming the two charges, J.B. turned and tossed them both just ahead of the bobbing raft. They sank without a trace.

"What do?" Jak demanded, holstering the empty blaster and swinging around the rapidfire to send a short burst into the mud. Rats moving below the surface squealed and died.

"We're picking up speed," J.B. said, counting on his fingers. As he reached the number six, he relaxed slightly. "Anything tossed in front of us, will soon be in our wake, and so…"

Double explosions illuminated the shallow river

and the surface roiled to vomit up rats, gators and eel-like snakes in every direction. Buffeted by the blast, the companions were hit by a wave of stinking filth, then an exhalation of stinking hot gas that stole the air from their lungs.

Coughing and hacking, the companions turned away from the growing fireballs in the boiling river, the twin thermite charges expanding and building in force as the nonstop chem reactions actually used the oxygen in the water to fuel the hellstorm of lambent annihilation. Smoke, flame, steam and screaming filled the passageway as impossibly brilliant light increased in brightness until the skin of the companions prickled from the raw energy reflecting off the muddy walls.

"Sweet Jesus!" Mildred cried, but there was no help coming from that direction.

With a groan beyond description, the ceiling gave way and the aft tunnel collapsed, rocks, bricks and boulders plummeting into the water.

Pivoting, Ryan gave a sharp whistle and threw Krysty the scattergun. "Start paddling!" he yelled, pulling the Steyr and turning it over to use the flat stock as a crude oar.

Kneeling, Krysty did the same, and the raft began to move slightly faster.

Spreading outward, the destruction increased in violence, cracks speeding along the earthen walls like dirty lightning bolts. Waves rose and fell around the homie craft as if it were caught in a squall at sea. A

swell threw them high enough that the companions
had to duck and the stacks of supplies smacked into
the irregular ceiling with a resounding crash.

When they dropped back down with a sickening
lurch, Ryan held on to the raft for dear life, but the impact broke his grip and he went flying. He landed flat
on his back at the edge of the raft, with Doc flailing
right alongside. Clawing to stay aboard, the two men
watched helplessly as a nuke lamp broke free of its
mooring and went over the side. The instant the hot
headlight touched the cold water, the glass shattered
and the light went out. Then the nuke battery crackled
and split apart. Blue sparks danced along the surface
of the river, and a score of rats went stiff before rolling over to float belly-up.

Grabbing on to the lashings, Ryan and Doc hauled
themselves from the brink and back to safety. The electric discharges continued for another few heartbeats,
then died out, leaving only a wretched stink in the damp
air.

"Tie that other lamp down tight!" Ryan panted,
pointing at the last nuke lamp.

Nodding, Doc got busy with both hands. If the second lamp died, the companions would be trapped underground in total darkness. Entombed alive.

Behind the raft, more rocks and debris poured from
the violated ceiling until a mound rose from the river
in a newborn island. A white gator waddled into view,
bawling its rage at the disturbance, then a boulder
squashed it flat against the loose material, driving it

below the muddy waves. Unexpectedly, the walls collapsed across the river, joining the island mound into a crude dam. Then a large slab of brickwork came crashing down like a guillotine, nearly closing off the underground passageway.

Unstoppable, the dirty water rushed through the small remaining crevice, the strength of the stream intensified from the contraction. A rat come through and hit the water with a tiny splash. Then a gator tried to pass and got jammed into place, as solid as a cork. With the rushing water spraying out all around it, the reptile bawled with frustration, its deadly jaws snapping at the universe in blind rage.

The rumblings of the destruction slowly began to fade as the companions continued to rush with the current. But the water level was dropping again and their speed was decreasing. While Ryan and Krysty renewed their efforts at paddling, the others reloaded their weps and checked for any damage. Everybody had bites and scratches, but none was serious, and Mildred passed around a double dose of antibio tablets from the Deep Storage Locker. The physician had no way of knowing if the medicine was still potent, but it was the best she had against the dire possibility of infection.

After a short while, the rumbling crashes were left behind and there were only a handful of rats swimming alongside the bobbing raft. In ruthless efficiency, J.B. and Krysty Doc took care of them, and soon the companions were alone in the slowing river.

Hours passed without any incidents, with everybody poised in combat readiness. After a while, Doc and Jak replaced Ryan and Krysty at the paddling, then J.B. and Mildred. In spite of the accidental dam in their wake, the river was still flowing, just noticeably lower than before. In the stark white beam of the last nuke lamp, they could clearly see a scummy green line along the smooth wall where the water level used to reach.

Warily, Ryan noticed there weren't any stalactites or 'mites anymore, or roots, festooning the ceiling, or mud on the walls. Just a seamless expanse of what seemed to be predark concrete, the material smooth and undamaged.

Pumping up her little flashlight, Mildred played the pale beam around for a better look. "This is a predark sewer," she stated in relief, then laughed. "By God, I think we've been traveling through one all of the time!"

"Good. Sewers always have manholes," Ryan said, watching the half-burned corpse of a dead rat float past. "Soon as we find a ladder, we can get out of here."

"And then back to redoubt?" Jak asked hesitantly.

"Mebbe," Ryan murmured, cracking his knuckles. "If we can find it again."

Chapter Eleven

Rolling out of the morning fog, the four big men riding the sleek black two-wheelers raised their predark rapidfires and opened fire at the line of wooden carts.

All along the caravan of pilgrims, people cried out in shock and fell over, ghastly wounds pumping red blood. The ragged line of wheeled carts came to an abrupt halt, and the men scrambled for weps while the swayback horses went absolutely still at the sound of blasters. The animals knew the noise always was a herald of death, and the only protection was to not move.

"Son of a bitch!" a sec man cursed, leaping out of a cart, a cloth napkin tied around his neck, his face and mustache smeared with greasy soup. Crouching, the sec man leveled a remade scattergun and cut loose with both barrels.

The thundering barrage of nails and broken glass missed the racing group of Rogan brothers, the makeshift ammo rattling the leaves of the nearby trees.

Braking to a halt, Edward grinned evilly and replied with the 40 mm gren launcher slung under the barrel of the M-16 assault rifle. The fat shell hit the sec man, but the range had been too close for the predark warhead to arm. Instead of exploding, the 40 mm round slammed into the chest of the man like a flying sledge-hammer. Ribs shattering, internal organs crushed, blood and viscous fluid sprayed from the mouth of the startled man, and he flew backward to land sprawling in the dirt. The broken form shuddered once, then went still.

"Too close!" Alan snarled, spraying a group of women and children fleeing into the bushes.

"Frag that," John commanded loudly, pointing a bony finger. "There he is!"

Snarling obscenities, a fat man with a patch on his right eye threw a hatchet at the coldhearts, and Robert barely managed to duck out of the way, the spinning wep clanging off the shiny chassis of his bike.

"Not good enough, feeb!" he retorted in dark amusement, and shot the man several times in the belly, opening the stomach like a can of spaghetti.

"We surrender!" a burly man shouted, throwing down a homie zipgun and raising both hands. "Take what you want! We surrender!"

"Fool," John said with a sneer, killing the coward on the spot. "Not taking prisoners!"

As the incredible truth became apparent, the rest of the pilgrims broke ranks and took off in every direction, casting aside their belonging to hasten their speed.

Revving the silent engines of the military two-wheelers, the laughing Rogan brothers started circling the screaming people, shooting them down as if ammo grew on trees.

As the last of the pilgrims fell, the Rogans returned to the fat man with one eye. Retrieving the thrown hatchet, Alan braked his bike to a halt, then climbed off eagerly. Testing the edge of the wep on a thumb, the man knelt by the corpse and started to hack away, soon removing the head to add it to the collection of grisly trophies nearly filling the cargo pods of his bikes.

"Think that's him?" Edward growled, reloading his rapidfire.

"No way," John said with a frown. "There's no women with black skin, albino mutie or redheads in this batch. And no silver-haired wrinklie."

"So we hit the next ville?" Robert asked, kicking over a pretty young girl.

"Soon as Alan is done with the harvesting."

John turned off the bike to let it recharge a little. The batteries still carried a half charge, but life had taught him the harsh lesson that survival often depended upon a bite of food, a single brass or a sip of water. Waste meant getting chilled, no more, no less.

Looking over the field of death, John rested the hot rapidfire on a shoulder as he studied the bodies stretched out in the grass like shrapnel from an explosion. Nobody was even vaguely close to the protection of the trees, and every body was clearly torn apart. There was nobody only pretending to be aced in this bunch, like the last group.

"All set," Alan said, tucking the one-eyed head into a cargo pod. Flipping the hatchet into the air, he caught it by the wooden handle, nodded in satisfaction, then tucked the wep into his belt.

"Then let's go," John ordered, revving the silent engine of the bike. The gauges fluttered alive and the dashboard became illuminated. "We've got a lot more chilling to do."

WITH A GRINDING NOISE, the manhole cover moved aside and J.B. crawled onto the cracked asphalt. Moving out of the way, the Armorer brought up the Uzi as he looked around for any danger. But the streets seemed clear, the ruins stretching for blocks in every direction.

A moment later Ryan levered himself out of the opening and slid the Steyr off his shoulder to work the bolt. The air was hot and dry, sweet nectar after the pungent stink of the sewer. Dilapidated buildings dotted the sandy landscape, along with fireplugs, mailboxes and all of the usual trappings of predark civilization. They had found the ruins of a predark city. It was about time their luck changed.

As the two men stood guard, Krysty came out of the manhole, her revolver sweeping for targets. Bending, she offered a hand to Mildred. The sweat-drenched physician accepted the help and awkwardly clambered onto the asphalt, hauling her canvas med kit.

Jak came next. But halfway out, the teenager sat on the rim of the hole and drew his Colt Python to aim the blaster into the darkness. From below there came the sound of blasterfire and the savage bawl of a gator.

Quickly, Jak moved out of the way and Doc climbed into the sunlight with the smoking Ruger in his hand. Together, they fired their weps into the blackness, the thunderous reports illuminating the subterranean passageway. Far below, an alligator screamed in mortal agony, then went ominously silent.

Grunting in thanks, Doc holstered the Ruger and released the rope tied around his waist. Passing the end to the others, Doc stood guard while the rest of the companions started pulling. Like fish on a stringer, one by one, the backpacks were hauled out of the sewer and laid on the cracked street.

"Anybody hurt?" Mildred demanded, looking over the group.

Thankfully, there was no fresh blood spilled and nobody was grimacing in pain.

"Good enough." Walking across the street, Mildred leaned against the rusted remains of a car and tried to catch her breath. She was exhausted, but stoutly refused to leave any of the important medical supplies behind. With the MP-5 and its spare ammo, the physician knew that she was carrying too much weight, but she just couldn't relinquish any of the antibiotic pills or surgical gloves. Gloves! No more bare-handed surgery. She would never leave *those* behind.

"Should we prepare an egress, my dear Ryan?" Doc asked, gesturing at the open manhole.

Frowning deeply, Ryan wasn't sure about what the word meant, but he understood the gesture. "No, close it up tight," he said gruffly, working the bolt on the

Steyr. "That blasterfire is going to summon all sorts of attention that we don't want. Get your packs and let's move."

The bolt-action longblaster had been thoroughly cleaned during their long journey through the sewer and was now in working order again. It had been a good thing that he'd been cautious and double-checked the longblaster before using it. The barrel had indeed been blocked solid with condensed fuel and mud. Pulling the trigger on the Steyr would have been disastrous. Strong is good, but smart is better, as the Trader liked to say.

Working in unison, Jak and Doc manhandled the heavy iron cover back into place, then J.B. attached a wire and rigged a Claymore mine under a nearby civie wag, the curved front of the directional charge pointing at the sewer opening. Anybody moving the manhole would get blown in two from behind.

"Thought we left the gators behind," Krysty stated, checking the rapidfire as she glanced around the ruins. She wasn't getting any feelings of being observed. However, that didn't mean they were alone.

"Gators track folks good," Jak replied, reloading his piece. Then the youth chuckled. "But taste even better!"

Sharing a weary laugh, the companions gathered their belongings and started along one of the dusty streets, carefully keeping in the sunlight and out of the dangerous shadows. Until they had done a recce, nothing was to be taken for granted. Their travels had taken them a long way in the dark, and there was no way of knowing where they were until J.B. had a chance to use his sextant.

"Anybody recognize the town?" Ryan asked hopefully.

But that only drew a chorus of negatives.

Most of the buildings in sight were pretty tall, five, six, some of them even seven stories. But there was also the remains of a skyscraper, or at least what Ryan could only guess might have been a skyscraper. The structure stopped at about the ninth floor, the marble exterior broken to expose twisted beams of rusty steel. They'd all seen that sort of damage before. Most likely, something large blown along by the nukewind of skydark had slammed into the building. Or even a missile. Ryan wouldn't be surprised if they followed the angle of the breakage and found a glass-lined crater in the ground. Quickly, he checked the rad counter on his lapel and was relieved to see only a normal background level of rads. The ruins weren't hot. More good news.

"Dark night, I really hate to leave all that food and brass behind," J.B. said, casting a sorrowful glance down the block at the manhole cover. A gust of wind was blowing some dust along the street, making the few partially intact windows of the buildings rattle in the frames.

"We'll come back and get the rest once we have a safe place to stay," Ryan answered. "No sense hauling it all up, just to lower it back down again."

"Safe where is," Jak said in dry humor. "Watchdogs will guard."

"You mean, the alligators?" Mildred asked askance. Then she gave a tired laugh. "Yeah, I guess they will protect our excess baggage better than having Mike Tyson as a skycap."

She waited for a laugh. But when none came, Mildred sighed. Too many cultural references were meaningless these days. Doc got some of her jokes, but many fell flat. Humor was a victim of the war as much as anything else.

Easing off her bearskin coat, Krysty tucked it through the canvas straps of her backpack and undid a couple of buttons on her shirt. In spite of the heavy clouds, the sun was beating down hard and the temperature on the open street was quickly becoming uncomfortable after the cool darkness of the flooded sewer.

Most of the buildings in the city were smashed to rubble, piles of debris that reached twenty feet high. In others, only the windows were gone, making the buildings hollow shells that moaned as the wind blew through. Oddly, most of the destruction was only on the upper levels. Here on the street, most of the structures were in decent shape, with some of the windows and most doors relatively intact.

"This is nuke storm damage," J.B. said, adjusting his glasses. "Something must have blocked the sky-dark winds from smashing the place apart."

"Mayhap there once were hills surrounding the

city," Doc suggested, craning his neck to see down a side street. In the distance, there seemed to be only barren scrubland, a mix of sand and scraggy weeds stretching to the horizon. He found the sight oddly disturbing. Have…I been here before? he wondered.

Nervously fingering the silver lion head on his cane, Doc started to speak, then stopped. There were so many jumbled memories in his mind that he could no longer tell which were true and which were only delusions from his days of madness.

"License plates rusted clean," Jak said, squinting at a nearby civie wag. "No read location there." The perfectly smooth fiberglass body rested on jumbled piles of rusted machinery.

All of the wags lining the sidewalks were in ragged condition, their tires long gone, most of the windows broken and the interior not much more than cracked plastic and bare metal springs.

Brushing back his matted hair, Ryan scowled at that. Even the store signs were clean. No way of knowing if they were even in a country that spoke English, although the architecture looked familiar. But they could be anywhere.

Loose sand blew freely among the buildings, mounds reaching all the way to the roofs in some of the lower sections. Every window was rubbed white from the grinding winds, and most of the frames were bare metal, every flack of paint removed long ago by the inclement weather.

The sun appeared and disappeared behind the heavy

clouds, casting dappled shadows across the nameless city, not allowing J.B. to get a read with the minisextant. As they prowled along the storefronts, the companions found that a few of the larger windows were smashed open, the dry sand covering the inside of the stores like a golden carpet.

Going to a rusted hulk parked alongside the curb, Jak tried to see inside, but the windows were solid white. Trying the handle, he was surprised to find it unlocked, and pulled open the door, warily stepping out of the way. But the vehicle was empty, stripped to the walls. The seats were gone, the safety belts, the rubber mats, and the dashboard was only a series of gaping holes where dials and controls had once been. Only a CD glittered brightly from the sagging dashboard, its shining perfection making the rest of the wag appear dowdy and wretched in comparison.

Closing the door, Jak started to scratch under his bandage. The teenager forcibly stopped himself and tucked his wandering hand into a jacket pocket. Wounds healed faster if left alone. It had been hard enough to wash it clean while in the filthy river below.

Quite unexpectedly, the sun broke free from the cloud cover and J.B. quickly reached under his shirt to pull out his miniature sextant. It took him a few moments to do the mental calculations, then check them against the predark map in his munitions bag.

"This is southeastern Arizona," J.B. said, tucking away the old battered map at last. "We're in the Zone.

Close enough to Tucson that it really makes no damn difference."

"Tucson," Doc whispered, as if the word had hidden meaning. A sick feeling blossomed in his stomach for no discernable reason.

"Or at least, this is where Tucson used to be," J.B. added casually. "Could be some other city, the way the nuke quakes moved some places around."

"Move cities?" Jak said in a disbelieving tone. Then he added, "Nukes moved mountains. Why not city?"

"Curious. Tucson was an important city in this state," Mildred muttered, removing the cap on her canteen. She took a small drink, trying to ration the water. "I'm startled that it wasn't nuked."

"Not enough bombs in existence to vap every city on the bastard planet," Ryan stated, looking down an alleyway. It was clean and empty, not even a rat was in sight. "If there had been, we wouldn't be here."

Tightening the cap, Mildred had to nod at the logic. Destroying civilization, and obliterating humanity, were two entirely different things. Thank God.

Turning a corner, the companions found a buzzing mailbox, the rusty container crawling with bright yellow bees.

Ryan marked the location of the hive uneasily. Those might just be bees, or they might be those killer bees Trader had told him about so long ago. Impulsively, he reached up to rub his missing eye. As a child, he'd tried to steal honey from a hive once, and a swarm of bees had stung him all over, one of the insects getting him just under the left eye. The flesh had swollen so much that he had been blind on that side for a week. An eerie harbinger of things to come.

"We should be looking for a place to stay the night," Mildred suggested, resting against the smooth metal post of a streetlamp. "A bank, library, police station, something solid like that."

Cupping a hand to her face, Krysty looked upward. "We should be able to get a good view of the whole city from the top of one of these buildings," she suggested, without much eagerness in the words.

"Indeed, madam?" Doc rumbled in hesitant agreement. "Just as long as you are not suggesting a stroll to the top of one."

Mildred took appraisal of the destroyed skyscraper. The internal struts and beams were visibly swaying in the warm breeze. The twisted metal was probably groaning like a nearly chilled man, but at this distance there was only the sound of the endless wind.

"Not up for it, eh?" She chuckled.

"Only in my youth, dear Doctor," Doc replied with a mocking bow. "Which at this point seems a million years ago."

Slinging the Steyr over a shoulder, Ryan took a long pull from his canteen, the flat sterilized water from the redoubt washing out the muddy flavor of the river.

"Strange," he said under his breath, screwing the cap back on the container.

Blaster in hand, Krysty turned. "What is it, lover?"

"The windows," Ryan replied slowly. "None of the store windows have their shutters down."

"Tucson had very little crime, if I remember correctly," Mildred said, hitching her heavy med kit into a more comfortable position. Her lumbar was starting to ache from the unaccustomed weight.

"Maybe they didn't have steel shutters the way Chicago and New York did."

"Deuced odd, I must say," Doc muttered, pulling out his LeMat pistol, only to holster the blaster again.

After being submerged, the black-powder charges were dead. The weapons would have to be purged and reloaded. Almost reluctantly, Doc hefted the Ruger .44 wheelgun and eased back the hammer, only to gently return it back into place. The stainless-steel blaster was a lot lighter than his cumbersome iron LeMat, and the bullets were waterproof. Both fine attributes. Then again, the LeMat was from his time period. A living piece of the past that he could hold. The touch of the Civil War blaster helped him to remember better times with his wife and children.

"This is a good area," Ryan declared, studying the intersection. "Mildred and Jak stay here while the rest of us do a fast recce."

"No prob," the physician replied, easing her med kit to the ground with a clunk. "Got you covered."

As J.B. and Krysty went in different directions, Ryan stepped around a pothole in the sidewalk to investigate a liquor store that seemed undisturbed. The grating was raised, but when he checked the door, it was open, the lock broken apart. For a split second he had a flashback to the city in his dreams, but then it was gone.

Shaking off the old memories, Ryan loosened the panga on his belt and gently pushed open the door with the barrel of the Steyr to walk inside. Illuminated by the milky window light, the interior of the store was empty.

Everything was gone. Every stick of furniture, every light fixture, even the carpeting on the floor had been removed. The place was stripped to the walls. The foam tiles in the ceiling had been pried loose, exposing the framework of aluminum struts hanging from the gray concrete ceiling.

Warily checking the bathroom, Ryan wasn't surprised to see that the sink and toilet were also missing, along with the wall mirror. The one-eyed man felt a cold chill creep along his spine at the sight. A looted city was to be expected, but not like this. This had been systematic, well organized. The sink hadn't been ripped out of the wall, but unbolted and carefully removed. Scavenged. The whole nuking store had been scaved.

Quickly stepping outside, Ryan found the other companions coming out of different buildings, all of their expressions similar: confused, concerned and slightly worried.

"Same thing here," Ryan said, resting the stock of the longblaster on a hip. "Somebody raided the whole damn city, didn't they?"

"Every bastard lock, stock, and barrel," J.B. replied, pushing back his hat. "As long as there was a barrel, in the first place."

"Bastard strange, that's for sure," Ryan said, walking to another store and pressing his face to the glass to try to see inside. From the faded lettering on the inside of the glass it seemed to be a bookstore, but it was difficult to tell for sure. The old glass was so badly roughed it was like trying to look through winter ice.

Just then a soft hooting sounded from inside the store, and the companions scrambled for their weapons. Safeties were snicked off and slides racked as they watched a humanoid figure move along the other side of the frosted glass. He was shuffling along the interior of the building with his shoulders hunched, long arms dangling and what seemed to be ragged clothing handing in strips off the bulky frame.

Tracking the murky shape with the muzzle of the SIG-Sauer, Ryan jerked a thumb to the left and began to retreat from the bookstore. Nodding in agreement, the other companions were close behind, moving as softly as possible. That was a stickie inside the building. The muties were the scourge of the Deathlands, hard to chill and often traveling in packs of dozens. The only reason the mutie hadn't taken over the Deathlands was that they were stupe and easily outmaneuvered.

Tightening her grip on the MP-5 rapidfire, Mildred wondered if she had inserted a full clip into the blaster after that last fight with the gators, or was it only partially full? But this wasn't the time or place to double-check. She would have to make sure to only fire in short bursts. As gently as possible, Mildred clicked the selector switch from automatic to single shot.

As if on cue, there came a musical jingling from a shop bell and the door to the bookstore swung open on creaking hinges. Blinking its oversize eyes at the sunlight, the big male stickie tilted his head to look directly at the massed companions.

Nobody moved or spoke for a single long second, the incredible sight of the mutie using a door just like a norm paralyzing the stunned companions into immobility.

It hadn't dumbly pushed the door open, Ryan realized in shock. The mutie had turned the knob first to disengage the lock. How was that possible?

Then the stickie gave a loud hoot, the end of the cry rising in pitch. Without warning, the window exploded, showering the companions in shards of milky glass, and out rushed a dozen of the humanoid creatures, uncaring of the sharp glass they raced over with bare feet. But even as the companions recouped from the startling arrival of the muties, they felt shocked at the sight of the stickies waving thick sticks with a sharp rock attached to the ends with ropes.

"No way!" Ryan shouted in disbelief, even as he cut loose with the Steyr. The 7.62 mm rounds blew away two of the stickies, the dying muties dropping their clubs as they slumped to the sidewalk gushing watery blood from the gaping head wounds.

"Son of a bitch!" J.B. cursed, hammering the muties with a long burst from the Uzi, the copper-jacketed 9 mm rounds punching through the heads of the creatures with grisly results.

But as the first wave of stickies fell, more climbed through the broken window and charged at the companions, waving their crude weapons. Then the one standing in the doorway reached back inside the store and pulled out a wooden spear, the tip blackened by fire to make the point hard and more lethal.

Fireblast! Ryan fired the SIG-Sauer once, blowing out the brains of that monster, then swung up the stock to smash the face of another as it tried to grab him by the throat. Incredibly, the next stickie backed away and tried to duck around the longblaster.

What the hell was going on here? These stickies were dodging an attack, almost as if they were intelligent. This was worse than any jump nightmare!

Jak cut loose with the Colt Python, blowing tongues of flame from the blaster, then flipped a knife into the eye of a second mutie. Both fell, oozing blood onto the sandy predark street.

Instinctively thumbing back the hammer on the Ruger as if it were the LeMat, Doc blew off the misshapen face of a stickie, the grisly remnant hitting a nearby wall with a wet splat. An eye clinging to the bricks stared blankly back at Doc, making the scholar shuddered in revulsion.

Ruthlessly, Krysty sent a fan of hot lead from the MP-5 across the shambling things, and Ryan put two more rounds into the bigger stickies to finish the job. But even as the last mutie kneeled on the broken asphalt, it looked up to croon at the cloudy sky in a new and different kind of hoot that none of the companions had ever heard before. Almost immediately, a distant hoot answered.

"Dark night, the bastard is calling for help!" J.B. gasped, dropping a spent clip from the Uzi and slapping in a spare. "What's going on here? Did we jump to another world?"

"Is Kaa back?" Krysty demanded, her hair writhing in fright at the terrible name.

Even as she frantically reloaded, Mildred considered the matter and knew that she had no possible answer. Nobody knew for sure where the stickies came from in the first place, whether they were accidents of Nature caused by the nuclear holocaust, deevolved humans, escaped genetic experiments, bioweps, or whatever. But there was one, singular, unarguable factor about the mutants. They lived, and anything alive always tried to improve itself, to make the next generation stronger, smarted, better. Perhaps the stickies had just taken the next step in evolution.

In spite of herself, Mildred shivered at the idea. Stickies with weapons.

"Into the store, fast!" Ryan directed the companions, pocketing an exhausted clip and sliding the Steyr off a shoulder.

"What was that?" Doc demanded, stupefied. "Are you mad, sir?"

"The call came from over there," Ryan stormed impatiently, walking over the chilled mutie. "So we know the store is empty, now move it or lose it, Doc!"

Hesitantly, the scholar did as requested, his face twitching with unease as they moved into the building. The interior of the store was the same as the others, stripped bare with nothing remaining. Why there would be stickies inside an empty building, Ryan had no idea, but these were new stickies. It would be impossible to guess their needs and goals.

As the companions checked their blasters, the hooting from outside was becoming steadily louder. And closer.

"Sounds like too many take out in stand-up fight," Jak stated gruffly.

"I'll agree with that," Krysty added, opening the bathroom door with her rapidfire. For a second, the woman almost fired at the sight of angry eyes on an inhuman face. But then relaxed when she saw that it was her own reflection in a broken mirror.

"Everybody out the back door," Ryan directed, pulling a gren from the pocket of his fur-lined coat. Very carefully, he checked the color coding on the military ordnance before removing the ring with a jerk, then casting it aside.

Already moving that way, Jak eased open the metal fireproof door at the rear of the store, peeking outside with his MP-5 rapidfire at the ready. The exit lead to an alleyway with a sagging wooden fence and a couple of rusted cars. An empty street showed at either end.

"Clear," Jak announced curtly.

"Move," Ryan ordered, flipping off the arming lever of the canister. As the gren began to trickle smoke, he rolled it into the middle of the store as the companions rushed into the back alleyway. Standing rearguard, Ryan added another smoke canister to the first just as a big male stickie appeared in the broken front window. Even through the billowing smoke, Ryan could see there was a necklace of human teeth around its neck, and the mutie raised a spiked club to shake it menacingly.

With a dry mouth, Ryan added a third gren, then moved fast, ducking out the back door, and kept going. His thoughts were chaotic, but cold. Escape. Keep moving, and get as far away from this pesthole as possible.

Ryan just reached the end of the alleyway when the door slammed open and a detonation shook the entire building. Waves of chem flame washed out of the doorway and from the windows, the heady blast rattling the wooden fence and setting it ablaze. Then the ancient partition fell apart, simply too old and weathered to withstand the raging thermite explosion.

The hooting from the store changed to inhuman howls as Ryan ran to rejoin the others, the heat rising steadily from behind. The thermite had gone off two seconds early! He'd have to remember that in case the others were malfuncs, as well.

Turning the corner, Ryan drank in the cool fresh air as the light and heat continued to intensify from the burning store behind. But the wailing cries were now mixed with angry hooting from elsewhere in the ruins. As Ryan reached the sidewalk, a stickie appeared and thrust a wooden spear at him. Dodging out of the way, Ryan fired the Steyr from his hip and cut the mutie down. Then another spear flew by the man, the wooden shaft flashing past his good eye.

Astonished, Ryan turned to see more armed stickies advancing around the burning building. They had come at him from two different directions in a flanking maneuver. Damn, the stickies were hunting him instead of the other way around! Normally, they loved fire and would always rush to investigate something ablaze before going after a person. But not these bastards.

Working the bolt-action as fast as possible, Ryan blew away the closest stickie, and charged out of the alleyway just as Jak and Krysty appeared, tossing grens. With his combat boots slapping against the loose sand, Ryan was almost across the street when the charges detonated, the combined blast of the antipers grens seeming to shake the universe.

Just then a sharp whistle caught Ryan's attention and he changed course to head for J.B. standing on the next corner. The Armorer was pulling something from his munitions bag, and when Ryan saw what it was, he redoubled his speed to streak right past the man in a desperate attempt to gain some needed distance. This was going to be close.

Ripping off the safety tape, J.B. yanked the arming

pin and flipped the lever, then threw the gren straight at the window of the corner store. It smashed through the snowy pane in a loud crash of glass and disappeared inside.

Pivoting on a heel, J.B. grabbed his hat and started sprinting after the other companions. Down the block, they had taken secure positions behind a rusted police car, and were all aiming blasters in his direction.

The mob of hooting stickies had arrived and started up the street. Counting under his breath, J.B. reached ten and dived for the sidewalk. When Ryan and the others saw that, they needed no further prompting and did the same, hugging the concrete as if their very lives depended on it.

Reaching the corner store, the stickies paused to look inside as if suspecting a trap...and were enveloped in a bright flash of light, followed by a muffled whomp.

A hard wind swept the intersection as half of the five-story building vanished, compacted into black lump by the irresistible force of the implo gren. The remaining walls cracked, and the rest of the structure tumbled into the street. The two stickies still standing hooted in horror as the falling debris of the building engulfed them completely, and the last vestiges of the armed mob disappeared from view, buried under the crumbling tonnage of stone, bricks and bent steel.

As the dust clouds from the destruction spread down the empty streets, the companions rose shakily to their feet and breathed a sigh of relief. Then more

hooting came from above, and the friends looked skyward to see additional stickies on the roof of a movie
theater.

"Shitfire, the town is infested!" Ryan cursed, blasting away with the Steyr. Krysty and J.B. were right behind with their own weapons, spent brass arcing
through the air.

But then a strange whistle came from out of nowhere, and a fireball of gargantuan size arched upward
to crash onto the theater in a blazing torrent. Burning
stickies flew off the roof to land in the streets in sickening smacks, the lumps of smoking flesh twitching
before finally going still.

Chapter Twelve

"By the Three Kennedys," Doc whispered in shock, even as another group of stickies loped around the corner.

Swinging around their weps, the companions braced for a fight. But these muties were facing down the side street and ignoring the armed companions. Seizing the moment, the friends backed away to gain more combat room while they reloaded with frantic haste.

Hooting nervously, the stickies waved their clubs, and one threw a spear. It went out of sight around the corner, and there came a loud metallic clang. A moment later a huge lumbering wag rolled into view.

The vehicle was a predark bus covered with sheets of corrugated metal. A grillework of thick bars protected every window, and a dozen armed men stood on the roof protected by a low sandbag wall, a crude iron-pipe railing holding the stout barrier in place.

A plume of dark smoke rose from behind the sandbags, but none of the men seemed concerned, so Ryan guessed whatever they were burning had something to do with the fireball launched the earlier. Probably a catapult.

However, the stickies went crazy at the sight of the lumbering wag, and insanely charged the vehicle. One mutie went under the spiked tires, torn apart even as it was crushed flat. Another stickie leaped onto the grillework covering the driver's-side window, and a scattergun roared from inside the wag, the fiery discharge cutting the mottled creature in two. As the legs fell off, the upper torso reached inside the wag, and a man cursed, the words changing into an anguished wail.

"The enemy of my enemy," Ryan muttered, finishing the ancient quote with a blast from the Steyr. A stickie on the sidewalk had its head removed, the body walking onward for a full yard before toppling over dead, the suckers covering the discolored skin opening and closing like dozens of silently screaming mouths.

Slamming the rusted wrecks of predark cars out of its way, the driverless juggernaut careened along the street, the man behind the wheel beating at the inhuman hand still attached to his bleeding face. Jumping the curb, the bus knocked over a lamppost, and a man went flying off the roof to hit the asphalt with a sickening crunch of bones.

As the stickies converged on the unconscious man, the companions peppered the hated creatures with their blasters, the MP-5 rapidfires hosing the foul muties with high-velocity lead.

Inside the wag, a large man with skin as dark as Mildred's, pulled a handcannon and aced the driver

with one expert shot. Yanking the body out from behind the steering wheel, the newcomer took the chilled
man's place and fought to bring the careening wag
under control. Directing the wag back into the street,
the driver slammed on the brakes. They squealed in
wild protest, but the rampaging wag shuddered to a
stop, rocking back and forth for a few moments before
coming to a complete halt in the middle of an intersection.

Shouting orders, the men on top rushed to the sandbag wall and sent a flight of arrows from homie crossbows into the wave of stickies. Hit twice, one of the
humanoid creatures leaped on top of a mailbox and
hurled a club. Notching a fresh arrow into his crossbow, a man got smashed in the temple with the flying
cudgel and his head cracked open wide, red blood and
gray brains gushing from the monstrous wound.
Shrieking in pain, the man dropped out of sight behind
the bags and two other men spun around to lower their
crossbows and mercifully chill their mutilated comrade.

Waving his arms, the stickie on the mailbox hooted
in victory, then a man on the roof of the wag threw
down a liquid-filled glass bottle with a burning rag tied
around the neck. The crude Molotov shattered on the
mailbox, the oily contents erupting into thick flames.
Covered with fire, the hooting stickie fell backward off
the mailbox and started blindly running about, waving its sucker-covered hands. At a full rush, the thing
slammed into a store window shattering the century-

old pane of glass and cutting itself. As it fell, the hooting stopped and the men on the wag feathered the smoking corpse with a dozen additional arrows purely for the sake of revenge.

As the men cheered, another stickie dropped its club to run at the wag, threw itself onto the side. The mutie stayed there for a moment as fresh gelatinous ooze poured from its multiple suckers, then the creature began to climb up the smooth metal.

Aiming carefully, Mildred put a pair of 9 mm rounds into its head, then Ryan blew off an arm, stopping its ascent.

Behind the steering wheel, the big black man stared at the companions in puzzlement as he hastily reloaded his own black-powder handcannon. Son of a mutie bitch, who the frag were these rists?

As the dying stickie reached in through the grille, a young man with a bushy mustache rushed over and shoved his crossbow into the face of the creature. The arrow went through the mutie's head, spraying out a ghastly mix of bones, brains and blood. Losing its grip, the stickie fell away, but the leg stayed attached and the corpse hung off the side of the wag, dribbling watery life onto the sandy street.

Another stickie turned to throw a spear at the companions. Krysty ducked out of the way, the shaft going through her living hair. She braced for the onslaught of pain, but apparently the spear had only parted the filaments, not broken any. Feeling sick at the thought of what might have happened, Krysty furiously swung her MP-5 to center on the thing, but Ryan beat her by a heartbeat. The booming Steyr SSG-70 sent out a single skull-shredding round. The stickie reeled away with its head blown open.

Meanwhile, a pair of stickies leaped onto the iron grille of the wag and started beating on the bars with their clubs, making a hell of a racket. The driver shot one with his blaster, then a man on top fired an arrow downward into the top of the stickie, the barbed end coming out between its legs. Gushing blood, the mutie went limp and dropped to the ground, twitching as if struck by lightning.

Then something moved in the sky, and Ryan cursed at the sight of a stickie leaping off the top of a nearby building.

Working the bolt to lever a fresh cartridge into the longblaster, Ryan tried to track the mutie, but it was too late. The hooting stickie landed on the roof of the wag among the men and lashed out with both arms. A man had his crossbow knocked away, the shaft going for the clouds, but another screamed as his face was ripped off, the pulsating red muscles under the skin stretching like warm taffy in the sun.

Pivoting fast, another man fired an arrow at the stickie, but the shaft went completely through the creature with no apparent effect. Reaching out, the stickie grabbed its new victim by the throat. Startled, the man tried to pull away while he fumbled for a knife. Then a thunderous report sounded and the arm of the stickie was blown off at the elbow.

Smoke pouring from the barrel of the .44 Ruger handcannon, Doc broke open the exhausted blaster and started reloading with fresh brass shells from the pocket of his frock coat.

Startled at first, the rest of the newcomers seemed to finally see the companions, and cheered at the unexpected support. Only now even more stickies jumped onto the vehicle and started moving for the men like ghastly spiders.

With judiciously placed rounds, Ryan and companions started picking off the things while the men pulled the sopping rag fuses from the Molotov cocktails and simply poured the oily contents onto the crawling stickies. Then the rags were lit and dropped onto the sodden attackers.

Bleeding, hooting and set ablaze, the remaining stickies finally jumped off the vehicle to start limping down the street in an effort to escape from their human tormentors.

"No survivors!" the driver shouted from inside the bus, and with a grinding of gears, the wag lurched into movement. "Chill every one of the rad-stinking freaks!"

As the armored vehicle banked into a turn, the men on top started to rain additional Molotov cocktails upon the street, creating a wall of flames. Blocked in that direction, the wounded stickies dashed into a nearby alleyway, only to stop as they reached a dead end, a brick wall twenty feet high. As they turned to leave, the armored wag angled into the mouth of the alley, the sides scraping along the cinder-block walls and throwing off sprays of bright sparks.

"Chill 'em all!" the driver bellowed, starting the wag rolling forward. "No survivors!"

Unable to zero in on the stickies anymore with the wag in the way, the companions took this opportunity to reload.

Hopelessly trapped, the terrified muties started to climb the brick walls in a desperate effort to escape. But the snarling men shot them with arrows until the feathered corpses dropped to the predark asphalt, then more Molotovs were unleashed. Black smoke rose from the twitching inhuman forms, but, not satisfied, the snarling driver rolled the wag all the way into the alley, crushing the burning bodies underneath the spiked tires. Reaching the end, he shifted the gears and backed out, then rolled back in again, before finally retreating into the war-torn street.

Stopping in the middle of the intersection, the driver nosily set the brake and killed the rumbling engine. Pulling a lever, the driver threw open the side door with a squeal of rusty hinges. In tight battle formation, a grim group of men exited the vehicle, armed with axes, and went into the gory alley to make sure each and every one of the crackling stickies was permanently chilled.

"Blood for blood," a gruff voice announced.

Turning from the sight of the slaughter, Ryan saw the driver step off the machine and start to approach.

There was no denying it, the driver was bigger than

Ryan, taller by almost a full four inches. His hair was close-cropped, too short for an opponent to grab, and his face was covered with small scars. His boots were the pebbled hide of a desert lizard, and he was wearing the ancient blue uniform of a civie police officer, although now there was a screaming eagle embroidered where the badge had once been located. A military gunbelt rode low around his waist, the big-bore revolver shiny with oil, the ammo pouched heavy with powder and shot for the black-powder wep.

Studying the array of scars, Mildred recognized the marks as second-degree burns that had been poorly treated. The physician was willing to bet there was a lot of scarring among the sec men using the Molotov cocktails.

"Blood for blood, could mean a lot of things," Ryan said carefully, resting the Steyr on his shoulder. His grip was loose, the barrel pointing away from the stranger, but Ryan kept his finger near the trigger. Just because the companions had helped take out the muties didn't mean the two groups were friendly yet. Even coldhearts would sometimes help people trapped by muties, then jack and ace them afterward. But as the Trader always said, it was easier to make deals than bullets. It never hurt to talk first. *Especially if you had a gren in your pocket.*

"Is that so? Well, it means a truce here," the man said, rubbing a scarred hand across his jaw. "You fight by our side against the stickies, and no sec man can raise a hand against you, until you break the baron's law. You savvy?"

Returning from the alleyway with bloody axes, the group of armed men started to gather behind the driver. They watched the companions with interested expressions, but the axes stayed tight in their grips, ready for fast action if it was deemed necessary.

"I savvy," Ryan repeated, then clicked the safety on the longblaster. "Blood for blood."

At the noise, the mob of sec men visibly relaxed.

"The name is Stirling," the big man said, jerking a thumb at his chest. "Steven Stirling, sec chief for Two-Son ville."

Ryan nodded at that. Two-Son, Tucson. Made sense. There followed a brief round of introductions, during which Stirling looked hard at Jak, then shrugged as if accepting that the albino was just a pale norm, and not a mutie.

"Hell of a war wag you got there," J.B. said politely, going over to the machine. This close, he could see that the strips of armor were actually the louvered gates taken from the predark stores. The LAV could have driven through the armored bus without slowing down, but the bus would be a juggernaut against mercies in civie wags.

"Yeah, she does the job," a grizzled sec man said, puffing out his chest in pride. "Aced a lot of stickies with the *Metro*."

"Good name," Jak said with a friendly nod.

"Thanks."

"I'm just glad that we could help," Krysty added honestly. "There are few people I'd let stickies get hold of alive."

"Well, I know a few." Stirling snorted in dark amusement. "Fragging things have chilled more of my men with their clubs and spears than I want to remember. Now they're leaping off the rooftops onto us! Blind norad, it's like they're getting smarter every nuking month."

"Yeah, about that..." Ryan started, when a low moan came from the top of the war wag.

"Corporal, who was hurt?" Sec chief Stirling demanded, looking in that direction.

"It's Daniel, sir," a burly sec man replied from behind the sandbag wall.

Adjusting his glasses, J.B. saw there was a red-and-white stripe sewn on the shoulder of the man's police uniform. The other sec men had only a white stripe there, while Stirling had a blue one, as well. Badges of rank for sec men? Interesting. Hadn't seen that in a long time.

"Is he burned badly?" Stirling asked, flexing his scarred hands. There was no emotion in the words.

"No, sir," the corporal replied. "A stickie touched him on the neck." He pointed at Doc. "The wrinklie blew off the stinking mutie's arm, but the hand is still attached, and, well..."

"The suckers are leeching out his blood," Stirling finished in a barely controlled growl of anger.

"Yes, sir."

Pulling out his blaster, the sec chief opened the chamber of the revolver and checked the load. Closing it with a snap, he cocked back the hammer. "Okay,

I'll do him myself. A blaster is a lot faster than slitting his throat."

"No, wait!" Mildred interrupted, hugging her med kit. "I'm a healer. Maybe I can save his life."

Murmurs rose from the rest of the sec men, softly counterpointed by a low groan of pain.

"Can you now?" Stirling muttered suspiciously, then he shrugged. "Well, I'll be nuked if I can figure out any way you can make him worse. What's your price?"

He turned to face Ryan. "Or do I talk to you?"

"Mildred is in charge of healing," Ryan answered bluntly.

The sec chief curled a lip. "And you're in charge of the chilling," he said, not posing the statement as a question. "Yeah, I can see that. Fair enough."

He turned. "Okay, Healer, what do you want for saving him? If you can, that is."

"A week's food and bed in your ville," Mildred replied, trying not to show her annoyance. These days, nobody did something free, unless it was to rob you afterward. If she didn't ask for payment, they'd never allow her near the wounded man.

Rubbing his jaw, Stirling chewed that over for a minute. "Done," he said at last, and gestured toward the wag. "Get moving."

Passing her MP-5 to Doc, Mildred clambered up the steps and entered the bus. With slow and steady moves, Doc checked the safety on the rapidfire, then cradled it in his arms, letting it stay in view as a warning, but deliberately keeping his finger off the trigger.

"Einstein, Carstairs, Clay!" Stirling barked. "Check our fallen and make sure they're chilled. Call out if anybody is still sucking air."

"Yes, sir!" Clay said with a salute. "Should we bury the bodies here or…" The teenager left the sentence hanging.

"Burn them," the sec chief ordered. "The stickies would only dig them up later. We don't feed them our dead, boy."

"Yes, sir."

"Be sure to save the boots and blasters! Those don't grow on trees, you know!"

Gathering a clinking sack of Molotov cocktails, the three sec men hurried off to their grisly task.

"Now, about you folks," Stirling said, turning toward the waiting companions. "How the frag did you get so deep into the Zone without horses or a wag? Or is it broke someplace?"

"We used boot leather, my good sir," Doc said, tapping his shoes with the ebony stick. "The essence of primordial locomotion."

Crossing his massive arms, Stirling frowned. "Come again?"

With a curse, Ryan drew and fired the SIG-Sauer, the blaster only a blur.

Before Stirling could react, there was a hoot of pain and a stickie dropped from the underside of a theater marquee. It hit the cracked sidewalk and sluggishly started to rise again. Both the companions and the sec men cut loose with their weapons in unison, and the humanoid creature was torn apart by the banging fusillade.

"Tricky bastards," Stirling muttered, starting the process of purging and reloading his black-powder revolver. "If only we could find their nest, we'd ace all of them in one shot."

"Stickies have nest?" Jak asked incredulously. Just how smart were these local muties?

"Bet your ass they do, and it's well hidden," Stirling said with a bitter laugh. "We've searched for years and never found their nest, and it's gotta be a big one. We have more stickies than scorpions, and we got a lot of scorpions."

Abruptly stepping to the side, something crunched under the teenager's combat boot. "One less," Jak said matter-of-factly.

Just then there came a blood-curdling shriek from the top of the wag, and something went flying over the roof. The object landed on the sandy street with a smack, the sucker-covered fingers twitching grotesquely a few times before the hand went still.

"She did it!" the corporal shouted, leaning over the top of the sandbag wall. His face was a mixture of delight and astonishment. "The lady healer did it! Cut the suckers off, easy as peeling back a scab!"

"He…he's going to live?" Stirling asked incredulously.

"Hell yes!"

The rest of the sec men broke into cheers as Mildred stood into view wiping the ooze and blood from her hands with a cloth. A couple of the men on top of the war wag started laughing and pounding on the physician in congratulations until it almost seemed like they were beating the woman.

"Son of a bitch, she saved him," Stirling whispered, pausing in the reloading. "The baron is going to throw a party when he hears about this!"

"Why is that?" Doc asked, arching a silvery eyebrow.

Giving a crooked grin, a sec man started to laugh. "Daniel is his son."

"The boy's a bastard, sure enough," Stirling admitted, ruefully rubbing his chin in embarrassment. "But still the only son he's got, and heir to the ville."

"And your baron sends him out to fight stickies?" J.B. asked incredulously.

The chief sec man shrugged. "Sure. Why not?"

Glaring angrily at the war wag, another sec man grimly added, "Good thing, too. Nobody wants a baron who faints at the first sight of blood."

Radiating suppressed fury, Stirling gave the man a hard look and he immediately went quiet. The companions noted the incident, and naturally assumed there was some sort of trouble in the baron's family.

As the son of a baron, Ryan could understand that problem better than most. Sometimes, Mildred and Doc talked about democracy, the republic, congress, parliament, and other such predark things. But these days only the strong ruled, and their successors were normally chosen at the end of a working blaster and not by the will of the people. Smart was good, but a baron had to be strong for the sake of his ville.

"Enough already!" Mildred finally shouted, pushing back the gang of joyous sec men. "I'm not a drum, you crazy bastards!"

That only brought louder gales of happy laughter. But the sec boss called a halt to the boisterous congratulations. Rubbing her stinging shoulders, Mildred gathered the med supplies and started down into the lower level of the bus.

"That was mighty good shooting there, rist," a blond sec man said, coming over to address the companions. "You're faster than even the baron with that fancy blaster!"

"You heard my name before," Ryan said in a voice as cold as a grave. "And unless you want to breathe dirt, stupe, you'll be triple-wise to remember it."

The blonde bridled at that, but when he meet the gaze of the Deathlands warrior, the man hunched his shoulders and moved deeper into the crowd.

"Pay no attention to Porter," Stirling said, tucking his weapon away. "He's young and got a big mouth, but he don't mean no trouble."

"I do," Ryan said bluntly, ending the discussion.

A few moments later Mildred hopped out of the vehicle and rejoined the companions. Oddly, her face was a somber study. The woman didn't feel like celebrating in the least. Ten people had died in less than an hour on this street, and she had only been able to save the life of one. Mildred felt physically tired and emotionally exhausted.

"You, you and you!" Stirling barked, pointing at some of the sec men. "Clear the dead muties off the wag and get ready to roll."

Hefting their axes, the sec men got busy chopping, the sound of metal on flesh making the intersection sound like a butcher shop.

"Where's your ville?" Krysty asked, looking into the desert. "Mebbe an oasis somewhere in the dunes?"

"Not far," Stirling answered cryptically. "Walking distance."

Keeping a straight face, Ryan said nothing at that. He had the feeling the ville would have been described as being walking distance away if it was on the other side of the continent. The Two-Son ville sec men might allow a strange healer into their war wag to save a friend, but no bunch of armed outlanders was going to stroll into their ville unannounced.

"All done, Chief," a sec man reported, his ax dripping clear ichor. "Stickies are a lot more cooperative when they're in pieces."

"You got that right." Stirling grunted, scanning the war wag. It was streaked with gore and burned black in spots, but there didn't seem to be any serious damage to the machine. Just to my troops, he added to himself sourly.

"Gill, front and center!" Stirling barked, looking around until he spotted a middle-aged man.

"Sir?" the sec man replied, approaching quickly.

His uniform carried the marks of a corporal. He was holding a crossbow and there was a large quiver slung across his back. Only two arrows remained.

"You're the new driver," Stirling said, motioning with his head. "Get the *Metro* moving, and stay out of the shadows."

"Me?" McGillian asked in surprise, then broke into a smile. "Yes, sir!"

Ambling into the bus, the fellow stored away his crossbow, then got into the driver's seat and started to work the controls. The engine misfired a few times. Frowning in consternation, McGillian fiddled with something on the dashboard controls. In rough order, the rest of the sec men climbed on board the bus. Only four stayed on the street with their sec chief. But Ryan saw that they all carried blasters. Smart.

Suddenly the heavy engine of the war wag rumbled into life. Bursting into a triumphant grin, McGillian shifted gears and the mammoth machine started to roll along the predark street. Yes!

"Okay, move out!" Stirling commanded, starting to walk alongside the slowly traveling wag. "Corporal, make sure the catapult is ready for action. Everybody else stay razor-sharp until we're behind stone! I'm not losing any more sec men today."

Which does not include us, Ryan mentally noted, sharing a look with Krysty. She nodded in understanding.

With the spiked tires digging into the loose sand, the *Metro* began to move smoothly along the predark street with Stirling and his escort at the side, and the companions right behind. Notching fresh arrows into their crossbows, the guards on top of the war wag rocked to the jerking motion of the machine as they studiously watched the shadows and rooftops for any suspicious movements.

Under his breath, Doc muttered something in Latin and Mildred hushed the scholar. Friendly didn't make the sec men friends.

Chapter Thirteen

Staying alongside the rumbling wag so they could have a good view of what was ahead, Ryan and the companions easily kept pace with the lumbering vehicle.

"Stirling, that word Porter used before," Ryan called, shifting his backpack to a new position. "I never heard it before. What is a 'rist'?"

"Eh?" Stirling seemed surprised by the question. "Well, it means outlander." Even while talking, his eyes moved on a regular sweep back and forth among the predark buildings, endlessly searching for enemies. "It is an old word, from before skydark."

"Rist," Doc said, mulling it over as he started to clean the LeMat. Could the root of the word possibly be tourist? When skydark hit, the people of Tucson would have banded together, family with family, the outlanders would have been the folks without kin, those just visiting the town. The tourists. Now it was a derogatory word for stranger.

"Tourist. So much for the legend of Southern hospitality," Doc murmured, packing each chamber in the firing cylinder individually.

"This is the west, not the south," Mildred shot back, pulling out a handkerchief to mop the sweat off her neck. "Besides, who could possibly be called a tourist anymore?"

After a few minutes Doc closed the cylinder with a solid click and holstered the blaster. "Indeed, madam, I stand corrected. We are all outlanders now, strangers in a strange land."

"Got that right," J.B. added, taking out a butane lighter. He applied the flame to the end of the cigar stub in his mouth, puffing it cherry-red, and exhaled a long rich stream.

"Got another of those?" a sec man asked hopefully, sniffing at the pungent fumes. "I'll trade ya fair for it."

"Sorry, last one," J.B. said, pulling out the cigar. Then he caught Mildred trying to hide her usual disapproving expression. The Armorer chuckled. Aw, what the hell.

"Want this one?" J.B. asked, holding out the smoldering stub.

"Thanks!" The sec man grinned and took the stub to start puffing away contentedly. "Nuke me, it's been a long time since I tasted tobacco. What do you want in trade? I got a good knife and some honeycomb."

"The 'comb will do fine."

"Deal!" And the exchange was made.

As the group proceed through the sandy city, the *Metro* took a slow turn around a corner and the sec men on top cut loose with a flurry of arrows at the sky. They were notching replacement arrows when a large bird fell to the ground in a feathery thump.

A young sec man darted forward to grab the chilled bird and scurry back to the wag. The older men complimented the speed of the teenager as the side door of the wag hissed open and he climbed inside with the prize. The door promptly slammed shut in his wake.

"Not very trusting," Krysty stated, pausing to take a sip from her canteen.

Keeping his voice casual, Ryan asked, "Would you be, with outlanders armed like us around?"

Capping the water container, the redhead took a minute before smiling. "No," she admitted honestly. "Not really."

Angling around two more corners, Gill shifted gears until the wag reached a section of street that was relatively clear of sand. The potholes in the asphalt were poorly patched in some spots, but much better in others, which seemed to indicate a learning process. The locals were doing repairs on the ruined city. This was something the companions had never encountered before in all of their travels. Just who was the baron here?

Reaching relatively smooth pavement, the wag picked up speed, while Stirling and the sec men began to look noticeably less anxious.

"We're close to their ville," Ryan stated.

"But they're not heading into the desert," J.B. said, shifting the Uzi slung on his shoulder.

Removing a spare clip from his jacket pocket, Ryan then worked the bolt to eject the partially spent rotary clip, then inserted the fresh 5-shot cluster. Satisfied for the moment, Ryan glanced at the ruined downtown skyscraper, trying to guess their location from the sloped angle of the building. "We seem to be going deeper into Tucson," he decided.

"Ville inside ruins," Jak said with a frown, stepping around a fresh pothole full of prickly cactus plants.

"Never did like those," Krysty added, gently massaging her cheek to try to soothe her sore gums. From the mad brother and sister of Nova ville to the redheaded monster in that nameless town they had nicknamed Zero City, villes inside ruins had always been trouble for the companions. When civilization fell, everybody smart fled the coming food riots. Only feebs and crazies stayed behind, many of them turning into cannies. Gaia, was this why they were being greeted so warmly? They were being led to the cooking pot?

Surreptitiously, the woman slipped a hand into her pants' pocket and checked the gren. If worse came to worst, she'd take a lot of cannies with her before they tasted meat.

"There!" a sec man cried, pointing in the weeds.

Going into a crouch, Stirling spun and fired his blaster at a dark recess under a loose pile of broken bricks. A high-pitched squeal rang out and a tan-colored rabbit bolted from the opening and raced away. Starting to reload, an angry Stirling cursed at the miss, and several of the sec men risked a brief smile behind his back.

"Damn wind must have taken my shot," the sec chief growled to nobody in particular.

Tactfully, nobody disagreed.

The *Metro* turned at the next corner, and the companions now saw only a vast open space that stretched for a good half mile. The concrete paths of ancient sidewalks were still in place, but the buildings that had been inside those cracked borders were gone, the smooth ground evenly packed with rubble and loose sand.

This is a shatter zone, Ryan realized. An open field with no place for attackers to hide. There had to have been some rough fighting here once for the locals to do all of this work.

In the midst of the wide expanse stood a formidable wall, the imposing barrier composed of everything imaginable: concrete sidewalks slabs, marble cornerstones, bricks, cinder blocks and rusty steel beams. The debris of a dozen buildings had been compiled to erect a massive fortification around a small section of the predark city.

Rising high behind the impressive shield were three old buildings, the glass in the windows just as milky-white as those in the ruins, but a few of them flashed mirror-bright. Ryan made a mental note on the location of those. That had to be the home of the baron.

Even from this distance, the companions could see guards walking along the top of the wall, and more of them standing on the roofs of the three buildings. The sec men on the wall appeared to be carrying crossbows, but the ones on the buildings held longblasters. Mildred noted with some satisfaction that women were also walking the wall. She was starting to like this new baron more and more.

"This is why the stores were cleaned out," J.B. said, breaking off a small piece of the honeycomb and tucking it inside a cheek like a chaw of tobacco. "A ville this size needs a lot of different stuff to keep working. Barracks, taverns, armory, stables…"

"Prisons, torture chambers, dungeons, slave pits," Doc added darkly in a whisper.

Sucking on the sweet honey, J.B. had no response to that because it was often true. He passed around the remaining comb to the rest of the companions. Everybody took a sticky piece until there was nothing remaining.

As Gill steered the *Metro* across the broken field, Ryan noticed that there was a second wall set about fifty feet outside the main barrier. It was only about three feet tall, and made of some sort of upright concrete.

"I don't understand this," Mildred said out of the corner of her mouth. "Those are K-rails, a kind of portable divider that repair crews used on highways during construction. But why are there two walls?"

"It's a buffer," Ryan answered bluntly. "Set to break the charge of coldhearts on foot or to slow down a rushing war wag."

Mildred pointed. "But they left a couple of gaps."

"Chill zones," J.B. answered, licking his sticky lips. "The sec men can concentrate all of their blasters on the gaps when the outlanders rush through and cut 'em down in droves."

"A killing field," Doc added, using a term he had once read in the newspaper about a battlefield tactic used in the Civil War. Then he frowned. A civil war. Bah, as if such a thing were possible!

"Good design," Jak admitted, kicking a stone out of his way. "Be bitch to get out."

"Think we're walking into a trap?" Krysty asked in concern, casting a sideways glance at Stirling and his sec men. The men were smiling broadly now that they were within sight of the ville, their hushed voices rising in volume.

"Not think so," Jak stated hesitantly. "But wrong before."

Nodding at that, Krysty surreptitiously checked the antipers gren in her pants' pocket. There was another in her bearskin coat, and more in the backpack, but this was the only gren she could reach with any speed. She wasn't getting any feeling of danger from the sec men or the ville. But as Jak said, they had been wrong before.

Shifting the weps in their hands, the figures of the guards on the wall watched closely as the war wag and the companions slowly approached. Clearly visible behind the barrier were a couple of angled wooden beams festooned with ropes and baskets at the end.

"Catapults," Mildred announced. "Just like the small one on top of the wag."

"That'd be my guess," J.B. agreed, wrinkling his nose to move his glasses. "And damn big ones, too. Right, Doc?"

"Good Lord, how should I know?" the scholar replied curtly. "I taught literature, not history. In my day, the Army of the Potomac used cannons, not siege engines."

"What talk?" Jak said with a scowl. "Just ropes and weights, no engine."

"A siege engine is another term for a catapult," Mildred explained. "Actually, it means any large device used to forcibly enter a castle."

The teen snorted at that. What a bunch of mutie drek. Predark whitecoats were crazy, and that was all there was to it.

The front gate of Two-Son ville proved to be a double set of metal panels that rose almost to the top of the masonry wall where a steel I-beam packed with adobe bricks bridged the sections. Rusty barbed wire covered the bridge and there were a few scraps of cloth, along with what appeared to be scalps, fluttering in the breeze from amid the endless coils—the grim remnants of an obviously failed attempt to gain entry.

A small door was set into the left side of the double panel, and for some unknown reason a band of corrugated iron ran along the bottom. The two sections of the gate itself were covered with multiple sheets of steel, iron, tin and aluminum, each riveted over the other in a crazy patchwork-quilt pattern.

Slowing their advance, Ryan and J.B. shared a glance. Those were obvious repairs done to the portal over the years. Two-Son ville had seen some hard battles in the past, and there was no way of knowing if the present inhabitants had been the defenders or the invaders.

Applying the squeaking brakes, Gill eased the wag to a rocking halt and sounded the horn four times, then three, then once.

That was clearly a code of some kind, Ryan realized, tensing slightly. But what was the message?

In response, a flap made of riveted steel fell forward to expose the car tires set along the bottom of the front gate. With ponderous creaking, the right side of the gate started to swing outward, the inflated tire crunching on the loose pebbles covering the ground as they rolled along.

The gate hit the wall with a resounding crash, and the *Metro* rolled on through, the sec men on top of the war wag having to duck behind the sandbags because the fit was so tight.

Instantly, Ryan could see why the gate needed a row of tires to move—it was over a yard thick and composed of three layers of telephone poles arranged in a staggered pattern, the first row set vertical, the second sideways and the third vertical again. The gate was well over a yard thick and had to have weighed a couple of tons.

"Need an implo gren to get through that," J.B. whispered, forcing himself to appear calm. "I'm not sure that even a LAW rocket launcher or an Armbrust could dent this thing."

Merely grunting in reply, Ryan flicked a finger and clicked the safety off the loaded Steyr.

Blowing dark fumes from the tailpipe, the battered *Metro* angled away from the gate and turned to go around a squat brick wall set directly in front of the entrance to the ville.

Damn, it's another a firing wall, Ryan noted. A place for the ville defenders to stand behind and shoot over the top at anything that managed to get through the colossal gate. Whoever designed this place really knew how to fight, that was for sure.

Beyond the firing wall, Krysty could see crowds of civies freely moving about, talking, laughing and shouting. There were rows of houses, huts and hovels mixed together with taverns, a horse stable and a tanner. Past those rose the slanted-glass roofs of a greenhouse, the three predark buildings towering above everything.

Greenhouses! Krysty felt a shiver run down her back. The rest of the companions clearly shared her feelings on the matter.

"All right, get moving," Stirling said, waving the sec men onward. "Clean up the *Metro,* and get her ready for another run tomorrow. I'm gonna intro our guests to the baron."

"What about the prisoner?" Porter asked with a sneer, running dirty fingers through his greasy blond hair.

The sec chief made a face as if he had just bitten into an apple and found half a mutie worm inside. "Yeah, bring him, too," Stirling ordered.

Prisoner? Ryan glanced at Mildred, who shrugged.

"At least it's not us," Krysty stated softly.

"So far," Doc whispered ominously.

Walking through the gateway, Ryan noted the solid construction of the gate and wall. From this angle he could see that the second door was a fake. It was backed by the concrete bulk of the main wall and was totally immobile. The door was merely a decoration to trick invaders into wasting time and effort to gain entry through something that couldn't be made to open.

"Okay, I'm impressed," Mildred admitted.

"Wonder which first," Jak added under his breath. "Smart stickies, or good wall?"

As the companions started around the firing wall, a shadow swept across them. They turned to see the gate closing. The locking mechanism was made of wrought iron, with only a few shiny steel parts. With a metallic clang, the exterior skirt was raised back into position to hide the tires, then was also locked into place.

"I love that sound," Stirling said, exhaling. "Always feels good to be safe at home."

"All right, drop those blasters," a stern feminine voice commanded.

Two sec men rose from behind the firing wall, each bearing homie scatterguns. A fat woman armed with an old Browning Automatic Rifle joined them. Mildred knew the blaster well. It had been an antique in her day, but these days the clip-fed, bolt-action weapon was a deadly marvel of mil tech.

"Not going to happen," Ryan said, keeping his hand relaxed on the stock of the Steyr. This whole thing didn't feel like a jack. There was the distinct reek of stupidity about the fat woman. He'd stay sharp, but let this play out before spraying lead.

"That was an order, not a request, rist," the corpulent sec woman snarled, working the bolt on her weapon. "Don't you worry, sir, I have the prisoners under control."

With that pronouncement, Stirling raised both eyebrows. "Prisoners? Did you say prisoners?" the sec chief bellowed, stepping in front of the companions. "Corporal, you're either drunk on duty, or a nuke-sucking feeb!"

"Sir?" the female guard asked in confusion. The two sec men behind her began to lower their weps, clearly telling which way the wind was blowing on this situation. Each of the men looked as if they would rather be swimming naked in a lake of rad water than involved in this present conversation.

Striding to the firing wall, Stirling slapped the long-blaster aside. "The prisoner has been taken to the Square, as per my orders," he shouted into her face. "These people are guests of the baron! Honored guests, I might fragging add, under my fragging personal protection!"

"Sir?" she repeated.

His burned face grim, Stirling leaned closer. "Besides, do you truly think that I would willingly let armed prisoners into the ville? *Do you?*"

Breaking into a sweat, the pudgy sec woman hugged the wep to her ample chest and forced a smile. "Ah, well, sir, I… That is…you…"

"Shut up, before I take that Browning and stuff it where the sun don't shine!" the sec chief roared, towering over the quaking guard. "These *people*," he said, stressing the word, "saved the life of the baron's son and are guests."

"Guests?" she asked, as if never hearing the word before.

"That's right! Now salute them in greeting, or I'll have your tits on toast for my breakfast!"

"Sir, yes, sir!" she replied, standing stiffly at attention and jerking the longblaster to her shoulder. "Hail, honored guests to Two-Son!"

The companions gave no response, but eased their fingers off the triggers of their assorted weaponry. Fools were like shitters, every ville had at least one.

"Sorry about that," Stirling apologized, hitching up his gunbelt. "The gate gang is always a bit twitchy. The stickies sometimes get inside, and they're the first ones to get aced."

"No prob," Ryan growled, feeling the fury pound inside him like the pistons of an engine. He knew it was a bad move, but he had no choice. Ryan tossed the Steyr to J.B., who made the catch and slung the rifle over a shoulder with his scattergun. He had been expecting something like this from Ryan after the fat bitch had drawn a weapon on him.

"All right, fatty, you want to try that longblaster

again?" Ryan said to the guard, a hand resting on the holstered SIG-Sauer.

"Sir?" she asked hesitantly, sweat forming on her brow.

"You heard me. Want to try to aim and fire that BAR before I draw this handcannon and blow your brains out the back of your nuking skull?"

Startled, the sec woman tightened her grip on her blaster. "Are you challenging me to a duel, One-eye?" she demanded in a cool voice, working the arming bolt.

"No, he is not! There will be no dueling in my ville," a deep voice boomed in command. "Put down those blasters!"

Pivoting, Stirling lifted the hand off his gunbelt and snapped a salute at the approaching group of people. Turning, the three guards behind the firing wall went pale.

The blood still pounding in his temples, Ryan forced himself to ease a hand off the SIG-Sauer and appraise the newcomers. Yeah, this was the baron. No doubt about that.

Surrounded by a cadre of armed guards, the tall, lean man was wearing old boots that were highly polished. His clothes were spotless, without a single patch, and the blue-steel blaster at his right hip was a Glock autoloader. The left sleeve of his jacket was pinned to his shoulder, the arm missing completely. A screaming blue eagle tattoo was on the side of his neck, talons splayed as it dived to attack.

Briefly, Ryan recalled the earlier comment on how fast the baron was supposed to be with a blaster. With only one arm? Interesting. If it was true.

Her long red hair waving about as if stirred by a breeze, Krysty studied the tattoo. The same design was embroidered on Stirling's jacket, and it was vaguely similar to the stitching on her boots. Luckily her pants were hanging on the outside, covering them at the moment. But from things Doc and Mildred once talked about, she knew that the eagle was the talisman of old America. But did it mean the same thing here, or something else entirely?

"So you're Ryan," the baron said, coming to a halt. "I'm Baron Petrov O'Connor, ruler of this ville. Thanks for saving my son, as well as Steven here. Good sec chiefs are hard to find as live brass these days."

"How do you know who were are?" Ryan asked suspiciously, looking for any of the *Metro* sec men in the group of bodyguards. None was in sight.

"I told him," Stirling announced unexpectedly. "If the weather is right, we got a way to talk over a distance."

Tilting her head, Mildred considered that. Couldn't be a radio, there hadn't been one in the war wag. But then she hadn't noticed a prisoner, either. And why would weather be a factor? Then she recalled the central buildings of the ville, the shiny windows brightly reflecting the weak sunlight.

"Mirrors," Mildred said impulsively. "You use mirrors to flash a code. Just like beeping the horn at the gate."

The sec men were clearly astonished, but the baron only raised an eyebrow.

"Well, nothing is a secret forever," O'Connor growled. "Or did you come up with something similar on your own?"

"Great minds think alike, sir," Doc rumbled, giving a half bow.

A crowd of civies was beginning to gather behind the bodyguards. They chuckled at the phrase, while the sec men blinked in surprise.

"Great minds think alike," the baron muttered, slowly smiling. "By the blood of my fathers, that's good. Triple wise. I can see why you folks travel with this wrinklie. Brains are just as important as blasters, I always say."

Did he now? Ryan's estimation of the baron went up a few notches. He knew that not every baron was a power-mad lunatic controlling his people by the whip and iron club. Most were, but not all. However, Ryan had also meet very intelligent barons before who still proved to be utterly ruthless coldhearts.

"My people!" the baron shouted, turning to face the crowd. "These outlanders saved the life of Daniel O'Connor and fought side by side with our brave sec men against the stickies today!"

That news generated an enthusiastic cheer.

Tucking a hand into his gunbelt, Baron O'Connor faced Ryan once more. "You are my honored guests, and will come to stay in the Citadel with me for the remainder of your visit."

Then the baron added in a sterner tone, clearly not meant for the companions. "And the hand raised against them will be treated as if its owner had attacked a sec man. Is that crystal?"

The attending crowd nervously murmured acknowledgment. It was obvious that the locals truly respected the one-armed baron, but feared his wrath even more. That was good to know. Ryan strongly doubted that anybody in this ville would be causing them any trouble again. At least, for a while.

"And that goes double for me," Stirling said, staring directly at a select few civies, all of whom immediately tried to radiate an air of innocence.

"All right, get back to work, the lot of you!" the sec chief added loudly, clapping his hands. "Water doesn't haul itself, and I want to see that new greenhouse finished by the full moon. Winter is coming, and sweat buys us food. Get moving!"

Muttering among themselves, the crowd started to thin, the people returning to their tasks, heading down the side streets into the ville, the sec men standing on the nearby wall going back on patrol. The brief break in their routine was over.

"Come, it's a short hike to the Citadel," the baron said, starting to walk. "And if I'm any guess of faces, you six have had a rock-hard day. I know tired when it stands before me."

"Well, we could use someplace to knock the dust off our boots," Ryan admitted, shifting his bulky backpack.

"And boil our clothes," Krysty added hopefully.

"That we can offer," O'Connor said with a grin. "I've smelled worse, but not from anything still walking."

"No argument there." Mildred sighed. Between the crud from the predark sewer, her own sweat and the blood of the muties, the physician was feeling rather ripe.

"Over dinner we can discuss the stickie problem," Stirling added, matching his gait to the stride of the rists.

"And where their nest might be," Ryan added sagely. "I have a few ideas on that."

"Excellent!" the baron said, casting a glance sideways. "The muties become bolder every year, and we constantly lose more troops. If we don't stop them soon, we'll have to burn down the ruins."

"But wouldn't that also destroy the ville?" Krysty asked.

"Most likely," Stirling agreed reluctantly. "But if we're going to eventually get nuked anyway, then we're taking the fragging bastards to hell with us."

"I eagerly look forward to hearing a third option," the baron said blandly, as if such a thing couldn't possibly exist.

Staying in formation, the bodyguards cleared a path through the crowded streets for the baron, sec chief and the weary companions. As they passed the homes and shops, people paused in their work to check out the strangers. Some of the oldsters scowled in stern disapproval, but the children watched in innocent wide-eyed wonder. Many of the younger people watched the companions with open hostility. Only a few looked on with frank curiosity.

"We're not very popular," Mildred commented on the sly.

"Indeed, madam," Doc intoned. "I know how a pork chop feels in a synagogue."

"Show 'em you like 'em, eh?"

That took a moment to unscramble, then Doc started to correct the mangled Hebrew phrase, before spotting her smile, and realized the physician was only teasing. He struggled briefly to come up with a clever quip in Latin, but failed completely.

"Quite so," Doc said in resignation.

The sun was starting to set behind the skyscraper downtown, casting its long penumbra across the ville, adding to the band of darkness thrown by the defensive wall. The air was rich with the smell of life, frying fish, boiling soup, unwashed bodies, leather, beer and hot metal. From somewhere, there came the sound of wood being chopped, and a woman began to sing softly, her voice clear and strong, rising to fill the approaching night.

Suddenly there was a movement underfoot. J.B. almost lost his balance as a small dog ran between his feet. In a snarling pounce, the dog leaped upon a rat, sinking its jaws into the back of the rodent and shaking it vigorously until the spine audibly snapped. Happily wagging its tail, the dog lay down in the middle of the street and began eating the corpse.

Fighting back the urge to pet the animal, Mildred heartily approved of its presence. Rodents carried a lot of diseases, and while cats were good for mousers, the house pets were completely outclassed in a fight with a full-grown rat.

"Do you use dogs to hunt muties?" Krysty asked the chief.

"Why, do stickies smell like rats?" Stirling asked in amusement. Then he saw that the redhead was serious. "Dogs?"

"Hopefully bigger than that," Ryan added, as the little canine struggled to haul away the fresh carcass from the companions' tromping boots. The two combatants had nearly been the same size. Unless the ville had a thousand such dogs, nobody sane was going to hunt stickies with these runts. The hounds at his old ville of Front Royal had stood half as tall as a man, and could bring down a full-grown bear.

"Nope, that's all we have," the sec chief said. "Are they too small?"

"Hell, yes."

"Pity."

Twirling his walking stick, Doc started to tell the others about how backwoods Mexicans used to hunt mountain lions with Chihuahuas, but held his tongue. The tale was outrageous, but true. However, few people ever believed that a huge lion could be brought down by the tiny, yapping dogs. Even when they attacked in packs of a hundred.

Passing by a tavern, a little girl sweeping trash out the door stopped to stare at Jak in growing horror. Dropping the broom, she made some sort of a gesture in the air that the teen recognized as a ward against evil. In his long travels, Jak had seen such things many times before.

"Nope, not ghost," the teenager said with smile.

Hesitantly, the child watched him walk by, then broke into a giggle and raced inside shouting for her mother to come see the snow-white man.

Jak chuckled at that.

"I always knew you had a good heart," Doc said, patting the teen on the shoulder.

Brushing back his snowy-white hair, Jak shrugged. "Like kids."

Several blocks later, a drunk staggered into the group and out again, never really noticing the baron even when he bumped into the noble. The sec men bristled, but O'Connor laughed the incident away.

"Been there, done that," the baron said with a tolerant smile. "Although I'm usually singing when I get that tanked." Then his face turned hard. "That wasn't a sec man, was it, Chief?"

"No, my lord, just a potter," Stirling replied, watching the drunk stumble into the tavern.

"Fair enough, then."

Keeping a private counsel, the respect of the companions for the baron increased once more. There were far too many rulers that would have chilled the drunk for a lot less of an offense.

As they approached the three predark buildings, the ground dipped slightly and the companions could see that the surrounding area was filled with greenhouses, easily a dozen of the structures, if not more. The transparent structures were placed to catch the southern exposure, and inside were rows upon rows of wooden tubs lush with growing plants, flowering vines climbing up a line of lattice trellises and bushes dotted with bright fruit. Off to the side stood the skeletal framework of two more greenhouses, only a few square panels installed in the roof.

Behind the sheets of glass, green plants grew in orderly profusion, the tiny dots of color among the greenery showing a wide assortment of fruit and vegetables.

"Where do you get your dirt?" Krysty asked warily, not sure if she wanted to hear the answer.

"Make it ourselves, but the crops yield less and less food every year unless we completely replace the soil," Stirling said with a sigh. "Must be doing something wrong."

Either that, or else they don't know anything about crop rotation, Krysty realized privately. Back in Colorado, her mother had taught Krysty much about plants and the cycle of life. Some plants took vital chems from soil, while others put them back in. Alternate the plants correctly and a greenhouse could triple its yield in a single year. Then again, mebbe they were using something that was contaminating the soil.

The bodyguards became alert as raised voices were heard down the street. The sec men closed ranks around the baron just as the group came upon an old mule that had decided to sit in the middle of street and refused to move. A swearing man was pulling on the reins with both hands, his sandals digging into the ground to no avail. Going around the obstruction, they left the farmer and his stubborn mule locked in mortal combat.

"Excuse me, Healer," the baron said, moving closer. "Mildred, correct?" She nodded. "Good. I have several healers, but none of them can remove a stickie's hand without also removing the limb it's attached to."

Unable to stop herself, Mildred looked at the pinned sleeve of the big norm.

"Yes, you are correct," O'Connor replied to the unspoken question. "It was my dear wife who took an ax and cut me loose. I damn near got aced anyway from the blood loss." Touching the empty sleeve, he frowned deeply. "Unfortunately, we haven't had similar good luck with other sec men and civies that we tried to save."

"I'll be happy to teach your healers what to do," Mildred replied without hesitation. "I happen to know a lot of tricks they can use to save lives. How to stop blaster wounds from festering, set broken bones so that the person isn't a cripple afterward, heal shine burns properly, all kinds of things."

As they walked along, the baron looked her in the face, carefully studying what he saw there.

"Blind norad, I believe you," he said with a faint smile. "Okay, Healer, name your price."

This nonsense again? "You really have nothing we can use," Mildred said politely. "We already have a week of room and board to our credit."

"Board?" the baron repeated puzzled.

"A week of beds and food," she translated.

Thoughtfully, O'Connor chewed over the odd phrase. Of course, beds were made of a mattress laid over a board. How obvious.

"That is true," O'Connor muttered, scratching at his cheek. "Well, you were walking through the ruins, so how about a horse?"

"Six horses," Mildred countered on impulse. "One for each of us."

The baron laughed. "You're not teaching us how to fly, Healer, or to make blasters out of sand. I'll pay no more than two horses. Take it or leave it."

"And I say five, and you say, three, and I say four, and then we dicker for a while, and agree on three with bridles and saddles," Mildred explained, making an impatient gesture. "So how about we shake on that, and skip all the haggling?"

"Done," the baron said, and held out his hand.

Shaking the man's hand, Mildred could feel his tremendous physical strength. The fingers were like iron. He could easily crush her fingers as if they were matchsticks, but instead he was gentle. Almost... tender.

Impulsively, Mildred meet the baron's gaze and saw something there that spoke of matters as old as time itself.

"Three horses, hey, that's great," J.B. said, adding his hand on top of their grip. "That's a fair deal, Millie. Well bargained, honey!"

Reluctantly releasing his hold, the baron diplomatically said nothing as J.B. slipped an arm around Mildred's waist. The beautiful healer was already taken. Such a shame. She was fit to be a baron's wife.

The rows of shops and homes stopped, and the group started along a flat road that led between the greenhouses, the slated-glass roofs sparkling in the dying sunlight. A wire-netting fence protected the greenhouses from windblown debris, along with any possible jacking of the veggies by rats. Inside the glass buildings, teams of civies watched the companions go by, and nervously tightened their grips on the crude tools used for tilling the dark loam.

"Greenhouses," Krysty said again.

"Eat nothing until we're sure there's no woodchipper," Ryan warned. The previous year, they had encountered a madman who ruled a nameless ville in the deep desert. The insane baron had also used window glass from some nearby ruins to build a score of greenhouses and protect the crops from the acid rain. However, he made the all-important dirt by mixing garbage with boiled nightsoil and human flesh minced in a predark woodchipper. Thankfully, there was no sign of a woodchipper in this ville. Then again, maybe it was just out of sight at the moment.

Leaving the questionable greenhouses behind, the group started across another flat chilling field. Circles of defense. Straight ahead, Ryan could see that the three predark buildings formed a lopsided triangle around the Two-Son Square. The open area held a stone well, a gallows and another firing wall. A scattering of people were lounging about, some of the civies rolling dice, others smoking corncob pipes, and a small group of sec men stood near a whipping post with a disheveled man, his wrists bound in heavy rope, his head lowered in submission. Close by there was a thick wooden post embedded into the ground with iron rings dangling from the rough-hewn top.

As the baron came near the group, the prisoner raised his head, and O'Connor stopped in his tracks.

"Explain this," the baron demanded, his voice strained.

There was no other way, so the chief sec man spoke bluntly. "Baron, Sec man Davies broke ranks and ran away during our fight in the ruins."

There was a long pause. "You mean," the baron said slowly, "that my nephew charged the stickies by himself?" There was hope in the words, but his expression beguiled the lie.

The bound man began to weep.

"No, sir," Stirling said, forcing out the distasteful words. "He dropped his blaster and ran away."

"I see," the baron said slowly, then added in a whisper, "Did you recover the blaster?"

"No, it fell down a grating."

"My hands…the stickies," Davies cried out, shaking all over. "My lord, they were everywhere! Uncle, they were throwing spears!"

The civies stopped rolling dice at that remark and looked about frantically.

"So the civies don't know," J.B. whispered. "That's mighty interesting." Ryan nodded in assent.

"My lord, are the stickies using spears?" a woman asked fearfully, wringing her hands.

"Yes, we aced them all!" O'Connor boomed proudly, then walked closer and took the prisoner by the collar to shake him hard. "Shut up, fool! Never speak of such things in public!"

Releasing the fellow, O'Connor stared at the bound man, his anguish and indecision plainly readable.

"It was all a mistake—" Davies started, but was promptly cut off.

"Fifty lashes for running away," The baron barked, spittle flying from his mouth. "And fifty more for losing a blaster!"

One of the sec men holding the prisoner gasped. "A hundred?" the corporal asked, then quickly shut his mouth.

"My lord, no one has ever survived that many strokes," Stirling interjected. "Perhaps, we could—"

"You heard the ruling," the baron said in a flat voice. "The same law is for all men. There are no exceptions. None! Not even for those of my bloodline.

"Such as it is," the baron added softly in disgust.

Saying nothing, Mildred and Doc both looked sick at the dire pronouncement, but the rest of the companions accepted it without a qualm. For sec men, discipline was a hard fact of life. When Ryan and J.B. traveled with the Trader, they had both chilled people for cowardice or some other crime—theft, drunk on duty, or rape. The weakness of one guard could get everybody else chilled in their sleep. The sec men stood strong, or the ville fell. The equation for life was as simple as that.

"Proceed with the punishment at once," the baron commanded, turning away. Then he added over a shoulder, "If...if my nephew lives, take him to the Citadel to recover. If not, inform my sister and burn the body outside the wall."

"Uncle!" Davies cried out, struggling against his bonds. But the sec men holding him were much larger, and both knew that if the prisoner should escape, they would take his place on the whipping post.

On the roof of the three buildings, sec men stood with longblasters in their hands. The scene occurring below was none of their concern. They watched the walls and the sky. Clouds were gathering on the horizon and rain was imminent. Whether or not it was acid rain, could only be told when the first telltale whiff of sulfur was carried on the heralding wind.

The baron started toward the central building. "This way to your rooms," he said, his pace neither quickening nor slowing.

Watching the one-armed man walk away, Ryan knew that the baron was trying to show he had no feelings on the matter, like any good ruler. The law was the law. Period. End of discussion. But O'Connor's posture told the world how deep was his sorrow at the craven act of cowardice. The one-eyed man tried to imagine what would have been his reaction if his nephew had run away from a fight, but found the idea impossible to conjure. Nathan was a Cawdor, and would gladly die to protect his ville.

"Uncle, please..." Davies whispered plaintively, the words dying on the desert breeze.

"Tie him to the post," Stirling ordered, going to the wooden stake and removing a coiled length of leather from a peg.

The two guards shoved the prisoner along and lashed his bound wrists securely to the iron rings. With his hands raised, Davies barely reached the ground, his boots resting on their toes.

Crossing to the whipping post, Doc pulled an empty leather ammo pouch from his pocket. "Bite hard on this," he suggested to the prisoner. "It will stop you from screaming."

Panic was wild in the sec man's eyes, but Davies opened his mouth and accepted the gift.

"Be sure to count between the strokes," Doc added softly. "Then tense before each one hits. It will make them hurt more, but do less damage. Be brave, and you will live."

Starting to drip sweat, Davies grunted in reply.

Darkness swept across the ville as the setting sun

moved behind some dark clouds, the shadows rich in wild hues. The civies on the Square started to leave, casting fearful glances at the rumbling sky.

"Sir, is that allowed?" a sec man asked frowning. "The outlander giving Davies—"

Flicking his wrist, the sec chief made the whip crack loudly on the ground. Dust puffed up from the hit.

"What outlander?" Stirling asked, coiling the smooth length. "Private, there is nobody here, but you two, me and the prisoner. Right?"

"Absolutely, sir," the second guard said stiffly.

"Good." Stirling tested the whip once more on the ground. "Okay, let's get this started."

Pulling knives, the two guards started to cut away the bound man's shirt, exposing a back already covered with old, badly healed scars. Obviously, this wasn't the man's first taste of punishment.

"Let's go," Ryan said, turning to leave.

But Doc stayed near the prisoner, watching the preparations. His hand began to move toward the blaster on his hip.

"Now, Doc," Ryan ordered in a tone he rarely used on a friend.

That jarred the Vermont scholar. Almost reluctantly, Doc let go of the LeMat and rejoined the others. "Barbaric," he muttered under his breath.

"And not necessary," J.B. added, starting across the darkening Square. "Davies should have been quietly aced in the ruins. A public beating like this only makes the civies nervous."

"Bad for ville," Jak agreed.

"Good God, sir, is that all torture means to you?"

"This isn't torture, Doc, but punishment," Ryan replied without any emotion. "Besides, I really don't give a flying fuck what they do to a bastard coward. A sec man who runs is worse than any invading coldheart."

Just then the crack of a whip split the air, closely followed by the muffled grunt of pain.

"I took sixty once," Doc said in a whisper, a hand going to touch his ribs. "Passed out at that point, and they let me be. Even Cort Strasser had a touch of mercy."

"Or mebbe it wasn't any fun for him without a scream," J.B. commented pragmatically.

Solemnly, Doc said nothing, but nodded at the possibility. That was a part of his life the time traveler would rather forget entirely.

"At least we can be sure there's no woodchipper," Mildred said with a sigh. "If they didn't feed the idiot into a grinder for this transgression, then we're safe enough."

"Guess so," Krysty added with a scowl. "But it's a hell of a way to find out."

The sound of leather on flesh came again, but there was no noise this time from Davies.

As the companions entered the front doors of the middle building, lightning flashed in the distance. Thunder boomed a few seconds later. There could be no doubt that a storm was brewing in the north and that it would arrive very soon.

Chapter Fourteen

A low hum could be heard as swirling electronic mists filled the mat-trans chamber, building, increasing, sparkling with a million tiny star points of bright light. Then just as quickly as it appeared, the quantum fog sank into the solid floor, exposing Delphi.

Striding from the chamber, the man briskly entered the antechamber, the bottom of his white robe moving around his moccasins like foaming water. Delphi had checked the chamber and couldn't find any trace of the jump sickness that hit unauthorized travelers, which meant that either Tanner and his people had solved the secret of a controlled jump or this was one of the many traps laid throughout the system for the escaped prisoner.

Checking his palm monitor, Delphi saw that this color redoubt was in Arizona. The Zone, as it was called in these barbaric days. He almost smiled. Excellent. The Rogans were very close. Soon, Tanner would be captured alive and then…

Delphi eagerly entered the control room and stopped. Kicked into a corner was the smashed remains of probe droid, a USB cable lying nearby.

Kneeling on the floor, he gently laid out the largest

pieces, trying to reconstruct the device. A lot of the camouflage chassis was reduced to pieces too small to utilize, but a few chunks were relatively intact. A neat hole penetrated the chassis on one side, the other totally smashed. Then among the circuit boards and thinking wires, he saw an irregular lump of metal that was clearly a bullet. The cyborg boosted his vision and swept the room, but couldn't find the ejected brass from a pistol. Didn't Tanner use a black-powder weapon? No, wait, the albino and redhead carried revolvers. Okay, mystery solved. The machine had to have found Tanner, but his companions shot the probe before it could link with the main computers and relay a message to Operation Chronos.

Slowly, Delphi stood. Excellent. The less Chronos knew, the better it was for TITAN, and for Department Coldfire.

Going to a security outlet, Delphi jacked himself into the system and his left eye began flickering through the video cameras secreted in every room. Soon, it was obvious that Tanner and his people weren't present. Then he found the broken Vulcan minigun, and checked inside the Deep Storage Locker. As expected, it had been looted. Double checking the inventory numbers of the munitions boxes, he scowled at the sight of the empty case that had once held implosion grenades. But if the test subject was armed with real weaponry...

Switching to an external view, Delphi cursed at the sight of the exploded U.S. Army Hummer inside the ruined tunnel, a Balisk-class guardian reduced to its smashed cybernetic framework. Oddly, the guardian hadn't been killed by implosion grenades. Then he realized the truth. They had sent the Hummer through the blast door loaded with high explosives. Damn, these people were smart! Perhaps too smart?

Changing to the exit door of the tunnel, Delphi couldn't find any indication that Tanner had departed the tunnel this way. Strange. Backtracking through the entire length of the access tunnel, Delphi paused at the sight of a ragged hole in the flooring. An explosion crater. He tried to get a view into the depths, hoping to find the rotting bodies of the people, but the angle was impossible. No choice then.

Disconnecting from the system, Delphi left the control room and headed for the elevators. Wherever Tanner went, he would follow. But first… Using his cybernetic implants, Delphi mentally sent a string of encoded commands to the main computer of the military redoubt.

A few moments later, a hidden wall panel slid aside on the bottom level, and another Balisk-class guardian rolled into view, the gelatinous biowep moving to rendezvous with its new master.

THE BRIGHT LIGHT of alcohol lanterns illuminated the interior of the Two-Son building. Ryan couldn't see the baron anywhere. Baron O'Connor either needed to be alone right now or he had more pressing business at hand. Most likely, it was a mix of the two.

"Good evening, honored guests," a wrinklie said,

shuffling forward with a lantern in her hand. She smiled, displaying a mouth full of missing teeth. "I'm Suzette, the head maid for the Citadel."

Her dress appeared to be made of window drapes and her moccasins were worn thin in spots, but she was clean, well-fed and carrying a large machete hanging at her side. Obviously, this was a highly valued member of staff. Few barons armed their maids.

"Good evening, dear lady," Doc replied, bowing slightly.

Unaccustomed to such things, Suzette blushed at the courtesy. "Please come this way," the old woman said, starting toward an open stairwell. The door had been removed and the concrete steps were covered with red carpeting that looked like it came from a movie theater.

"The baron has given you a room on the second floor, which is quite an honor. That's where his family lives," Suzette said with obvious questions in the words. Who were these ragged rists to receive such an honor?

Brushing back his thick black hair, Ryan snorted in reply. Honor, his ass. The truth was that the baron just wanted to keep the companions under observation. Keep your friends close, but your enemies closer, as the ancient saying went.

At the first landing, Suzette pushed open a door adorned with a painting of a screaming eagle, then entered a hallway well lit with lanterns set into wall niches with pieces of mirrors behind. The reflected light filled the hall bright as any halogen or fluorescent tube inside a redoubt.

"Somebody must have read the biography of Thomas Edison," Mildred said out of the corner of her mouth.

"I can only agree, madam," Doc replied.

At the far end of the corridor were several armed men behind a sandbag bunker. A pair of drapes were pulled apart to reveal a door bearing the eagle design, only done in more colors and in much greater detail.

"Ah, the west wing." Mildred chuckled, shifting her backpack.

"Oh, no, madam, that's the southside," Suzette corrected primly, going to a door bearing the hand-painted sign Royil Gest Rom.

Ill amused, Doc exhaled at the horrible spelling, but said nothing. That wouldn't have been polite for a "guest" in any century.

Going inside, Suzette hurried about lighting more lamps, then removed several tiny predark bars of hotel soap that she laid reverently on the washstand next to a crystal punchbowl, along with a matching carafe filled with clean water. The walls were covered with paintings of Two-Son when it had been called Tucson, as well as a collection of portraits of unknown people. A sideboard had several liquor bottles without labels, and a dozen slightly cracked drinking glasses on a silver tray.

Immediately, Jak began a sweep of the wall, studying the pictures very closely.

"If you need anything, just ring the bell," Suzette

directed, gesturing at a brass fixture that had to have been liberated from a firehouse. "Dinner will be ready soon. Baron O'Connor requests your presence at your earliest convenience."

"Thank you, that will be all," Ryan told her, looking around the place. The woman gave a curtsy, something the man hadn't seen in some time, and left the companions alone.

The internal walls had been removed from the office to make one large room. There was some brickwork along the former divisions, and Ryan could only hope the people who did the modifications knew what they were doing and the whole place wouldn't come crashing down on their heads in the middle of the night. A long row of ten beds lined the opposite wall, piles of sheets, pillows and blankets already laid out and waiting. A plastic bucket with a snap-on lid was placed discreetly under a wooden stool with a hole in the middle. Its purpose was obvious.

"Not exactly trying to impress us with their wealth, are they?" Krysty said, gratefully dropping her backpack onto the floor.

"Actually," J.B. answered slowly, chewing a lip, "I think they are."

"No spy holes," Jak reported, doffing his own backpack. The teenager straightened his shoulders, then gently rubbed the bandage on his head. "Starting itch," he complained.

"I'll fix that," Mildred replied, searching in her med kit.

Sitting the teen down in an office chair, she got busy with the bandages and soon the bloody wrapping was replaced.

"Better," Jak said in relief. "Thanks."

Taking turns, the companions washed as best they could in the punch bowl. Ryan went last, carefully removing his gloves before gingerly washing his red hands clean, then applying more lotion before donning the leather gloves again. Mildred had been right. His fingers were feeling better every day, and once his arm healed, he would be in good shape.

Ringing the bell summoned a young serving girl. Doc asked for more water, and she returned with a full bucket. Thanking her profusely, Doc tried to shoo the servant away, but she kept smiling shyly at the scholar and pretended to misunderstand him until Krysty took the girl by the collar and marched her out of the room.

"I think you made a conquest there, you silver-tongued devil." Mildred chuckled in amusement.

"What? Do not be absurd, madam," Doc admonished, carrying the bucket to the washstand to exchange the used water for fresh. "I am old enough to be her father, grandfather!"

"Which only means you're smart enough to stay alive, and rich enough to have two blasters," Mildred teased, trying to hide a grin. "That makes you quite a catch these days."

Turning his back on the physician, Doc merely grunted in reply, not trusting his tongue to discuss the matter. He was married back in his time, but had been with several women in the present.

Taking turns, the companions rinsed their clothing, then hung the garments over the frames of the portraits to dry, and to cover any possible spy holes they might have missed. After putting on fresh clothing, everybody checked their weps.

After adjusting his fedora, J.B. placed his backpack in the middle of a bed, then rigged a gren underneath.

"Antipers?" Ryan asked with a scowl, buckling his gunbelt.

"Nope, just a stun gren," J.B. replied, minutely adjusting the spring trip taken from a mousetrap. "But we'll be able to hear the bang outside, and the flash will blind anybody in the room."

"Good enough. We don't want to blow the rest of our stuff to hell and gone just to sound the alarm."

"I got it covered."

Leaving the guest room, the companions found Suzette impatiently waiting for them in the hallway.

"This way!" she announced, leading them up a flight of carpeted stairs to what seemed to once have been a suite of conference rooms but was now the baron's dining hall.

This carpeting was a rich blue, clean and in good condition. More alcohol lanterns lined the walls, but this time full mirrors had been placed behind them to double the brightness. The wallpaper was slightly faded, but the elaborate design was still discernable, and there was an enormous skylight in the center of the ceiling. Luminescent clouds were flowing past the twinkling stars, and lightning flashed somewhere off to the side.

There were no armed guards in here, but plenty of longblasters rested in open gunracks for fast access. Bare swords decorated every wall, along with Medieval shields and a couple of full suits of armor.

"Those must have been scaved from some museum," Ryan guessed softly. "Probably where they got that first catapult, too."

"Well, it's not the Beverly Wiltshire Hilton," Mildred observed dryly.

Set in the middle of the room was a long conference table covered with a clean white cloth and intact china plates. Silver candelabra held clusters of sputtering tapers, the soft yellow light mixing with the alcohol lantern to give a pleasant combination of illumination.

Privately, Doc wondered if everybody in the ville lived in such sumptuous plenty, and wisely decided that it wasn't likely. Rank did have its little privileges.

"Good evening," Baron O'Connor said, gesturing from the head of the table. "Please, be seated."

As the companions walked closer, they studied the other people watching their approach. Sec Chief Stirling was to the left of the baron, and alongside him was a dour-faced man of indeterminate age, and several woman. Across from them were two children barely into their teens.

"This is the Baroness Amelia," Baron O'Connor said, gesturing with an open hand. "And that is her sister, Catherine. Down there is Steven's wife Jan, their daughter Simone, and our Brewmaster, Cauldfield."

"Brewmaster?" Jak asked, furrowing his brow. "Cook shine for ville?"

"Shine? Blind norad no." Cauldfield snorted as if such a task was beneath the dignity of a mutie. "I—"

The baron loudly cleared his throat.

"Yes," Cauldfield recanted quickly. "Yes, indeed, I make shine for the ville lanterns."

Mutie shit. He cooked the fuel for the war wag and Molotovs, Ryan translated privately. He'd known it wasn't alcohol, or gas, or condensed fuel, but other than that he hadn't been able to identify the oily substance. Mebbe some sort of chem mix?

As greetings were exchanged, the companions took chairs and got comfortable. That was when they noticed a huge flag on the wall behind the baron's ornate wooden chair. The flag was made of red and white stripes, with a screaming eagle replacing the usual array of white stars on the field of blue.

"The family crest," the baron said proudly, observing their shift of attention. "It has never seen defeat."

"Nor will it ever," Catherine added haughtily, touching her riot of blond curls. The busty woman was wearing a predark dress that had been altered to show additional cleavage. The satin was cut almost down to the point of exposing herself like a gaudy slut. There were two handcannons in the gunbelt hanging from her chair, and when she bent forward a small blue tattoo could almost be seen hidden between her ample breasts.

Since neither statement seemed to need a reply, the companions didn't make one, and set about hanging their gunbelts over the backs of their chairs the way everybody else had done. Armed, but polite. The baron ran a tight ville.

A few moments later, a servant wearing welding gloves brought out a simmering iron pot and carefully ladled stew into stone bowls. Pitchers of frothy beer and carafes of water were placed around the table, along with wooden plates stacked with loaves of fresh bread hot from the oven. Then came a platter of small roasted birds, dozens of them all stacked on top of one another: crows, hawks, wrens, and what seemed to be an owl, although it did have four sets of wings. The smell was delicious, and everybody dug in with gusto. After living off MRE packs for the past week, the heady aroma of fresh-cooked meat was intoxicating to the companions.

"This is a very impressive home," J.B. said, removing his fedora and hanging it on the arm of his chair.

"Thank you," Amelia said woodenly. The slim woman picked at the food on her plate and kept shooting hostile glances at her husband.

"By the way, my dear," the baron said, pulling out a belt knife to hack a wren in two. "This is the healer who saved our son." Then he stabbed the bird with the blade and started eating it right off the bare steel.

Obviously startled, Amelia looked at Mildred and forced a polite smile. "For that service, I thank you," she said wearily. "Daniel is my only child."

"So I heard," Mildred answered, taking some bread. "And I can teach your other healers how to do the operation. It's not that difficult."

"Then you shouldn't have been paid so much," Catherine retorted, attacking a robin as if it were a charging stickie. "But then, a deal is a deal, as the sec men say. I'm sure you are very clever for a rist."

Dropping her fork with a clatter, Mildred hunched her shoulders at the insult and looked as if she was about to spring on the busty woman when J.B. laid a hand on her thigh under the table and pushed the physician back down into her chair.

"I also have only one child," Catherine continued, muttering under her breath.

Laying down his bare knife, the baron kept his face impassive as he used his good hand to pour a round of beer for everybody at the head of the table.

Gaia, so that was what was wrong with the sister! Krysty suddenly realized. They're worried about Davies. Rad blasting hell, if the feeb got aced, things could get ugly around here. There was nothing worse than a civil war.

"Hell of a war wag, too," Ryan said, using the panga to cut the heel off a loaf. A change of topic was clearly in order fast. When his own family members clashed, it often ended in a chilling. "It's one of the biggest I have ever seen."

"Bet your ass it is." Stirling chuckled, spooning some soup.

"My grandie found it in the ruins, and my father got it running," O'Connor added, spearing a hawk with the knife. He dipped it into the soup and started chewing on the wings.

"Took him years," the baron said with a full mouth. "Years! But it's the best wep we have against the stickies."

"Now about that," Ryan started when the door slammed open and a panting sec man rushed into the dining hall.

Laying down their knives and forks, Amelia and Catherine watched the man as if he were a messenger from the gods.

"My lord," the man gasped, clearly out of breath. "Your...your nephew lives."

There was an audible sigh from the people at the table, and even the companions relaxed slightly.

"Told you he was too stupe to buy the farm," Simone said, facing her bowl of stew.

"Hush, child," Jan ordered softly.

"Was it an old whip?" Mildred asked unexpectedly.

The baron raised an eyebrow at the strange remark.

"And what possible difference could that make?" Catherine snapped irritably.

"Yes, it was an old whip. Why?" Stirling asked, leaning forward. Was she asking it if was used and soft, and that he had disobeyed the baron by being gentle with the fool?

"A new one would have been better," Mildred said thoughtfully, stirring the stew with a spoon to check for anything unhealthy in the depths. But she could only find meat and vegetables. "Somebody should wash his cuts with shine and water. Boil the water first, let it cool and then mix the two half and half."

"They have already poured a bottle down his throat," Baron O'Connor stated. "To help kill the pain."

Going pale, Catherine stiffened at the word and muttered something too low for anybody to hear.

"That's good," Mildred replied. "Now put the rest on the outside, and he won't get an infection."

"Shine stops infections?" Amelia asked, her voice rising in shock.

"Nonsense," Cauldfield stated. "Never heard of such a thing. Ridiculous!"

"You don't know everything," Mildred countered tolerantly. "And yes, shine helps a lot. Not with everything, but with most infectious diseases."

"What about the Black Cough?" Jan asked urgently.

Sadly, Mildred shook her head. "Nothing stops that but death."

With that pronouncement, all conversation stopped for a while as folks concentrated on their meal. Doc looked around hopefully for a salt shaker at one point, but didn't see one. There were several in the MREs in his frock coat, but to display such wealth would invite a barrage of questions the companions didn't want to answer.

When the soup was gone, the old servant took away

the dirty dishes, and a young girl came in carrying a massive plank stacked with more tiny birds artfully arranged around a large poached lizard, the dead white eyes staring out above the lolling tongue.

"More meat, sir?" a serving girl asked in a husky voice, leaning close to Jak.

The teenager's jacket was draped over the back of the chair, so he could feel the delicious weight of her breasts pressing warm against his shirt.

"Ask you the same," Jak said with a smile, taking an eyeball.

Laying down the new platter, the servant moved against the teenager a little harder. Jak pressed back, and she bumped him with a hip and went on to serve the other guests in a less intimate fashion.

"Veni, vidi, vici," Doc muttered, raising his mug in salute.

Popping the orb into his mouth, Jak scowled at that in puzzlement as he chewed the delicacy. It was good and salty.

"I came, I saw, I conquered," Mildred said, translating the Latin. "That means the old coot thinks she likes you."

"Just new flavor, is all," Jak replied with a shrug. Lots of women were interested in the albino once they understood he wasn't a mutie. Afterward, they always seemed a little disappointed that he wasn't strangely built, or anything like that.

"So you're not going to…" J.B. didn't finish the sentence.

Across the table, the girl slapped the hand of Cauld-field from about her waist. Then she looked directly at Jak and beamed a smile. Frowning darkly, Cauld-field took the lizard's other eye and chewed it with a suppressed fury.

"Sure. Dinner first," Jak said wisely. "Need strength."

"So what were you saying about the stickies?" Stir-ling asked, breaking some bread and mopping up the grease on his plate. "Aren't they the same where you folks come from?"

"Stickies are stickies," Cauldfield said as if it were a law of the universe.

"The same? Dark night, no," J.B. replied with feel-ing. "Our stickies are dumber than a sack of rocks. We almost crapped at the sight of stickies armed with spears."

"Really?" Amelia asked, her demeanor cracking slightly with the disclosure.

"These stickies are abominations!" Doc added pas-sionately, dunking a slice of bread into his beer and waiting for it to soften. Two-Son ville had wheat, but their millstone had to have been a couple of house bricks rubbed against each other, because the bread could have been used to patch tank armor.

"No other stickies we know about are like these," Mildred translated, shooting the Vermont scholar a stern glance.

"Lucky us," the baron said in a mocking tone. "So only ours are smart?"

"Mebbe some other ville will wanna swap," Stirling said with a hard grin. "Trade 'em two for three."

Everybody laughed a little at that, but it faded away and everyone returned to the meal with dour faces.

Draining his mug, Ryan looked over the assembled people. The earlier mood was fading. These people paid a high price for their lifestyle. Mebbe too high a price.

Overhead, the storm clouds rumbled and boomed, but no rain was hitting the glass skylight yet.

"Anybody here a hunter?" Ryan asked, refilling his mug from the pitcher.

"What the hell has that got to do with stickies?" Catherine demanded, nearly showing her tattoo.

"No, we're not," the baron replied. "We fish in the river north of here, raise veggies and catch a few lizards and birds when we get lucky. There's really not much else around here to track down and hunt."

"Too many stickies!" Cauldfield snorted, ripping off a wing and chewing it savagely. "Anything large enough to be worth hunting has already been eaten by the muties!"

"Oh, I see," Stirling said slowly, laying down his knife. "Yeah, of course. That's triple smart. Hunters, eh?"

Sipping his beer, Ryan nodded. "That's right. You're handling the stickies like they were coldhearts, not as if they were animals. Mebbe they got weps now, but they're still just dumb animals."

"Why do you mean?" Jan asked, clearly puzzled.

"You don't chase a rabbit," Ryan explained. "That's the stupe way. You lay a trap and make it come to you."

Just then, the door swung open and a man strode into the room, every step releasing a small cloud of dust from his clothing.

"Sorry, I'm late, my lord," he said, the spurs on his boots jingling. "But I ran into some stickies upriver and had to jump a ravine to escape."

"Just glad you're alive, Taylor," the baron said, gesturing at an empty chair. "Stickies is what we're talking about. Have a drink! Looks like you need one."

"Thank you, my lord, I do," Taylor said, dropping into a chair and making it creak dangerously. Grabbing the pitcher, he poured a beer and drained the mug in a single draft, then poured another, letting the foam slosh onto the white linen.

"Taylor, these are some friends who I hope are going to help us with the stickies," the baron said, pointing with his knife. "And this is Asaro Taylor, our top scout. Rides the desert to watch for caravans, traders, slavers, and such, to warn them about the muties."

"Takes messages to other villes, too," Stirling added, pushing away his plate. "We've been trying to build an army to go after the muties, but nobody else is interested in our problems. Just their own."

"Which is as it should be," Cauldfield stated forcibly, pouring some water into his beer and taking a sip. Bah, still terrible. "Each ville should stand alone! That's how it has always been, and always will be."

"I disagree," Taylor stated, then paused to stare at Ryan.

The one-eyed man returned the gaze. "Yeah?"

"Son of a bitch," Taylor muttered softly.

"Problem?" Ryan asked, dropping a hand to the panga on his belt.

"You're from the south," Taylor said, as if the fact could not be disputed.

That brought all of the companions alert. As far as they could tell, Blaster Base One was to the south, but how could this scout possibly have known that?

"Actually, sir, we are from the east," Doc lied, chewing a small piece of the tough bread, his face the picture of innocence. "A delightful meal, Baroness O'Connor."

"Well, you can't be from the north," Taylor said, setting down his empty mug. "That's for triple damn sure. No way."

"And why is that?" Mildred asked in forced casualness.

Inhaling sharply, Krysty sat bolt upright in the chair, her animated hair starting to wildly move and flex as if a window had been thrown open.

Catching the motion, Ryan quickly set down his mug. The woman's mental powers didn't always work, but when she did something like that, all nuking hell was about to break loose.

"What unusual hair," Catherine murmured, closing her eyes to mere slits. "Is there a breeze blowing only on her or…"

Any further questions were interrupted by a muffled clang coming from the roof directly above.

"What is?" Jak demanded, pushing away his plate.

"The alarm bell!" Stirling cursed, shoving back his chair and grabbing his gunbelt. "The ville is under attack!"

Chapter Fifteen

Lifting his head toward the stars, a child baron looked into the infinite blackness of the universe with knowing eyes.

"They're coming," Baron Harmond said, hugging himself with thin arms. "By the blood of my fathers, I can almost see them moving through the night...."
Reaching out, the boy flexed his fingers in the chill air, trying to touch the intangible.

A dozen people stood on the roof of the baron's house, a predark bank converted into a formidable fortress. The walls were draped with sand bags, the windows covered by wooden shutters and iron bars. A high defensive wall of adobe brick studded with glass surrounded the desert ville, and armed sec men walked along the wide top, always on patrol against muties and coldhearts. Down among the many homes, cooking fires made the curtained windows glow warmly red, and there was a rich smell in the air of frying fish, sassafras tea and baked taters.

Standing close to the small boy, the adults waited patiently to hear more. At first, many of the people had resisted having a mutie as a baron. But soon the obvious military advantages of having a doomie plan out the defenses against an enemy that hadn't even arrived yet was clear to all. The young baron would have them digging new wells before the old ones went dry, and warned of acid rain storms days early. The isolated ville still existed only because of his advance warnings, which always came true. The sec men would die at his command, and the civies all but worshiped the child as a god.

"And what should we do about that, my lord?" a fat sec man asked urgently, wiping his mouth with the back of a hand. There was something in the air; everyone could feel it. The cropland and hills outside the ville were too quiet this night. There didn't seem to be anything else alive in the world except the tiny ville. Only the western Mohawk Mountains seemed normal, the jagged peaks framed by the rolling banks of fiery clouds that blanketed them every night.

"Frag that drek. What direction are they?" Chief Bateman countered, resting a hand on the grip of the wep at his side. A double-barrel scattergun had been cut down to just large enough to fit into a holster. The sec chief carried it instead of a handcannon, and the notches on the wooden grip weren't decorations, but the tally of the chills he had made with the blaster.

Unable to put the feeling into words, Baron Harmond turned to face the southeast section of the Zone. The one-eyed man and the timewalker, they were in that direction, with two brothers, no, two sons? But that made no sense. The doomie baron shook his head, trying to dispel the confusion. Everything was in flux. It was always difficult to clear-see into the future, but now it was pure chaos, as if the universe were unraveling. Had time come undone? Was the casement of reality cracked apart? Could this be the Second Apocalypse?

"Sir?" Chief Bateman asked nervously, stepping closer.

Breathing deeply, the baron turned away from the south and scowled at the north.

"They're coming," the doomie repeated softly. "Four norms on coal black steeds. One is tall, one cannot speak well, one is large as a bear, and the last carries death in his sleeves. They had different fathers, but consider themselves blood brothers."

"I'll sound the alarm," the fat sec man suggested, edging for the gate. "Charlie! Hey, Charlie!"

"Do nothing!" Harmond order brusquely. "There is nothing that we can do." Then he added, almost as an afterthought, "At least, there is nothing we can do at the moment." But soon, oh so very soon…

Shivering from the icy thoughts forming in his mind, the baron turned away from the blood-soaked desert—was it blood soaked or was that another hallucination?—and started toward the wooden flight of rusty iron steps that led down the side of the predark bank. Death was coming from the north and the south. This was where the future would be forged anew. Many would be chilled; he could see it, almost hear the screams. But afterward, the world would be forever altered.

Hugging their longblasters, the sec men formed a tight group around the child baron as he wearily walked to the paved street of the ville. A group of workers were patching a large hole in the ground in front of the gate, sprinkling sharp pieces of glass into the crude concrete for unknown reasons. But orders were orders, and nobody questioned the dictates of the baron.

Nodding satisfaction at the work, Harmond shuffled back to his bed and, hopefully, a long and dreamless sleep.

Tugging on his droopy mustache, Sec chief Bateman stayed on the wall. Red Dust, he hated waiting! However, when it was time to act, their baron would say so. Then his army of sec men would unleash all kinds of fragging hell.

Until then, they could only wait, and prepare for war.

At Two-Son ville, Ryan and the other companions quickly gathered their blasters as Baron O'Connor snatched a lever-action Winchester from the gunrack on the wall. The carrying strap was lined with loops full of brass that shone greasy and golden in the light of the alcohol lanterns, the hollowpoint lead tips a smooth gray satin. Flipping the longblaster over by its hinged lever on the bottom, O'Connor chambered a round and caught the wep in his waiting palm.

"Let's go," the baron said in a low growl.

"Are we in danger, Father?" Simone asked in a small voice, sliding closer to her mother.

"Of course not," Catherine snapped, reaching for another roasted bird. "This is just one of their silly drills. I have always said that—"

"Shut up, bitch!" the baron barked, raising the Winchester high as if he were going to strike the woman. "You will be quiet, or the last thing I ever do will be to throw you naked to the muties myself!"

Going pale, the trembling woman dropped the food and went very still in her chair. She could see in his face the man meant the threat.

"Triple red, people," Ryan ordered, rising from his chair and drawing the SIG-Sauer to check the clip.

As the companions checked their weps, Stirling went to the nearest window and threw the wooden shutters open wide. The ville spread out below in shadowy peace. Everything looked fine. Then he noticed the sec men on the wall scurrying like beetles. Dimly, he could be hear an alarm bell ringing from the direction of the front gate. But there was no sign of a fire or the headlights of an invading army of coldhearts.

"Something is happening, that's for sure," Stirling rumbled, squinting into the darkness. "I just don't see anything wrong."

"No signs of blasterfire," the baron added, leaning halfway out of another window. Lightning and thunder sounded from the sky above, masking the sound of the alarm, then the clarion warning came back loud and clear.

"Mebbe it's a mistake," Cauldfield suggested hopefully. The brewmaster was still sitting at the table, his gunbelt hanging from the back of his chair.

Standing guard near the door, Taylor gave the man a look of disgust that could have broken concrete.

"Nuke that drek." Stirling spit. "My troops don't ring the alarm bell for a bar fight. Blood of my fathers, what I wouldn't give for a pair of binocs!"

J.B. whistled sharply. The sec chief turned just as the Armorer threw the Navy longeye. Stirling made the catch and extended the collapsible device to its full length and started sweeping the landscape.

"Where did you get that?" Catherine asked in wonder.

Not bothering to reply, Ryan worked the bolt-action on his Steyr SSG-70 and joined the big man at the window. Bringing up the longblaster, Ryan squinted through the telescopic sight. The optics of the predark scope were nowhere near as powerful as the antique Navy telescope, but still better than nothing.

Five stories below, people were pouring from the homes, huts and ramshackle houses in various stages of undress. But every one of them carried a weapon of some sort: blaster, crossbow, longbow, knife or ax. On the wall, the sec men were pelting along, fixing bayonets onto the end of their longblasters or ripping open plastic boxes full of Molotov cocktails. More and more torches were being lit, along with dozens of lanterns. Near the gate, a woman was steadily beating on a large hoop of iron with a hammer, the clangs echoing across Two-Son.

With the MP-5 in hand, Krysty joined Ryan at the window and looked out into the night. Her hair was still agitated, ruffling and moving against the breeze coming in through the window. Something was wrong, something triple bad. But what the nuking hell was happening?

"Something strange is going on in the Zone," she whispered so softly only he could hear. "First, that jump at the redoubt and then the armed stickies…"

Checking his blaster, Taylor perked up his ear at that, and Krysty went silent. The man had to have unusually sharp hearing to have caught her words. No wonder he was a scout.

"Damn," Stirling muttered, both hands on the longeye. "Mebbe it's all a mistake."

Just then, a motion caught Ryan's attention in the scope and he leaned farther out of the window. A spark floated in the darkness, a firefly moving above the ville, flying through the air. The jot of light rose and fell, bobbing and moving seemingly at random.

But as Ryan's vision became adjusted to the darkness he could see the dim outline of the greenhouses. Fireblast, somebody was running along the top of the greenhouses carrying a torch. He grimaced. No, *something* was sprinting across the sloping glass as if it were level ground.

"Baron, you may have waited too long," Ryan said, lowering the longblaster. "See there? I think the stickies are now hunting you."

"Well, blast it!" the baron ordered, shouldering his way into the window. "Shoot, I say! That fancy long-blaster of yours should be able to ace that thing from here."

"Yes, it should," Stirling said in agreement, looking away from the longeye. "But we don't want that. Not yet."

For a long moment O'Connor stared in barely controlled rage at his sec chief, then slowly nodded. "Smart," he growled. "Dangerous, but if it works…"

"Yeah. If."

Ripping the napkin from around his neck, the grim baron strode back to the table. "Amelia, get into the safe room. Take Catherine and the others with you. Lock the door and wait for me. Don't leave until I personally say so."

"Do you really think that it's wise?" the woman said hesitantly.

But the baron was already at a gunrack on the wall. He took down a Browning, the carrying strap lined with ammo loops full of fat brass.

"Here," O'Connor said, passing her the autofire. "Now move."

Wordlessly, Lady Amelia looked at her husband, then took the longblaster and led the others from the dining hall. Only Cauldfield stayed, grumbling in annoyance while he strapped on a gunbelt and fumbled with the handcannon in the holster.

"I'll stay with them," Cauldfield said, checking the load in the wheel gun. The brewmaster was no sec man, but had grudgingly done his share of chilling over the years.

"No, you stay with me," O'Connor ordered in a no-nonsense tone. He returned to the gunrack.

"My lord, should I make sure they're safe?" Taylor asked, half turning toward the door.

Stuffing a box of brass into his pocket, the baron nodded as he picked up the Winchester once more. "Do it," O'Connor said bluntly, then cast a sideways glance at Cauldfield. "However, nobody goes near my family but me. Savvy?"

Giving a brief salute, the scout slipped out of the dining hall as quiet as a knife in the night.

Returning to the window, Ryan tried to find the shambling figure again, but the firefly was gone. Had it only been a trick of the light? No! There it was again, a stickie running along the roof of the greenhouses, jumping from one to the next, carrying a burning torch. Not just a stick on fire, but a bastard torch with a thick wad of flaming material on the end.

"Sons of bitches know how to get fire," Stirling said unhappily, lowering the longeye. "If that thing sets the barracks ablaze, the armory could catch. There's enough black powder and brass there to blow this entire ville off the nuking map!"

With a tense expression, Jan looked hopefully at the skylight. "Mebbe the rain would stop the fire?"

"If comes in time," Jak replied succinctly. His ruby eyes could see clearly in dim light, but the stickie had gone into hiding somewhere. The torch was nowhere to be seen on the roof of the greenhouses. Impatiently, the teenager shrugged his shoulders, checking the position of the knives hidden up the sleeves. They could save the ville by attacking, but waiting was the only way to protect the ville from further attacks. *Damned if do, and damned if don't.* Just like in a Tex-Mex standoff, the first to flinch would get aced.

On the wall, nervous sec men were firing into the night, the muzzle-flashes of the black-powder weapons sending out bright yellow daggers of flame. More sec men raced along the ville streets, checking every alleyway, the bayonets on their blasters reflecting the torch light like slivers of fire.

"Tell me, is the armory where you have the refinery?" Mildred demanded, going on a hunch. "The place where you make the fuel for the war wag and the Molotovs?"

"Don't know what you're talking about," Cauldfield said uneasily, his gaze sliding away.

Mildred looked directly at the man. "What comes out first is best," she said bluntly.

Whatever they were making for fuel in there, that statement should hold true. The most volatile compounds would be the first to distill. That was just basic chemistry. Although, that was mighty close to wizardry in these unenlightened days.

Dropping his jaw, the brewmaster recoiled from her statement as if physically struck. "Who are you people?" he demanded softly, a hand going for the blaster by his side.

"Allies," J.B. replied, working the bolt on the Uzi.

Then Jak did the same for his MP-5 submachine gun, followed by Krysty, and Doc clicked back both hammers of his two handcannons. Every blaster was aimed at the brewmaster.

Ever so slowly, Cauldfield raised both hands, palms turned outward. "Allies, yes, of course," he muttered quickly. "Sorry, I just… A reflex, you understand…."

"Cauldfield, go get the *Metro* running and pass out all of the spare Molotovs we have," the baron commanded, brandishing the Winchester. "We'll meet you at the gate."

"As you command, my lord," the brewmaster agreed, and hurried from the room.

Using the lever action, the baron loaded the Winchester with a flip of his one good hand. "You really know how to make juice?" O'Connor demanded of the physician, resting the longblaster on a shoulder.

Mildred nodded her head. "It's simple, really."

"Good. Then we don't need that shitbrain anymore."

Saying nothing, Ryan looked at Krysty. If the baron figured that out, then so had the brewmaster. Could be trouble coming that way. Good thing Taylor was guarding the baron's family. A coldheart had once gotten control of Front Royal by seizing the pregnant wife of the baron. That had turned into a real bloodbath. Hopefully, that scenario wasn't going to be repeated here.

"Okay, let's go hunting," O'Connor said grimly,

starting for the door. He knew the danger of getting caught outside in a storm if the acid rain came. But there was always a telltale reek of chems first that would give them a few minutes' warning. Among the ruins, there would be plenty of places to find safety. At least, from the rain. They might also get trapped in the stickie nest, but that was a chance the baron was willing to take to rid his ville of the lethal muties forever.

Suddenly the firefly appeared again, zigzagging along the side of the greenhouses, the stickie moving parallel to the ground.

"Move! I'll meet you at the gate," Ryan replied, resting his elbow on the windowsill and adjusting the focus on the telescopic sight. "First, I have to stop that nuke-sucker."

"Follow me!" the baron boomed, charging into the hallway.

In a ragged formation, everybody left with the baron. Except for Krysty. She knew that the rapidfire and her revolver didn't have the range to reach the stickie. Only the Steyr could chill it from here. But she wasn't going to leave Ryan alone with nobody to guard his six.

Sweeping the darkness with the crosshair scope, Ryan found the firefly once more and tried to get a bead on the racing mutie. Unfortunately its natural shamble made it difficult to target, and the lack of decent light wasn't helping any, either. He had to stop the creature from reaching the armory, but not by chilling it. That was the key to finding the nest. A stalking horse. If he could simply chase the mutie away, and it would lead them straight back home to the nest. Hopefully. However, to nick it in the leg was a hard shot even with good light and a stationary target. But there wasn't any other choice.

"Shoot the glass," Krysty suggested, her breath warm on his cheek.

"Smart." Growing a hard smile, Ryan shifted his aim from the moving stickie and onto the roof of the greenhouse. Stroking the trigger of the Steyr, he sent a 7.62 mm round into the glass and a panel shattered.

Startled, the stickie jerked back from the explosion, the report of the longblaster lost in the cacophony of the ringing alarm bells. On the streets and wall, nobody glanced up at the blaster shot from the Citadel.

Hesitantly, the confused mutie started forward again, and Ryan took out another panel. Then three more in rapid succession, as fast as he could work the bolt. Jerking out the rotary clip, Ryan stuffed it into a pocket and shoved in a spare. The one-eyed man had plenty of ammo, but only four more of the loaded rotary clips.

"That did it, lover." Krysty grunted, sounding oddly pleased. "See? It's turning back."

Checking through the scope, Ryan saw that the stickie had stopped and was looking around, clearly afraid to go in any direction out of fear the glass would erupt again. Taking a chance, Ryan aimed at the stickie's shoulder, then moved down its arm, waiting for the inhuman hand to come into the cross fire. Holding his breath, Ryan moved the crosshair along the mottled flesh past the elbow, to the wrist, and then he fired.

Five hundred yards away, the wooden torch exploded into splinters and went flying out of the stickie's grip. Hugging the limb, the mutie instantly turned to race along the roof toward the nearest part of the wall.

"Eastern wall, about a hundred yards from the gate," Ryan snapped, carefully marking the direction. "Let's move, lover. We got our stalking horse."

"Now we attack," Krysty finished grimly, her hair tightly curling as peals of thunder rumbled loudly in the cloudy skies.

Chapter Sixteen

Swiftly exiting the Citadel, Ryan and Krysty found a sec man waiting for them with a pair of saddled horses. Vaulting onto the animals, the two companions took off at a full gallop through the ville, and soon reached the front gate.

Fifty armed sec men were waiting there, the *Metro* poised at the barrier, its badly tuned engines rumbling and coughing, black smoke blowing out the tailpipes.

"East by southeast!" Ryan shouted, reining in his mount.

"About a hundred yards along the wall," Krysty added, "if the mutie runs straight."

"Open those gates!" O'Connor shouted, nudging his horse in the rump with his boot heels. The Winchester was tucked into a holster attached to the saddle, clinking bags full of Molotovs draped behind the one-armed baron.

As the gate lumbered open, Gill turned on the headlights of the *Metro,* flooding the area with white light.

"Turn those off!" Stirling yelled furiously. "We want to track this fucker, not make it run away to the mountains!"

Instantly, the headlights winked out and darkness returned.

Grinding gears, Gill got the war wag rolling and proceeded through the gate, radiating noise and fumes. In loose formation, the baron and his sec men followed close behind, the companions bringing up the rear.

Riding alongside the baron, Ryan said, "Jak should take the lead. There's no better tracker."

"The man could follow piss in the ocean," J.B. declared confidently. The munitions bag was resting on the saddle, the Uzi hanging free at his side, ready for action.

Holding the reins tightly, O'Connor waved his hand in consent.

Bending, Jak chucked the reins and his mount put on a burst of speed as it moved in front of the ponderous *Metro*. The albino teen had gotten the best of the horses, a young palomino mare, bridle-wise and strong. The beast was well-trained, and he felt himself starting to match her movements with his own body.

As the mare galloped along the bottom of the wall, Jak strained to detect any sign of the escaping mutie. He didn't have to try very hard for long. The horseback riders were doing a sweeping arch around the ville to reach the eastern point of the perimeter, while the stickie was running pretty much in a straight line. That gave the advantage to the mutie. But the horses were a hell of a lot faster, and Jak actually saw the stickie run down the side of the wall and charge across the shatter zone toward the ruins.

"Banzai," Jak muttered, remembering the word from when the companions had once jumped to Japan. Hell of a place. Sheer heaven for any blademan.

The unshod hooves of the palomino made dull thuds on the sandy street of the predark city as Jak carefully slowed the horse to a trot. He didn't want to get too close, or the stickie would attack, but he didn't want to fall behind and lose the mutie, either. This was a razor walk. One wrong move and the blood would flow.

Thunder rumbled overhead as Jak scanned the street with a sinking feeling that the mutie had somehow given him the slip. Then an inhuman footprint in the sand made him turn down a side street, and a moist handprint on a brick wall sent him along a dark alleyway.

Squinting to see in the midnight shadows, the albino teen drew his Colt and eased back the hammer. If the stickie knew it was being trailed, this was a perfect place for an ambush. But the teenager knew that he couldn't risk a light of any kind. Sound and smell, that was all he had to go on for the moment.

Unfortunately, the approaching storm was covering the sound of suckered feet running, and the faint smell of a chem storm was masking the rank body odor of the unwashed stickie. Suddenly, a flash of lightning split the night, and the teen saw a flicker of movement

on a rooftop, hand and footprints dotted along the side
of the stucco wall. Shitfire and honeycakes, it had
taken to the rooftops!

Having no choice, Jak kicked the mare into a gallop and circled the crumbling predark store. He
reached the other side of the building just in time to
see the leg of the racing stickie vanish around a corner.

That was when Jak noticed the street was clear of
sand. Instantly, the teen reined in his mount. The
hooves of his horse would sound like blaster shots on
the hard pavement. Having no choice, Jak then slipped
out of the saddle and proceeded as quickly as possible on foot. Now with both hands free, Jak holstered
the Colt and swung up the MP-5 rapidfire. If things
went to hell, he wanted to ace the mutie as fast as possible. And from a distance. One swipe of its hands
could remove his face.

Only then did he remember the bandage on his
scalp. Could the mutie smell the dried blood? Did it
know he was near? Jak had to remember that these
were smart stickies. All of the years chilling stupe muties was working against him.

A fluttering piece of thread on a splintery wooden
fence told of the mutie's passage. Warily peeking over
the top, Jak saw the thing standing in the middle of an
open field piled with mounds of rubble. Poised motionless, the stickie just stood there, seeming to wait
for something. Mebbe another stickie? Then thunder

rolled in the sky, and it darted into a dark alcove to vanish from sight. Easing his stance, Jak fought back a grin. Smart, but not smart enough.

Climbing over the fence, the teen crept across the slippery rubble, his heart pounding louder than the building tempest above. Reaching the alcove, he found it oddly blocked by a closed wooden door. But he had seen the stickie… This had to be it! The nest! There was no other possible explanation for the mutie going to the trouble of waiting for thunder to mask the sound of the closing door.

Staying low to the ground, Jak moved into the middle of the nearest intersection and impatiently waited for the rest of the sec men to arrive. A few minutes later, the hulking *Metro* rumbled into view, filling the street with its imposing bulk and noise.

Close behind, Stirling appeared, leading the small army, along with the palomino mare. "Lose something?" the man asked, offering the bridle.

"Don't need," Jak spoke urgently. "Found nest."

"Where?" the baron demanded, pulling out the Winchester.

As the teen quickly explained, all of the sec men got their blasters out and started to check loads for the assault. From the top of the *Metro,* there came the squeak of rope as pulleys hauled the wooden arm of the catapult, the plastic milk box at the end jammed full of Molotovs.

"Hell's fucking bells, no wonder we could never

find them," a sec man stated, studying the nondescript building. "We kept looking for rad pits or blast craters, some kind of covered hole in the ground, when the bastards were hiding in plain sight."

"Mighty clever for muties," another sec man agreed nervously, tightening the grip on his crossbow. The arrow, or rather, the quarrel, was tipped with a barbed head, the kind used to catch fish. Once it went into a stickie, there would be no way the mutie to get it out without ripping itself apart in the attempt.

"Bah, nothing clever about 'em," another sec man rejoined. "Just a bunch of feeb stickies. Dumber than rists."

Inserting a clip into the rapidfire, Mildred couldn't believe her ears. *They're just stickies.* That could easily be the death song of humanity.

"Okay, let's burn the place down," Stirling growled, taking a butane lighter from a shirt pocket.

"Sorry, but we can't do that just yet," Ryan stated firmly.

Pulling out a Molotov, the sec chief paused in the act of flicking the lighter alive. "And why not?" he demanded.

"Because, we don't know if they are all in there," Krysty said, checking the load in her S&W .38 revolver. Tucking away the blaster, she looked up at the old dilapidated building. It was just a half-fallen down ruin located among many others, indistinguishable from the rest. That fact didn't make her feel any easier. According to Mildred, nonmutie spiders built traps to capture their food alive. As did monkeys, and some lizards, snakes, birds… There were a lot of animals besides man that knew how to hide and ensnare their enemies. And this had all of the earmarks of a trap.

"You mean, there could be several nests," O'Connor huffed, the leather saddle creaking from his weight. "That's a hellish notion."

"The windows are white," Cauldfield said in annoyance, sliding off his mount to lash the mare to the bumper of a predark car wreck. "We could smash those open, but then they'd know that we're coming and escape out the back door."

Stroking the neck of his stallion, a sec man snorted. "Back door? Just how smart to you think these nuking things are?"

"Smart enough to know which building is the armory and try to set it on fire," Ryan retorted. "Too damn bastard smart, that's how smart."

"Dark night, this is like facing Kaa all over again," J.B. said, removing a strip of duct tape from the arming handle of a thermite gren.

"Kaa," the baron repeated. "The king of the muties? But that's just a stretch, a tall tale to frighten the littles. No mutie ever raised an army to fight norms."

"Oh, yes, he most certainly did," Doc stated resolutely. "We were there. We saw it all." Lightning flashed in sinister harmony to the stark pronouncement.

"So you think this Kaa is back?" the sec chief asked

as the thunder echoed among the predark buildings. The pause between the light and the sound were getting constantly closer. The storm was fast approaching.

"No, Kaa is gone forever," Ryan stated bluntly.

"Okay, so he had a son, or brothers," the baron relented. "Or whatever made Kaa smart is happening again."

"Evolution," Mildred said unhappily. "Life finds a way."

"Then what's the plan?" Cauldfield demanded petulantly, sliding a longblaster from the holster set next to his saddle.

"Got no choice," Ryan said, lifting the saddlebags and draping them over a shoulder. The leather pouches clinked in a satisfactory manner. "We have to know if this is the entrance to the nest, one of several nests, or even if the muties are there at all."

"Yeah, and how you gonna do that?" a sec man demanded hotly, protected by the shadows of the coming storm.

Sliding off his horse, Ryan scowled as he recognized the voice of Porter.

"How? That's simple," he said, turning to face the old building. The dead-white windows seemed to stare back at him like the eyes of a corpse. "We go inside and find out."

Silence engulfed the sandy street, with only the

puttering of the war wag and the shuffling of the nervous horses to disturb the night air. Even the storm seemed to be holding its breath.

"We…go into the nest?" Cauldfield repeated weakly, his voice strained to a hoarse whisper.

"Yeah, but we can't take everybody," the baron said, grabbing the saddlehorn and lowering himself to the ground. "We might as well shoot off fireworks first than do that."

"We six travel together," Ryan stated bluntly.

"I expected no less," O'Connor said, then he gave a chuckle. "You'd make a mighty good baron."

Ryan shrugged off the comment.

"Well, frag that drek," Stirling declared roughly. "No offense, but I'm not letting my baron go into a nest of stickies with only outlanders for companions."

"Didn't think you would," the baron said with a half smile. "I'll take along six men, as well."

"Lucky thirteen." Mildred sighed, using a strip of cloth to tie the beaded plaits off her face. "There's an omen for you."

"Well, let's get started," the baron said, slinging the strap of the Winchester around his neck. "Steven, you stay here with the rest of troops. Get ready to give cover fire if we come out running."

"What? I'm not one of the six?" the sec chief demanded. "No way, sir, I—"

"Save it," the baron snapped, cutting off the discussion. "These things took my arm, and I want to return the favor. Besides, one of us has to stay with the war wag." He paused. "For the sake of the ville. Savvy?"

A long minute passed. "You're the baron," Stirling said reluctantly, then added, "My lord."

"Glad you remembered. If I don't come back, then Daniel is in charge," the baron said, clumsily taking his own saddlebags full of Molotov cocktails. He couldn't light and throw the firebombs at the same time, but the baron had a strong feeling that wouldn't be a problem tonight. Death was in the air, thicker and more pungent than any acid rain. It was almost a tangible thing blanketing the predark ruins.

The sec chief said nothing.

"Steven, will you stand by my son?" the baron asked in the rumbling darkness.

"I…yes, I will, my lord," the sec chief promised. "He'll ride the eagle throne, and I'll chill anybody who says different."

Stepping closer to the sec chief's horse, the baron offered his hand and they shook. "Good enough, old friend." Then he added in a tense whisper, "Just watch your six for Cauldfield."

"He'll be the first man I chill if you don't come back," Stirling answered softly, casting a glance that way. "He wasn't my childhood friend, and I don't owe him jack, or shit."

"So I have gathered."

Choosing only the most loyal sec men, Stirling picked six to accompany the baron. Nervously looking at the predark structure, the troopers climbed off their horses and handed the reins to friends, then proceeded to double-check their handcannons and longblasters. A few of the sec men exchanged weps, so that the people going in would have a better blaster. One corporal passed over a handcannon to a cousin already armed with a homie scattergun.

"I want that back," he stated gruffly, emotion tightening his throat.

"No prob," the other sec man said, tucking the blaster into his wide belt.

"All right, let's move out," Ryan said, drawing the SIG-Sauer. "I'll take point."

"Like hell," the baron growled angrily. "I always take the lead."

As a chill wind blew along the street, Ryan patted the blaster. "This shoots barely louder than a cough. How about your longblaster?"

Leveling the big-bore Winchester, the one-armed baron started to object, but then considered the logic of the man with the silenced blaster going first. He didn't like it, but accepted the hard reality. Blind norad, O'Connor wanted to do some chilling tonight! It was like a hunger in his belly.

Readying their explosives and blasters, the companions started across the street when a sudden flash of lightning cast the world into stark relief for a single long heartbeat. It made the building strangely resemble a human skull. Then the diffused light faded and darkness returned.

"If you hear explosions…" the baron added over a shoulder.

Stirling grunted. "We'll come running. Yes, sir."

"Good man. See you in Hell, Steven."

Detouring past the field of rubble, Ryan went stealthily by the snowy windows and up a short flight of granite steps to the front door.

"I thought the stickies used the side door?" a sec man asked, both hands worrying the stock of his longblaster.

"Which is why we're using the front," Ryan whispered back, watching the roof for any unnatural movements. "Now, pipe down. This is a recce, not a bloody gaudy house orgy."

Going to the door, J.B. quickly checked for any boobies, but it was clean. He picked at the lock with a couple of steel probes. The rusty tumblers were stubborn, but finally yielded.

As the weathered portal swung aside, there came a dry exhalation from the building carrying the smell of mold, decay and something else. This was a sharper smell, nasty and unclean.

"Stickies," the baron breathed, thumbing off the safety of the Winchester. "By gad, this really is their fucking nest."

Pointing at two men to stay and guard the exit, Ryan led the way inside. The dank air was thick enough to chew, and the norms pulled neckerchiefs over their mouths as if caught in a sandstorm.

As the front door closed, candles were lit. In the dancing light, the norms could see that the peeling walls were bowed slightly, as if sagging under tremendous weight or just from sheer age. The terrazzo floor was cracked and stained, and the front desk of the office building was coated with layers of thick cobwebs. Apparently, this had once been an office complex. A directory on the wall listed all of the companies here, a single plastic headstone for the hundreds of people who had once worked here, now long gone, deader than the grit under their boots.

Judiciously, Mildred scanned the list of names, but none of them were familiar. Then again, any of them could have been a covert front for some government agency from of her time.

Going to the left, Ryan easily located the side door that the stickie had used to enter the building. Jak pointed at the loose sand mixed with the dust on the floor. Multiple tracks overlapped one another. Ryan frowned at that. These weren't enough footprints for a horde of stickies. If this was their nest, it hadn't been here for very long. Mebbe only a couple of months. Were the stickies moving around in the ruins? Just how smart were these bastard muties?

Following the trail, Ryan watched for traps as he slipped through the still building, the accumulated cobwebs covering everything like a blanket of freshly fallen gray snow. The detritus of time lay heavy over the office building, solemn and implacable.

As the group of companions and sec men returned

to the lobby, Ryan saw marks along the wall where the stickies had gone around the stairs and climbed directly up the wall to the landing on the next level. Were the stairs a trap?

Relaying his suspicions to the other with sign language, Ryan studied the marble stairs for a minute, then slowly started to ascend. Almost instantly, a stickie lunged out of the gloom with both hands raised for a chill.

Chapter Seventeen

Spinning out of the way of the rush, Ryan smashed the mutie in the face with the barrel of his weapon. It staggered but didn't fall.

Moving fast, Baron O'Connor kicked it in the belly, then Doc whipped out his sword and lunged forward. The silvery length of the Spanish steel pierced the stickie through the mouth, pinning its forked tongue into place. As the other sec men stepped away from the lashing suckers, Ryan fired twice, the SIG-Sauer coughing 9 mm death into the monster's head. The stickie rocked from the impact of the hot lead, almost coming free from the sword. Then it shuddered all over and went still, dropping limply to the filthy floor and stirring up a small gray cloud.

Distastefully, Doc retrieved his sword and wiped it clean on a nearby curtain bearing the monogram of some predark company.

While Krysty and Mildred scanned overhead with their MP-5 subguns, Ryan dropped the clip of the blaster to replace the two spent rounds.

"Think there's more of them hiding?" a sec man whispered from behind his mask, worrying the checkered grip of his scattergun. In his mind, the darkness was alive with stickies.

"Better safe than chilled," the baron replied softly, using the long barrel of the Winchester to probe the alcove that the mutie had been hiding in. But there were no other stickies present, only a rusted candy machine, the confections behind the ancient glass as inedible as the dead stickie.

"No talking," Ryan admonished in a harsh whisper, starting up the stairs once more, the canvas bag of Molotov cocktails at his side clinking softly.

The next floor was the mezzanine, with all of the closed office doors facing the railing that looked down onto the lobby. Here the dust was disturbed, and the norms proceeded with extreme caution. If more stickies were hiding, there was no telling from which direction they could charge.

A set of escalators waited motionless at the far end of the mezzanine, and the group split apart in unspoken consent. The companions took the left, the baron and his sec men going up the other. Here and there they noticed old bloodstains on the serrated metal steps, and Ryan kept a close watch on the drop ceiling. The feeble glow of the tallow candles barely reached outside the group, and it was as if they were traveling inside a bubble of light through a black ocean.

At the top of the escalator, Ryan paused to try to hear if anything was moving in the building, but there was only the breathing of the other norms. No creaking water pipes, moaning wind or scuttling mice. Not even the rumble of the coming storm outside could be discerned.

The armed group of hunters moved onward. Eventually, the top floor became another reception area, the floor a decorative tile mosaic. Huge green plants filling wicker pots in the corner were obviously plastic, and there was a line of phone booths with what looked like vid screens. Those made Ryan tense. Yeah, he knew those from the Anthill. Very high-tech in its day. Just drek now, not worth scavenging. Then he saw Krysty go stiff.

"Trouble?" Ryan demanded in a tense whisper.

Her hair flexing and waving nervously, Krysty didn't reply at first. Just for a moment, the woman could have sworn that she heard a hoot.

Noticing the agitation of the redhead, Mildred pumped the handle of her flashlight and moved the weak yellow beam along the pay phones. The dulcet illumination was reflected off the vid monitors, magnifying the light into a golden wash that revealed a nightmare.

Just down the hallway to their left were dozens of stickies. The entire third floor seemed to be packed full of the sleeping muties, jammed together solid like brass in an ammo clip. The muties were lining the walls in resinlike cocoons, probably made from the hardened residue of their own gelatinous ooze. Baron O'Connor had used the term nest, but Ryan hadn't expected it to be accurate. This was a beehive, just like

the mailbox near the manhole cover. It was a honeycomb full of sleeping stickies!

Inhaling sharply at the sight, the baron waved the
Winchester at his sec men to order them back down
the escalator. If this wasn't all of the stickies, it was
enough. Time to burn the place down. But it was vital
that his troops didn't see the nest. Somebody was sure
to panic, and with one loud noise they would all get
chilled. There wasn't enough live brass in the whole
ville to stop this inhuman horde.

As the anxious sec men followed their baron, one
of them gurgled loudly and grabbed his throat, blood
gushing from a gaping wound.

Firing from the hip, Ryan fanned the nearest alcove
with the chugging SIG-Sauer. The 9 mm rounds torn
off the leaves of the plastic plants and smacked hard
into the marble wall to ricochet away. Then a stickie
fell forward, bleeding from the arm. Then another
mutie appeared, carrying a heavy wooden club. The
sec men braced for a rush, but instead of attacking the
norms, the stickie began beating the cudgel against the
marble wall, the booms echoing through the entire
building.

An alarm! Snarling a curse, J.B. mercilessly cut it
down with the stuttering Uzi. Silence didn't matter
anymore. The recce was over.

"Light 'em up!" the baron ordered, firing the
Winchester, then flipping the arming level of the longblaster to shoot again and again.

A dozen stickies died in their cocoons before even

knowing there was anything wrong. But a score more of the creatures jerked awake and stared at the little band of humans as if unable to comprehend the sight. Then the stickies started to swarm, their deadly hands stretched out toward the invading norms.

Everybody opened fire, the multiple muzzle-flashes strobing in the dusty darkness. Shuddering into death, stickies fell to the floor, only to be replaced by more. Leaping over predark furniture, some of the creatures started to crawl along the walls, their sucker-covered hands reaching down from above.

"Molotovs!" Ryan shouted, swinging a saddlebag onto the floor with a strident crash. "Block the stairs! Use the flames as cover!"

Letting go of the Uzi to let it swing from its canvas strap, J.B. yanked out a willie pete gren and flipped the sphere into the nest. Only a heartbeat behind, a sec man lit the rag on a Molotov and threw it against the ceiling. It crashed into a fireball, the contents dripped down onto the leather and the saddlebag instantly caught, the rising well of flame filling the landing. The shadows were banished, showing only more stickies, along with woven cages full of human bones.

Shooting in short, controlled bursts, Mildred was hit by the shocking realization that these stickies kept captives. Prisoners of muties, to be eaten at their convenience. A hellish larder worse than the butcher shop of any cannie tribe.

With the first shattering glass, the stickies charged.

But still they made no noise, the lack of their usual hooting giving the rush a terrible dreamlike quality.

Even though he was shocked to the core, Ryan still managed to ace two muties before spinning around and dashing for the escalator. What kind of muties were these? The things had almost norm intelligence!

As the conflagration began to die down, J.B. added another willie pete gren. The second flood of burning white phosphorus completely filled the landing, setting several stickies ablaze. Minus their usual hooting, the muties dashed madly about, waving their arms wildly until crashing into the walls or tumbling over the balcony and plummeting out of sight.

"Eat this, ass-sucker!" a sec man snarled, throwing a Molotov.

Darting around the pool of willie pete, a stickie incredibly caught the thrown bottle in a suckered hand, and made to heave it right back when Mildred triggered her rapidfire and blew the container apart. Covered in burning oil, the stickie backed away, waving its arms, still terribly silent.

"Why aren't they screaming!" Doc demanded, the LeMat and Ruger performing a duet of death. The black-powder blaster was throwing out clouds of smoke that soon mingled with the thickening clouds of reeking fumes from the burning dead.

"Shut it and run!" Jak commanded, burping his rapidfire into the muties.

A dull series of explosions came from the sec force's longblasters, the rounds hitting with deadly accuracy. But the closed office doors suddenly were thrown open and more stickies joined the mob. The army of them seemed endless.

Taking the awkward metal steps at a run, the companions and sec men retreated fast, firing every step of the way. The grim norms had to concentrate on not tripping down the escalator. The serrated steps were larger than regular stairs, and one wrong move would send a man tumbling, which would start a cascade of bodies falling down the motorized stairs, easy prey for the slavering muties.

And those little cages. J.B. grimaced hatefully, pulling another gren. About to yank the pin, he scowled at the charge and tucked it away to rummage for another. An implo gren would remove half the building, acing the norms along with the stickies.

Turning to shoot, a sec man tripped and staggered, immediately knocking over two other men. As the trio went tumbling, a blaster discharged, the lead ricocheting off the marble walls, a light fixture exploding on the ceiling.

The stickies charged at the fallen men, as if sensing these enemies were less of a threat than the others.

Jumping off the escalator, Ryan turned and fired at the mob of armed stickies boiling down the stairs like some jump nightmare. The first one toppled over in death, but the second was only wounded, and it started hooting insanely. Now all of the others took up the cry, and it was answered by countless more from the floors above until forming a deafening chorus of madness.

Working together, Krysty and Mildred raked the creatures with their rapidfires, while Doc's handcannons unleashed volleys of death. Pulling a Molotov cocktail from the bag at his side, Ryan held the oily rag in front of the sound-suppressed gun muzzle and stroked the trigger. The muzzle-flame ignited the rag, and he heaved it onto the metal steps. The firebomb hit and shattered, forming a crackling pool. A few of the sec men added their own bottles to the conflagration until it was a roaring bonfire, the bright orange flames licking upward.

Hooting wildly at the sight, some of the stickies charged through the flames, setting their ragged clothing ablaze. Others leaped for the walls and started shimmying along the decorative marble slabs in an effort to get past the fiery obstruction. Even as he chilled them, Ryan again noted that the muties didn't seem fascinated by fire anymore. That had been their greatest weakness, and now that was gone.

Suddenly a wooden spear came through the flames and chilled a sec man. A scattergun boomed in response, followed by another. Molotovs went flying, and the MP-5 rapidfires chattered way, spent brass arching through the air to fall musically to the cold stone floor. More spears were thrown, along with wooden cudgels. A sec man cried out as his wrist was smashed and his blaster was knocked to the floor to discharge into his own leg.

Acing a mutie on one of the walls, Ryan felt his blood run cold at the terrible look of cold intelligence in their furious eyes. Hot plague, some of them are smarter than others, the one-eyed warrior realized even as he ruthlessly gunned them down.

Backing for the stairs, the two groups stopped to reload, the baron tucking the Winchester between his legs to thumb rounds into the breech, when a flight of spears streaked into the crowd of norms. Nimbly dodging, Doc smacked a spear aside with his sword. But a sec man fell, the wooden shaft going completely through his chest to pin the startled man to a chair. Screaming obscenities, another sec man fired blind into the writhing flames and threw more Molotov cocktails, while the companions concentrated on taking out the stickies on the walls. But the fighting was pandemic now, all pretense of order gone, and none of the norms were sure that they would ever escape alive. Unstoppable, the waves of stickies kept coming.

Chapter Eighteen

Blood and brass, screams and smoke filled the dusty air, and breathing became difficult. A rain of clubs took another norm, and J.B. threw an antipers gren at the muties. The staggering blast rocked the building, and pieces of bodies went flying everywhere. But another flight of spears pelted the group, and more norms were chilled. Red blood and gelatinous ooze seemed to be everywhere.

Fighting their way to the stairs, the companions and remaining sec men ducked again as thrown clubs came spinning out of the dwindling pool of fire, closely followed by spears. Another man fell, mortally wounded, his belly ripped open wide, the intestines slithering onto the floor like greasy rope. Dropping his blaster, the dying man grabbed the internal organs with both hands and began to wail as he tried to shove them back inside his body. With calm deliberation, Baron O'Connor flipped the lever of the Winchester to chamber a fresh round and shot the sec man in the heart. The piteous shrieks stopped instantly.

"Keep it up!" Ryan shouted, dropping a clip and slamming in his last spare. "They can't see us any more than we can see them!"

"Use all of the bombs!" the baron shouted, dropping the spent Winchester and pulling out his handcannon. The old Glock .44 pumped copper-jacketed bone-shredders into the stickies, and every round chilled with gory efficiency.

Coughing from the thickening smoke of the chem fires, sec men obediently threw more bottles into the blaze, the crashing of the glass causing a gush of heat and noise. The smell of the roasting stickies was worse than cooking sewage!

Suddenly there came the sound of boots on the stairs and Sec chief Stirling appeared with a dozen more sec men brandishing weps and bottles. At the sight of reinforcements, everybody cheered and redoubled their efforts, the barrage of homie scatterguns, black-powder blasters and yammering rapidfires, reaching a deafening crescendo.

Temporarily out of brass, Ryan holstered the SIG-Sauer and did a fast side arm throw of a high-explosive gren onto the escalator. Releasing his rapidfire to hang by its strap, Jak did the same, and Baron O'Connor unexpectedly added a short pipe bomb.

"Move!" Ryan and the baron shouted in unison.

But the groups needed no encouragement, they were already pelting down the steps at a breakneck pace. Seconds later, the assorted mil ordnance cut loose and concussion shook the building, shrapnel from the staggering detonations throwing shards of broken floor and twisted metal everywhere. Breaking apart, the escalator groaned as if it were dying, then something loudly snapped inside the machine and metal parts sprayed out in every direction. Hit in the head with a spinning gear, a stickie perished trying to stuff its own brain back inside the broken skull.

With a cry, Stirling fell to one knee, a dagger of blue stone jutting from his shoulder. But the tough man rose and stumbled away, dribbling crimson in his wake. Reaching for the Steyr, Ryan felt white-hot pain along a forearm, and saw that he was pumping his lifeblood. Hugging the wound to his chest to try to staunch the blood loss, Ryan fumbled for the Steyr. Only five rounds left in the longblaster. He had to make every one count.

Just then, the foam tiles lining the ceiling collapsed and a half dozen stickies fell upon the group of sec men. Caught completely by surprise, the startled men began to fire among themselves, hot lead smacking into other sec men in their blind haste to chill the hooting muties. Ryan got the longblaster up in time to ace a stickie in the throat. Then another monster made a swipe at him, and Krysty hammered it to hell with her barking rapidfire. Doc shot one in the face with both handcannons and blew off its head, the skull shattering like an egg under the double assault.

A stickie grabbed Porter by the sleeve and yanked, but only took away the shirt. Unharmed, the man emptied his blaster into the mutie, shouting curses. Swinging his handcannon, Baron O'Connor pumped two booming rounds into the thing, and it went sailing backward over the railing to crash onto the reception desk in the lobby on the ground floor.

"Everybody outside!" Ryan bellowed, heading for the open doorway. He could see the two sec men there, shooting into the chaotic lobby, their black-powder blasters sending out plumes of acrid smoke that temporarily masked the exit.

Incredibly, more muties appeared at the top of the stairs. Their rags were smoldering, and many oozed bodily fluids. But their eyes were fierce and they moved without a sound, aside from the slap of bare feet on the shattered floor.

Spinning, one sec man tripped and another ran over his fallen comrade, uncaring of the trampled man. The baron gunned down the coward, and grabbed the sec man on the floor to haul him up, then shove him toward the door.

Desperate to buy seconds for the others to get out, Ryan and J.B. both flipped grens across the lobby, and the entire area was filled with the searing flash of willie pete. In response, the stickies hit the walls and crawled past the hellzone the same as before. Now they dropped to the floor, and, amazingly retrieved their thrown spears, then rushed at the norms in a picket charge, all the while hooting as their staring eyes choose victims.

A wounded sec man was slow to reload, and as he closed the wheelgun, a spear took him through the chest. The norm stood there for a long moment, staring in stark disbelief at the wooden shaft sticking through his blue uniform. Then he sighed deeply and lay on the filthy floor as if merely going to sleep.

Somebody else grabbed his fallen blaster and emptied it into the stickies, before turning to run away.

Pouring outside, the companions and the few remaining sec men scrambled down the stairs and across the foyer to explode out the front door. As they dashed across the sandy street, the *Metro* went into action. The catapult thumped and a dozen Molotovs rained upon the granite steps, erupting into a huge fireball.

Trapped in the foyer, the stickies hooted angrily and threw some spears at the war wag. Those only bounced off the armed sides, and the sec men behind the sand bag wall returned fire with crossbows. A dozen muties fell, their mottled bodies feathered with arrows. The ville sec men took heart at the display. The muties might have weps, but they couldn't aim worth drek. Time to press the attack.

"Cover the rear!" the baron shouted, firing his revolver. "Make a ring of fire! Use every Molotov!"

A spear flashed by his head just then, but the one-armed norm didn't even flinch. "Every Molotov! Save nothing!"

Hoisting clicking bags, a team of sec men rushed to obey, while the rest continued to shoot from the sandy street. High overhead, the dark clouds roiled in mounting fury and a strong breeze blew along the street, kicking up a stinging cloud of loose sand.

The catapult peppered the front of the building with another firestorm, setting the bottom level ablaze. Spears came out of the front door and a sec man fell, most of his face removed by the barbed point.

Suddenly the glass windows on the second floor shattered and a score of armed muties popped into view. But expecting that tactic, the furious sec men forced them back inside with crossbows and hot lead.

"Don't let anything get out!" Ryan shouted, clumsily trying to load the SIG-Sauer. But his hands were slick with blood, and he dropped the clip.

"Burn it to the ground!" Baron O'Connor added loudly. "Use everything we have. It's now or never!"

Rallying to the cry, the sec men began shooting at anything that moved inside the writhing flames. A window shattered on the third story and a stickie jumped out to land sprawling on a dead sec man. Waving a club, the mutie weakly tried to rise in spite of the fact that both of its legs were clearly broken. Caught reloading, Jak dropped the rapidfire and put two .357 Magnum rounds into its head, blowing out the back of its skull. Something moved in the sky, and a sprinkling of spears came flashing down from the roof. The wooden shafts hit the *Metro,* and another norm screamed into death.

Red light flickered into life from behind the infested building, and there could be heard the steady crashing of glass from the thrown Molotovs of the sec men. The ring of fire was expanding, slowly forming an impassable barrier around the nest.

Carrying two spears, a huge stickie tried to run through, and came out sheathed in red flames. Totally blind, the hooting creature raced across the street and smashed into the brick wall of a predark movie theater. The mutie stopped making noise and went still, but didn't fall, the burning corpse stuck in place to the rough brickwork by its array of oozing suckers.

Covered with sweat and soot, Krysty and J.B. peppered the open windows to drive back a stickie trying to reach the side of the building. Then another window was smashed open and a stickie jumped onto the sill, then slapped a hand onto the outside wall. Swinging around, it pressed flat against the surface and began to scuttle around the corner of the building just as Krysty sent a long burst of 9 mm rounds at the thing, and missed. Then two arrows from the sec men on top of the war wag caught it in the back, and the mutie went limp, nailed in place by the wooden shafts.

Gouts of orange flame were licking out of the windows by now, and the ring of fire was completed on the ground. Charred bodies dotted the landscape, a mix of norms and stickies.

More spears came arching down from the roof. Easily avoiding those, the ville sec men continued their assault, shooting and reloading their blasters as if this were the end of the world. Changing angles, the catapult thumped again, and the roof exploded in flames. A stickie tried to jump to the next building, but only made it to a tilting telephone pole jutting from the sand. As the thing braced for another jump, Ryan finished reloading the Steyr and fired from the hip. Hit in midair, the stickie was thrown sideways and tumbled lifeless to land in the vacant lot.

Thunder rumbled ever louder from above, and the

sec men's horses were nickering in fear at the mounting fire. Spears and blasterfire peppered the night, the increasing wind carrying away the horrible reek of the cooking corpses.

"Let's end this!" Ryan snarled, firing into the blaze.

"Bet your ass!" J.B. answered grimly, throwing a gren.

Flying through the smoke, the mil sphere went in through the smashed remains of a second-floor window. A heartbeat later, the implo gren activated. With a dull thump, a huge chunk of the predark building vanished, contracting to the size of a lump of coal. The ville sec men paused in their shooting at the sight of a thousand more stickies exposed along the bisected flooring. The hundred on the second floor had to have only been the guards. The third and fourth floors were a solid honeycomb of the weird cocoons. It was a mutie army!

"Hit 'em again!" the baron ordered as he advanced closer, firing his handcannon nonstop. His features were illuminated by the crimson light, making the one-armed giant appear to be a war god from predark mythology. Madness filled his eyes, but the blaster boomed in deadly accuracy.

Heartened by the sight of the baron taking the lead, the sec men rallied and double their assault on the burning structure. But then a low groan came from the building as the interior beams started to bend, stretching like warm taffy. The walls cracked, floors broke apart, and the upper levels of the office building col-

lapsed onto the lower stories in a prolonged avalanche
of crumbling masonry.

Anguished hooting could be heard from within, but
nothing tried to escape, and as the blaze spread
throughout the shuddering ruins, the cries slowed until
there was only the loud crackling of the rising flames.

BY DAWN, the structure was reduced to a smoldering
skeleton of twisted steel beams with a few sections of
broken masonry at the cornerstone.

"Well, that should do it," J.B. declared, sipping a
cup of cold coffee sub. With his hat pushed back, a pale
streak of clean skin was visible on the Armorer's forehead. The rest of his face was almost black from the
windblown soot.

"Yeah, they're all chilled," Ryan said, clumsily holstering the SIG-Sauer with his left hand.

Sitting on the curb across the street from the building, the one-eyed man had stayed through the night to
watch the structure burn to the ground, then he and the
baron had lead a recce into the cellar to make sure none
of the stickies had escaped into the warren of sewers
below the predark city. But the manhole covers had
been undisturbed. Perhaps the stickies had been afraid
to use the sewers because of the gators. Mebbe they
didn't know what the metal disks covered. It didn't really make a difference. The new breed of stickies was
gone, burned out of existence.

"Will you please stop moving?" Mildred ordered irritably, digging her fingers into his arm.

Snorting in reply, Ryan did as requested, coolly watching as the physician finished stitching shut the gash in his right forearm. As Mildred bit off the fishing line, Ryan tried not to grunt from the tug on his raw flesh. Pain was part of life; only the dead didn't bitch.

"You were lucky," Mildred said, tucking the supplies into her canvas med kit. "No tendons were damaged and no nerves cut. Rest for a couple of weeks, and you'll be good as ever."

"Wish we could say the same for everybody else," Ryan said, trying to make a fist. His hand was weak, and the sown gash in his arm throbbed painfully at the attempt.

"Lots of folks dead," Mildred said, forcing herself to stand. "But a lot more saved. Try to remember that."

Gingerly flexing his fingers, Ryan only grunted in reply.

Without further comment, Mildred turned to walk away, looking for anybody else whose wounds she could mend. A couple of healers from the ville had arrived during the night. But there were a lot more bodies to bury than patients to fix. A lone sec man with a canvas bag was already moving among the corpses, gathering boots and blasters. The grisly work of staying alive.

"Nuke storm of a night, eh, lover?" Krysty asked, squatting on the nearby sidewalk. The MP-5 subgun hung at her side, the weapon dotted with ooze and dried blood. Her clothing was ripped in numerous locations, and her skin showed a lot of bruises, but the gentle waving of her hair told him that the woman was undamaged and healthy.

"Had better," Ryan stated, placing the aching arm across his lap.

"I guess we took some losses," Baron O'Connor said, walking closer. The big man was chewing a piece of jerky, the motion making the tattoo on his throat seem to fly. A scattergun was slung across his back to replace the Winchester. "I guess your healer was right. A lot more survived."

"Depends on whether stickie, or not," Jak drawled, casually stropping a knife on a piece of whetstone. Satisfied with the result, he tucked the blade up a sleeve of his jacket and pocketed the stone. "Better for us than them."

"Yeah, don't think we'll be troubled much by muties anymore," Stirling added, his left arm in a sling, the shirt caked with dried blood and crystalline ooze. "Even if some got away, we aced the bulk of them, and there'll never be another nest like this rad pit again. We know what to look for now."

"To do is to learn," Doc agreed in his stentorian voice, watching the clouds move by overhead. The storm hadn't broken the previous night, but the sky was still overcast. The rain, acid or not, had held off just long enough for the fire to do its job. Every now and then, the scholar almost believed in luck.

There came the sound of hoofbeats, and everybody jerked up their heads, hands going for weps. Then Taylor came into view, riding a chestnut mare. Everybody relaxed and several sec men waved in greeting as the man reined in his mount and walked her over to the baron.

"Trouble?" O'Connor asked, squinting hard. "Is my family safe?"

"Mount up!" Stirling bellowed, pulling a blaster.

Stopping whatever they were doing, the battered sec men grabbed blasters and raced for the *Metro*.

"No, no! Everything is fine, my lord!" Taylor hastily corrected. "Your kin and the ville are perfectly safe."

"Then what the frag… At ease!" Stirling shouted. "False alarm!"

Grinding to a ragged halt, the exhausted sec men allowed themselves to slump, and most just sat on the sandy street wherever they stood.

"Then why are you here?" the baron demanded, scrutinizing his troops. The sec men were exhausted, but still willing to charge into battle. That was what came from ruling a ville by laws and not from whim.

"Saw the fighting was over and decided to come over. I was watching the fight through binocs," Taylor explained, hitching up his gunbelt. "Thought you'd like to know that the ville was hit last night by a dozen stickies armed with torches. Four bunches of three."

"They came in waves?" Ryan demanded suspiciously.

"Shit yeah. Damnedest thing. One had a torch, and the others carried spears, almost as if they were guards for the first."

"Combat formation," Stirling muttered, casting a backward glance at the destroyed nest. Shitfire, the ville was lucky they had managed to nightcreep the muties. This could have been a lot worse.

"Did they try for the armory again?" the baron asked, scratching at the end of his missing arm.

"Yes, they tried. But after the first attack, I had all of the black powder and predark brass moved to the safe room with the baroness. The next three times the nuke-suckers only found barrels of dirt—and us waiting in the shadows." The scout grinned.

"Excellent news!" the baron boomed, slapping the sec man on the back. "Well done, indeed!"

The man grinned at the pounding. "Thank you, my lord. The way I figure, if they stopped after four tries, that should mean you got them all and can come home again."

"We were coming back anyway," Stirling replied gruffly, hawking and turning to spit into the sand. "We're out of lead, powder, arrows and Molotovs. We'd have to start kicking the muties if we found any more."

"Got you covered there," Ryan said, patting the SIG-Sauer at his side.

"Well, you certainly have earned my personal thanks after the fight in the nest," the baron said. "And what the frag was that thing your man threw? The gren that blew up half the building?"

"Just something I found in a wrecked APC," the Armorer lied, forcing his hand away from the munitions bag at his side. "Sorry, that was the last one."

"Damn."

"Is that what happened?" Taylor asked, sounding impressed. "Some predark mil bomb? Well, shit…" Turning to face the smoky ruins, the scout gave a low whistle. "Blind norad, I'm glad you're on our side. And triple glad those mercies up north of the Zone didn't get you."

"Mercies?" the baron asked.

Just then, the corner of the burned-out building collapsed in a deafening crash, sending out a billowing cloud of soot and burning embers. Armed sec men rushed to the spot to check for stickies, but they found nothing.

"What mercies are you talking about?" Ryan demanded, massaging his forearm.

"Bunch of wild-ass coldhearts running just north of here," Taylor replied, rubbing his unshaved face to the sound of sandpaper. "That's what I was starting to say at the Citadel last night. When I was talking to the other villes about the muties, I heard about some coldhearts going around chilling everybody with one eye."

Wrapping a bandage around the head of a wounded sec man, Mildred jerked about at the remark. "Everybody?" she demanded, deliberately repeating the word. A feel of cold dread started to fill her stomach.

"Anybody and everybody," Taylor agreed. "Men, women, children. It's the damnedest thing."

Slowly, the baron turned to look at the companions.

Saying nothing, Ryan fumbled with his gunbelt, attempting to buckle it on backward and put the SIG-

Sauer on the left side where his undamaged hand could draw the wep.

"Those coldhearts are sending out a message, a blood warning to somebody," Stirling stated, running stiff fingers through his dirty hair. "Keep out of the Zone, or die."

A warning? No, it was an invitation, Ryan mentally corrected, tightening the gunbelt into place. And an unmistakable one at that. The only question was, who had sent it? The whitecoats from Operation Chronos? Some old enemy returned for vengeance?

"Tell us more about these strange deaths," Doc urged. "Tell us everything."

Just then, a blinding burst of sheet lightning crashed overhead, thunder rumbled and the dark clouds broke, pelting the predark ruins with a cold, hard rain.

The storm had finally arrived.

Chapter Nineteen

Grunting from the effort, Alan and Robert Rogan swung aside the disguised gate, and a dusty Edward rolled into the woodsy glen on his motorcycle.

Directing the purring machine across the compound, Edward skirted the campfire, circling once around Lily and nearly knocking her into the flames. But the sullen girl concentrated on stirring the taters frying in an iron skillet and gave no reaction to her tormentor. Revving the bike, the laughing man drove away at a slow pace.

Placing the frying pan on a flat rock set near the fire, Lily took a stick with some cloth tied to the end, dipped it into a plastic bucket of honey and shine and swabbed down the sizzling haunch of meat roasting above the flames. Pretending to ride her down was their second favorite game. But after the first few days of being their slave, she really didn't give a nuking damn about anything that happened anymore. Their brutality was beyond words. Dirty tech lovers. When she was sure her brothers weren't looking, absolutely sure, the girl would liberally season their food with spit. The coffee was especially good for that.

But not this night, Lily added privately. There was a large bone running through the hindleg of the griz bear, which meant that she might get something to eat after they were done stuffing themselves. Mebbe. Hopefully.

Braking to a halt near the concrete bunker, Edward pushed down the kickstand and climbed off the dirty two-wheeler. Reaching into the saddlebags, the barrel-chested man pulled out a leather eyepatch and a human scalp dripping with long silvery hair.

"Was it them?" John asked, glancing up from his work. The tall man was sitting on a rock covered with the furry hide of a recently chilled bear. On the metal table in front of him was a clean piece of white cloth covered with a disassembled combo rapidfire.

"Nope, another bust," Edward said.

"Good." John smiled without warmth, his hands moving with intimate sureness as he lubricated the recoil spring of the rapidfire and slipped it into the housing. "I want to be the one who puts Ryan on the last train west."

"Not going to happen," Alan said, puffing on a hand-rolled cig as he walked over. "Unless they're stupes, these outlanders will run for the end of the world once they hear that the Rogans are hunting them."

Making a detour past the campfire, Alan slapped Lily on the rear, the blow causing the girl to stumble and almost go into the flames. With a gasp, she drew back and started to turn toward the man with the basting stick brandished in her fist as if it were a hatchet.

He grinned at the action, and Lily slumped, turning back to work with an expressionless face. If she only had a knife, or a blaster…!

"Well, bro, Delphi says that once this Ryan hears about what has been happening here in the Zone, the one-eyed bastard is going come after us with every blaster firing. And right behind him will be the real prize. Tanner," John commented, glancing down the inside of the barrel. "To find Tanner, we hunt Ryan. Easy pie. And so far, Delphi has been right about everything else."

"Yeah, sure, makes sense," Alan grudgingly admitted. "But the son of a bitch is sure taking his sweet bloody time getting here!"

"Ain't nobody in a hurry to get aced." Edward chuckled, going to the waterfall. Dipping a bucket into the pond, he went back to the bike and started to wipe it down with a cloth. The water flowing off the front fender began to run crimson as the dried blood washed off.

"Food's ready," Lily announced, demurely stepping away from the campfire.

The girl stayed out of the way as the four coldhearts gathered around to use their eating knives to slice off thick pieces of the bear, and fill their tin plates with mounds of taters fried in lard, and canned beans.

"Mebbe we need to take the chilling up a notch," Robert suggested in his horrible voice, using the blade to scoop up the beans dripping with hot fat.

"Whatcha mean?" John asked, biting off a piece of

meat. The animal had tried to get into their base through the trees and gotten tangled in the barbed wire. He and his brothers had first cut the tendons so it couldn't fight, or run away. Then they had skinned the bear alive. Damn, that had been fun, the griz had lasted a hell of a lot longer than any man or mutie.

"How about we don't just scalp the corpses, anymore," Robert croaked, taking a sip of the coffee. "We could do worse to them first. A lot worse. You know, to help spread the news around faster."

"Now, you're making sense, bro." Alan grinned, a knife slipping out of his sleeve and into a waiting hand. He turned the blade in the firelight, inspecting the edge. "The bloodier the tale, the more often it gets told."

"Sound good to me," Edward agreed, smiling, picking up a sizzling tater with his fingers. He ate it slowly, as if the heat meant nothing. "By the time we're done with him, the chilling of Ryan will become a nuking legend that folks will tell for years!"

"Forever!" Alan laughed, his insane eyes twinkling at the unspeakable visions of bloody torture.

Raising their tin cups, the Rogan brothers toasted the idea and drank to seal the deal.

"More coffee, bitch," John said, tossing his empty cup at the girl. "And if you spit in it again, we'll do you like we did the bear."

Going deathly pale, Lily rushed to obey.

Grinning at her response, John went back to the meal. Hmm, a spectacular chilling. Something so horrible that the news would spread across the Zone and force Ryan their way. A red night of screaming worse than getting caught by stickies, and even more terrible then being captured alive by cannies. An interesting problem. Could it be done? Then the answer came to him in a flash.

Yeah, John Rogan thought, looking skyward at the merciless sun. That'll do just fine.

Chapter Twenty

The rain storm had lasted for days and flooded whole sections of the predark Two-Son ruins. But eventually, the sun came out and for a week slowly baked the landscape dry with unrelenting heat.

"I hate to see you folks go," Stirling said, frowning as he adjusted the sling supporting his bandaged arm.

Nobody knew what the squat building had been in the predark day, but it was now a horse stable. A row of windows lined the wall, set just below the ceiling. The glass panes had been carefully removed to use in the greenhouses, the openings giving some much needed ventilation. Adobe brick walls sectioned off the open area into stalls for the horses, and big steel barrels had been cut in two to hold their feed and water. A thick layer of sand covered the floor, and two young boys were sweeping up the manure to be used in the greenhouses. The baron wasted nothing.

"Hate to leave," Ryan said truthfully, carefully using both hands to tighten the belly strap of his mount. "But we have to find out if these rumors are true." The chestnut stallion was young and strong, its eyes bright with intelligence. These were the best animals the ville possessed, two of them from the baron's private stock.

"Could be a trap," Stirling suggested with a frown.

"If is, bad news for them," Jak said, climbing into the saddle. The teenager had kept the same mare from before, and the animal moved her neck to brush against the hand of her new master.

"Especially with these," J.B. said confidently, patting his munitions bag.

Most of the predark grens hauled from the redoubt had been used in the fight with the stickies, so the companions had waited until after the rain to retrieve the rest of the supplies stored in the sewer. Unfortunately, the sewer had flooded and the precious supplies were gone, washed away to someplace downstream.

After some heated discussions, the companions came to a decision, one they had never made before in all of their travels. Over the past week, Ryan and J.B. had shown Baron O'Connor and Sec chief Stirling the secret of making guncotton, a simple explosive that was more powerful than C-4 plas. The stuff was utterly useless for blasters, as it was just too strong. It always blew the gun apart, often chilling the person pulling the trigger.

However, guncotton was perfect for making pipebombs. Any further invasions of stickies could easily be handled by simply blowing the infested building into a million pieces with a wooden barrel of the homie explos. The precious knowledge had bought the companions three magnificent horses—in addition to Mildred's three—and all of the food they could carry. Plus, a full bag of the new pipebombs.

Formerly a teacher, Doc had been inspired by that event. Since paper was unknown, the scholar spent a rainy day sanding a plank smooth and then carving the alphabet into the wood. Surprisingly, the baron's wife had picked up reading relatively quickly and promised to pass along the knowledge of "the marks of sound" to every child in the ville.

As the word of these deeds spread, the rep of the companions grew, and so Krysty took this opportunity to instruct the greenhouse farmers about crop rotation, and how to get a maximum yield from the greenhouses. The farmers seemed highly doubtful of the idea that less work would deliver more food, but reluctantly agreed to give it a try. The rists knew old tech that bordered on magic. Old coins, boiled water and bed sheets had been used to make the stuff called guncotton. Mebbe rotating crops really would work!

Knowing how to make shine from his days on the bayou, Jak had gone with Cauldfield to visit the distillation unit for the fuel, but found nothing there that could be improved. That made Cauldfield furious, and the man had demanded advice, thinking the youth was holding out on him for some reason. A heated argument followed, and Jak was about to draw down on the fool when the baron interfered and forced them apart.

"Some folks born knowing nothing," Jak muttered afterward, "and get more stupe every year."

While tending the wounded from the ferocious battle, Mildred had shown the midwives and healers everything she could about basic medicine. They had absorbed the information and started setting most of it to rhythm so that knowledge could be easily remembered. Quickly seeing the logic of this in a world where reading and writing were unknown by most folk, Mildred used some radio and television commercials from the twentieth century to offer musical suggestions. The catchy jingles were gratefully accepted. But later, the physician had to stop herself from laughing at the sight of the somber healers chanting about basic hygiene, birth control and battlefield surgery based upon advertising slogans.

"Madison Avenue at its best." Mildred chuckled in remembrance, and started humming famous chewing gum lyrics while checking the lashing on the saddlebags.

"How do you double pleasure, Millie?" J.B. asked, puzzled, leaning over in his saddle.

"I'll show you later," the physician promised with a chuckle, climbing onto her horse. The Appaloosa gelding nickered softly as she settled into place, and stomped the sandy ground, making a chomping sound with its hooves.

"Let's get moving, people," Ryan directed, awkwardly grabbing the saddle horn and swinging a leg over the stallion to settle into the hard leather saddle. "Mount up! I wanna be far from these ruins when nightfall comes."

"And may Gaia guide us along the way." Krysty sighed, a small bandage covering a wound on her cheek from a stickie spear that had come too nuking close for comfort.

The day was warm, and the redhead had her bear-skin coat tied about her waist, the S&W revolver riding high on her gunbelt in front, and the MP-5 hanging in the middle of her back. The rapidfire held a single full clip of predark brass, and there were no more spares. After that, Krysty would be down to the revolver and a few pipebombs.

Privately, she also would have preferred to stay in Two-Son ville for another week, and teach the locals how to convert black powder into gunpowder. Then J.B. could have made reloads for the MP-5, and they could go north packing heavy iron. But there was no holding back Ryan. The companions all rode with him, or the man would have gone alone.

"Well, if I can't change your mind," Stirling said, walking over. Hitching up his gunbelt, the sec man offered his left arm. "Good luck."

Without hesitation, Ryan reached down and the two men shook. Then Stirling did the unexpected and squeezed with all of his strength. Ryan frowned at that, then did the same back. A minute passed with the two maintaining the grip, until sweat appeared on Ryan's brow and a red stain started to spread on Stirling's bandaged shoulder.

"Cut that shit out, right now!" Mildred snapped, startling her horse. It whinnied in surprise, starting a chain reaction of snorting from the other horses in the stable.

Finally, the two men let go, each trying not to show how much pain he was experiencing.

"Nuking hell, Ryan, your healer did a terrif job on the stitching, but that arm isn't completely healed yet," Stirling stated bluntly, ignoring the throbbing ache in his shoulder. "Your blaster hand is stiff, and nowhere near as fast as it used to be. Let it heal for fuck's sake. Wait another week! What difference can that possibly make?"

"Can't." Ryan grunted, casually resting his right arm on his leg. "Folks are getting aced to get my attention. I've got to stop it."

"Fair enough. But why not wait a while longer? What's the damn hurry?"

Tugging his gloves on tighter, Ryan really didn't have the words to explain why. It certainly wasn't because of pride, or honor. It was something else, something impossible to explain. This was just something he had to do, even if it wasn't a smart move. When a man looked in a mirror, he damn well better like the fellow staring back, or else he might as well just eat his blaster. Life was more than a matter of survival at any cost. There was more. Traveling with the Trader, a young Ryan had learned that the hard way over the years. Would he have died to save his son, Dean? Hell, yes. What about J.B. or Krysty? Sure, without pausing for a tick. So what about himself? Now that question took some deep thinking, but the answer came back the same. He had to ride north, and as soon as possible.

In reply, Ryan shrugged, unable to put the complex emotions into mere words.

Frowning, the sec chief sighed in resignation. "Well, at least don't take any chances with those cold-hearts," Stirling advised sternly. "Just ace them on sight. Or better yet, shoot them from behind. Savvy?"

"I savvy," Ryan replied, turning his horse toward the open doorway of the corral and kicking it into a trot. The rest of the companions followed.

Shaking his head, Stirling closed the swing door to the corral and went to check the other animals.

As the companions rode their horses through the ville, the civies came out to line the street and wave goodbye. A couple of young girls blew kisses at Jak, and several woman bowed slightly as Mildred passed.

"You know, I can't remember the last time we left a ville and were still friendly with the reigning baron and his sec force," J.B. said, adjusting his fedora. "Heck of a nice change, I must admit."

"Well, at least Front Royal in the east, and Two-Son here in the West," Krysty added, her hair flexing and waving. "That makes two."

"Two villes out hundred," Jak snorted, brushing back his snowy-white hair. "Not much."

"No, indeed, Mr. Lauren, it is not," Doc rumbled, squinting at the sec men standing on top of the approaching wall. The armed guards were also smiling and waving. "But then, at least this was a safe haven."

"For once, I agree with you," Mildred said, rolling her hips in rhythm to the animal between her thighs. Two villes out of a hundred. Not much at all. But the desert ville offered them a vital fallback position, someplace to use as a retreat if the hammer fell. Retirement was an unknown word in this dark time, but Mildred had been taught to look ahead, to plan for the future, both good and bad. Deep down in her heart, she had already decided that if something ever happened to the others, this is where the physician would make her new home. A place to write down her medical knowledge for future generations, a journal of what she had seen, and done in her travels with the companions. She'd jotted down a few ideas already, but there was so much more to record.

Plus, there was always the nearby redoubt, Blaster Base One. Given enough people and supplies, Mildred felt positive it would be possible to dig through the collapsed tunnel and reclaim the redoubt with its cornucopia of weapons, medicine, electricity and food. With those supplies, Two-Son could become the capital of a new America. A land without slaves, warlords, cannies, or death areas.

"Millie?" J.B. asked, riding closer. "You okay, honey?"

The woman dried the moisture off her cheeks with a sleeve and nodded quickly in reply. "Just some sand in my eyes," she lied as the vision of the future faded away into a dream. But the physician knew that dreams were important. The wheel was born in a dream, the radio, penicillin, plumbing, the Magna Carta, the Constitution... Even after everything else was cold ashes blowing in the wind, dreams still survived.

Approaching the front gate, Ryan could see there were several folks waiting for them near the firing wall. Baron O'Connor was standing with his wife and son, as well as Jan and Simone Stirling and a scowling Cauldfield. Only Catherine was missing, and Ryan really didn't give a damn. That bitch was going to be real trouble someday.

"I see that Steven couldn't change your mind." Baron O'Connor's voice boomed.

"Nope," Ryan said.

The baron waited for more, but when it wasn't forthcoming, he shrugged. "Well, can't say that I really blame you," O'Connor admitted. "Come back if you can. You'll always be welcome."

"Not if I have anything to say about it," Cauldfield muttered softly.

"Good luck," Daniel said, stiffly rising.

Ryan nodded. "Same to you,"

"Open the gate!" the baron commanded, and the guards rushed to obey.

As the companions rode out of the ville, Ryan tensed as the alarm bell began to ring. He reached for his blaster. Then he eased his stance at the realization that it was just the baron's way of saying goodbye. Son of a bitch, that was certainly a first! A royal farewell.

Starting across the shatter zone, Doc cast a brief glance backward, and saw the huge gate ponderously swing closed. Then a light began to flash from the Citadel, and he smiled. Doc didn't know their mirror code, but he understood the message. Good luck. Come back alive.

Shielding the toy compass with a hand, J.B. checked the swinging needle. "North is that way," the Armorer said, pointing.

"Okay, get razor-sharp, people!" Ryan shouted, leading the way through a gap in the row of K-rails. "It's a two-day ride to the next ville, and the coldhearts know we're coming. They might attack us from anywhere along the way."

"Then why are we heading due north, straight into their arms?" Krysty demanded. "You planning a suicide charge?"

Adjusting his eyepatch, Ryan gave a half smile to the woman as he kicked the rump of the stallion with his boot heels, and the animal responded by breaking into a full gallop.

STANDING ON TOP of the wall, the sec men of the ville watched as the companions moved into the ruins and out of sight. A corporal then faced into the ville and made a chopping motion.

"Are you sure about this, Father?" Daniel O'Connor asked, dropping back into his chair. The young man was still very weak. "This not our way."

"There is no other choice," the baron replied, the folded cloth of his empty sleeve flapping in the breeze.

Suddenly there came the sound of galloping horses, and Daniel turned to see Sec chief Stirling come riding up with five mounted sec men. All of them were armed with longblasters, crossbows, quivers of arrows and bags of the new pipebombs.

At a gesture from the baron, the massive gates rumbled aside once more, and the grim pack of riders galloped out of the ville heading into the desert on their dark mission.

James Axler
Outlanders

An ancient Chinese emperor
stakes his own dark claim to Earth…

HYDRA'S RING

A sacred pyramid in China is invaded by what appears to be a ruthless
Tong crime lord and his army. But a stunning artifact and a desperate
summons for the Cerberus exiles put the true nature of the looming battle
into horrifying perspective. Kane and his rebels must confront a four-
thousand-year-old emperor, an evil entity as powerful as any nightmare
now threatening humankind's future….

Available November 2006 wherever you buy books.

THE DESTROYER

DRAGON BONES

Living forever totally rocks...

The strange-looking animal touted to be a real live dinosaur was a bona fide apatosaurus. Unfortunately, the dino has been stolen, flash frozen, locked away in secret, awaiting its personal contribution to creating a formula for immortality. Suddenly everybody is a believer in the longevity offered by the poor dead animal and CURE has a crisis on its hands. Smith orders Remo to find the thing and incinerate it before fountain-of-youth seekers rampage the world. But Remo's got bigger problems. Chiun is acting a little off, a little tired—and single-mindedly determined to enjoy a restorative cup of immortality tea brewed with dragon bones....

Dragon Bones is the last installment of The Destroyer published by Gold Eagle Books.

Available October 2006 wherever you buy books.

A global nuclear meltdown is ticking toward reality...

HELL DAWN

Project: Cold Earth is a malignant computer worm capable of destabilizing nuclear reactors to the point of meltdown. It's the brain child of a CIA freelancer who's become a high-value target for the good guys and the bad. Now the virus is in the wrong hands, along with its creator, and everybody—the hunters, the buyers and the sellers—are crowding the front lines. It's a desperate countdown for Stony Man, a nightmare made in the U.S. but poised to take down the rest of the globe....

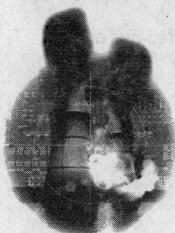

STONY® MAN

Available October 2006 wherever you buy books.